BEELZEBUB SONATA

Plays, Essays, and Documents

Stanisław I. Witkiewicz

Edited and translated

by

Daniel Gerould and Jadwiga Kosicka

Performing Arts Journal Publications
New York

Library of Congress Cataloging in Publication Data
Beelzebub Sonata
CONTENTS: Chronology, *The Beelzebub Sonata, Tumor Brainiowicz, Dainty Shapes and Hairy Apes*, Documents.
Library of Congress Catalog Card No.: 80-81998
ISBN: 0-933826-08-7
ISBN: 0-933826-09-5 (pbk)

Graphic design: Gautam Dasgupta

Printed in the United States of America

———————————

Grateful acknowledgement is made to the following for help and advice in preparing the translations, obtaining the photographs and gathering materials dealing with Witkacy's life and works: Stuart Baker, Bernard Dukore, Michael Earley, Louis Iribarne, Jan Krynski, Zbigniew Lewicki, Glenn Loney, Anna Micinska, James Parker, Konstanty Puzyna, Grzegorz Sinko, Lech Sokol, Rosemary Weiss.

An earlier version of the Chronology first appeared in *Theatrefacts*, II, No. 2 (1975).

These translations have received an award from the Translation Center at Columbia University, made possible by a grant from the New York State Council on the Arts.

Publication of this book has been made possible in part by a grant from the National Endowment for the Arts Washington, D.C., a federal agency.

Contents

PERFORMING ARTS JOURNAL PLAYSCRIPT SERIES

General Editors: Bonnie Marranca and Gautam Dasgupta

Stanisław Ignacy Witkiewicz

A Chronology

1885

Born 24 February in Warsaw, in the Russian-occupied section of Poland; son of Stanisław Witkiewicz, well known painter and author, and Maria Pietrzkiewicz, music teacher, who were married in 1883. The Witkiewicz family originally came from Lithuania where they were land-owning nobility. The playwright's great uncle, Jan Witkiewicz, was arrested in 1823 for revolutionary anti-Tsarist activity, first condemned to death, then stripped of his title, and finally forced to become a common soldier in the Russian army. However, due to his brilliance in learning Persian and other Near Eastern languages, he became a trusted Russian secret agent in Central Asia and Afghanistan, operating under a number of disguises and pseudonyms. In St. Petersburg in 1839, on the eve of an audience with Tsar Nicholas I, Jan Witkiewicz committed suicide after having become dissatisfied with life and feeling himself a spy and a traitor to Poland. The playwright's grandfather, Ignacy Witkiewicz, was exiled to Tomsk for participating in the insurrection of 1863 against Russia and was accompanied to Siberia by his twelve-year-old son, Stanisław, the playwright's father.

1890

Family moves permanently to Zakopane in the Tatras mountains, in the Austrian-occupied section of Poland, because of Witkiewicz senior's poor health. There, Witkiewicz senior became one of the principal creators of Polish intellectual and artistic life at the turn of the century, promoting the new Impressionist movement in the arts, and extolling the values of the folklore, handicrafts, and architecture of the peasant mountaineers.

1891

Baptised with the Polish-American actress Helena Modjeska present as his godmother. Encouraged to develop his talents in many directions as he grew up, young Witkiewicz began to paint and play the piano; collected insects and built "museums"; was educated entirely at home by his father and various private tutors. Believing that all formal schooling produced only mediocrity and conformity, Witkiewicz senior made his son's education an unusual experiment in the application of his own ideas about art, culture, and civilization to form a unique and exceptional individual destined to become an outstanding artist.

1893

Wrote *Cockroaches* and other childhood plays and published them on his own printing press as Volume I of his comedies. "He's terribly interested in everything that's written in dialogue form," his father wrote. "If you take into account that this 'author' is eight years old, you must admit that he's got an awful lot of talent! Lope de Vega wrote his first play when he was 10 years old."

1900

Close friendship developed with Leon Chwistek (Polish mathematician, philosopher, and painter) and Bronisław Malinowski (the anthropologist). Together they read plays and poetry, wrote mock-scientific treatises, and invented bizarre names for one another such as "Edgar, Duke of Nevermore," "Baron Brummel de Buffadero de Bluff," and "Dorian Fidious-Ugenta," which Witkiewicz would later use in his plays, reflecting the strong appeal of Poe, Oscar Wilde, and the dandies and decadents. "If we manage to hold on here another year without yielding to school — it would be most fortunate both for the boy's soul and for his health," his father wrote. Although never sent to school, he regularly took the end-of-the-year examinations so as to receive his diploma.

1901

Made his first trip to St. Petersburg, where he stayed with an aunt and visited the Hermitage; painted actively, mainly landscapes from the Lithuanian countryside where he frequently visited another aunt. "As your painting progresses, you're going to be a marvelous proof of the truth of my theories of art, and during the years when others are learning their ABC's in incomprehensible school exercises — you'll be an independent master of your art," his father wrote in one of the more than 500 letters Witkiewicz senior sent to his son during the period from 1900-1915.

1902

Took part in his first exhibit in Zakopane. "Stasiek's two landscapes look extremely good and are considered the best works in the judgement of the public," his father commented. Wrote his first philosophical treatises, *On Dualism* and *Schopenhauer's Philosophy and his Relation to his Predecessors,* and worked out the basic principles of his theory of Pure Form in conversations with his father, a proponent of realism in painting and a skilled aesthetician. Young Witkiewicz's aim was to put painting back in the realm of art, a position which he felt it had lost in the epoch of realism.

1903

Obtained his secondary school certificate by final examination in Lvov; studied languages (English, French, German, and Russian) and higher mathematics. Continued to write philosophical treatises. In his artistic endeavors, he was stimulated by the intellectual and artistic elite who visited the Witkiewicz household. Sholem Asch, a protégé of Witkiewicz senior, became a friend and enthusiast of the boy. In letter after letter, interspersed with citations from Nietzsche, the father constantly exhorted his son to be free, independent, lofty, sublime, creative, and untrammeled: "In intellectual concepts reach into infinity, in social ideas go to the ultimate extremes of boundless universal love. Don't become encumbered by any caste limitations, by any professional prejudices, by any petty-minded forms of individual class egotism. Live in the future. Constantly stand on the heights from where you can observe the farthest horizons and spread the wings of thought and action for flight beyond them."

1904

Completed *Daydreams of an Unproductive Man: Metaphysical Palaver,* never published philosophical essays. Visited Vienna, Munich, and Italy. Particularly impressed by the symbolic paintings of Arnold Bocklin. "As for Böcklin," his father wrote, "if only it grabs you by the throat right from the start — then it's fine. Those are just the impressions and opinion that I was hoping for." In October went with his father to Lovranno, a health resort on the Adriatic in what is now Yugoslavia. Met the pianist Arthur Rubinstein, then visiting Zakopane on a concert tour, and began a long friendship lasting until 1931 when they met for the last time.

1905

Discussions with his father about the Russian revolution of 1905 which Witkiewicz senior hoped would topple the Tsarist Empire, leading Poland to freedom. His father wrote, "I'd like you to take the most radical position — that is, the position for absolute social justice, which is the expression of the sole force worthy of honor which can unite mankind — love. Of the social systems that exist today nothing can remain. We must fight against this with complete intransigence." Enrolled in the Cracow Academy of Fine Arts against his father's wishes. His father reacted, "Don't think my precious I want to restrict you. I want you to progress as individually and as independently as possible... What I'm concerned with is not your finishing the University, but the total development of your soul... You, who as a child were independent and proud of your self-sufficient spirit, now would have to hand over responsibility for your own art to some lousy school — yes, all schools are lousy! You won't go along with the herd — you'll go alone." This decision became the cause of the first major overt conflict between father and son. In May took a short trip to Italy with the composer, Karol Szymanowski, who dedicated his first piano sonata to Witkiewicz.

1906

Due to his father's influence dropped out of the Academy and returned home to Zakopane.

1907

Attended extensive Gauguin exhibit in Vienna. Took private painting lessons with Władysław Slewiński, a pupil of Gauguin.

1908

Turned from landscapes and began painting portraits and making grotesque charcoal drawings ("monsters") with titles like "The Prince of Darkness Tempts Saint Theresa with the Aid of a Waiter from Budapest" and "A Man with Dropsy Lies in Wait for His Wife's Lover." Saw Fauves and early Cubists in Paris, exhibited in Cracow, and began a long and anguished love affair with the celebrated actress, Irena Solska, who specialized in playing demonic women in the modernist plays of such writers as Ibsen and Przybyszewski. Witkiewicz senior moved permanently to Lovranno on the Adriatic for his health. Visited in November by his son who had enrolled in the Cracow Academy of Fine Arts for a second time.

1910

Wrote *The 622 Downfalls of Bungo, or The Demonic Woman*, autobiographical novel about his romance with Solska and his development as an artist. "I have written more than 800 pages, and now I'm painting most industriously so as finally to improve my position in the world and shut the traps of my lousy enemies." This youthful "Portrait of the Artist as a Young Man," with its *fin de siècle* atmosphere and frank treatment of sex, remained unpublished until 1972. Went to Zagreb in May with Irena Solska who was making a guest appearance in the theatre. Finally abandoned once and for all his formal study of painting at the Academy.

1911

Visited Brittany (Pont-Aven) invited by Slewiński. Saw Cubist exhibit in

Paris. Stayed in London for two weeks with Bronislaw Malinowski.

1913

Still without a profession or genuine direction in life, solely preoccupied with the enigma of who and what he was, incapable of supporting himself and forced to live at his parent's expense, underwent a severe mental crisis and was analyzed by a Freudian psychiatrist, Dr. Karol Beaurain, in Zakopane where his mother still lived. Witkiewicz wrote, "I experienced a monstrous feeling, the feeling that I was going mad — but this time not figuratively, but really..." In spite of this mental disruption, kept working on his painting and writing (in his correspondence mentioned a new novel about which nothing is known). He wrote further, "I feel madness very clearly and I'm frightfully afraid of it. A pile of drawings will be left behind after me. I'm the most unhappy of human beings. I've got to move mountains." Exhibited many works in Cracow and Zakopane. Felt his psychoanalysis had been unsuccessful, although he developed a life-long interest in Freud and his discoveries. He related, "I had a session with Dr. Beaurain — my psychoanalysis is now nearing completion. But I haven't acquired any faith in it. If I come out of this, it won't be due to my realizing that I have an embryo complex." In December visited his father in Lovranno for the last time.

1914

In February his fiancée, Jadwiga Janczewska, committed suicide probably due to a tragic imbroglio involving Szymanowski who was then visiting Zakopane. Plunged into despair and brooding grief, accepted Malinowski's invitation to join the British Association for the Advancement of Science and traveled with him to Australia via Ceylon to attend the annual scientific conference held that year in Adelaide and Sydney from August 8 to 12. This trip opened Witkiewicz's eyes to the beauty and mystery of the East and became the basis of his lasting interest in non-Western cultures. The intense color and strangeness of existence which he experienced in the tropics had tremendous impact on his painting and perception of the world, and furnished him with material for many plays and a philosophical viewpoint for judging European civilization, as in the parallel cases of Gauguin, Conrad, and Artaud. Contact with primitive art and religion helped Witkiewicz formulate his own conception of a theatre with magical and ritual functions. Possibly planned to take part afterwards in Malinowski's projected first anthropological expedition to New Guinea and the Trobriand Islands as photographer and draftsman. But at the outbreak of World War I quarreled and broke with Malinowski, possibly over political issues, and left for St. Petersburg where as a Russian subject he enrolled in officers training school — although exempt from service as an only son — thereby wounding deeply his anti-Tsarist father who eventually received word of his son's decision.

1915

Underwent a radical transformation in the army. His aunt wrote his mother from St. Petersburg: "The way he is now he never was before. Calm, almost joyful, he holds himself straight with his head raised high—he's completely shaken off the despairing state of apathy in which we saw him when he came back. He's preparing for his theoretical examinations remarkably well, and he's holding up under the rigors of army life splendidly. He looks very well in his uniform, neither the heavy boots, nor the thick coat, nor the sabre bother him in the least." After finishing training school served as officer in the elite Pavlovsky Regiment, wounded at the front at Molodechno (Vitonez), near Minsk. In September, Witkiewicz senior died at Lovranno without seeing his son again, and was given a national hero's burial in Zakopane.

1917-1918

In Russia, painted extensively (according to some estimates perhaps as many as several thousand portraits and compositions); developed a life-long enthusiasm for Picasso whose works he viewed in Moscow at the Shchukin Gallery. For Witkiewicz, Picasso's works expressed what Witkiewicz meant by Pure Form: "There is no 'essential' difference, for example, between ancient Chinese art (it is the most beautiful art that ever existed) and Picasso." Experimented with drugs for the first time, worked on philosophy and aesthetics. At the time of the February Revolution was supposedly elected political commissar by his regiment. He wrote: "During those final days I had much food for thought in the spectacle of the Russian Revolution from February, 1917, to June, 1918. I can't call it anything but a spectacle since unfortunately I watched it as though from a box at the theatre, not being able to take an active part in it due to my schizoid inhibitions. I observed that unparalleled event at absolutely close quarters, as an officer in the Pavlovsky Regiment which began the Revolution. Later, I had the honor of being elected by my wounded soldiers from the front (I was in only one battle, at Stokhod) to the 4th Company of the Auxiliary Battalion of that Regiment, the same company which actually started the Revolution. I owed that honor to my own weak negative qualities: I didn't smack my soldiers in the face, didn't swear at them 'po matushkie,' I gave lenient punishments and was fairly well-behaved—nothing more; 300 men, enclosed in a huge, round regimental stable, fought for several days against the whole of Tsarist Russia." In late June, 1918, returned to independent Poland; associated with the group of painters known as Formists. Wrote his first mature plays, *Maciej Korbowa and Bellatrix* and *The New Homeopathy of Evil*. In September finished his main theoretical work, *New Forms in Painting and Misunderstandings Resulting Therefrom*, which he had begun in St. Petersburg in 1917. Part IV, entitled *On the Disappearance of*

Metaphysical Feelings Due to the Development of Society, contains all of Witkiewicz's fundamental social and philosophical theories in three chapters: 1) "The Development of Society," 2) "The Suicide of Philosophy," 3) "The Downfall of Art." Exhibited widely with the Formists and was accepted by them. For the only time in his entire life felt that he was not isolated artistically. In order to distinguish himself from his late father, began signing his works "Witkacy."

1919

New Forms in Painting published in Warsaw. In it he wrote, "I consider that art, along with religion and metaphysics, has been one of the means by which man for centuries has tried to free himself from the anguish of existence in and of itself, the anguish of day-to-day existence. In the past that torment was fear in the face of the unknown and the menacing, today it is rather fear in the face of the pettiness and every-dayness which deluge us from all sides and cover us completely...Art is an escape, the noblest of drugs, which can transport us to another world without bad effects on the health of the intelligence and without a hang-over." Completed *The Pragmatists,* a short Pure Form play. Began translating Joseph Conrad's *Almayer's Folly* into Polish with the help of Conrad's cousin Aniela Zagórska, and under the influence of this novel, sets Act II of his next play, *Tumor Brainiowicz,* in the Malay Archipelago.

1920

In a wild burst of productivity wrote ten plays in one year, including *Tumor Brainiowicz; Philosophers and Martyrs, or the Harlot from Ecbatana; Mister Price, or Tropical Madness; The New Deliverance; They; The Frightful Tutor;* and *Miss Tootli-Pootli* (an operetta). *The Pragmatists* was published in a literary magazine. Exhibited his paintings frequently, developed and published his theory of Pure Form, *An Introduction to the Theory of Pure Form,* which attempted to liberate drama from realistic psychology and story-telling and put it on the same bases as modern art and music. He wrote: "I have the impression that the theatre hasn't yet gone through the period of formal exuberance that the other arts have passed through. It's not dying a natural death but being done in systematically by a kind of monstrous mafia of directors, actors, and managers who give it punishing blows, maltreat it viciously.... In my opinion the task of the theatre is to put the audience in an exceptional state...a state where the mystery of existence can be apprehended emotionally."

1921

Continued playwriting at a feverish pace: *The Anonymous Work* (dedicated to Malinowski); *Kind-Hearted Auntie Walpurgia; Gyubal Wahazar, or Along the Cliffs of the Absurd; Metaphysics of a Two-*

headed Calf; The Water Hen; The Independence of Triangles; and In a
Small Country House. First performances of his plays, Tumor
Brainiowicz (Cracow) and The Pragmatists (Warsaw). Tumor caused a
scandal and was subjected to ridicule by the critics: "It seems that we
are watching and hearing the ravings of a syphilitic in the last stages of
creeping paralysis...Witkiewicz's play is a total absurdity from which
nothing can ever arise. It is an unnatural clinical abortion. It should be
put in alcohol and studied by psychopathologists." Despite the hostility
of critics and the indifference of spectators, Witkacy tried to stage his
plays according to his principles. At various times he wrote, "I'm having
great fun reading the reviews; I'll answer them and crush them as they
deserve." "My contention is not that a play should necessarily be non-
sensical, but only that from now on the drama should no longer be tied
down to pre-existing patterns based solely on real life meaning or on
fantastic assumptions." Published several articles (mainly polemics with
critics), participated in avant-garde exhibits, and painted a large
number of fantastic compositions in which the explosion of colors re-
called tropical foliage. "My paintings," he said, "were not painted in
cold blood, but quite the contrary, in a state of total unconsciousness."

1922

Wrote Jan Maciej Karol Hellcat; Dainty Shapes and Hairy Apes or The
Green Pill; The Cuttlefish; and Aesthetic Sketches. The Water Hen produced professionally in Cracow for only two performances. Argued with
the critics, attacked the Futurists for not being interested in creating
"great and condensed constructions, often being just satisfied with small
compositions and defective forms..."

1923

Married Jadwiga Unrug who lived in Warsaw. Alternated between living
in Warsaw with her and in Zakopane with his mother. Wrote three plays,
Janulka, Daughter of Fizdejko; The Crazy Locomotive; and The Madman and the Nun. Together with his wife, translated The Pragmatists
and The Crazy Locomotive into French. Theatre published a collection
of miscellaneous essays which had appeared in various magazines from
1919 to 1922. Discussed with Szymanowski the possibility of his writing
the music to an opera based on The Madman and the Nun.

1924

Abandoned painting as a pure art forever; felt that this phase of his
artistic creativity was over, writing: "I completed my artistic work in
painting, after I realized that further efforts in that direction would be
fruitless, totally regardless of whatever might be the circumstances of
success or failure, to which I've never paid any attention." Wrote The
Mother and Persy Bestialskaya. Earned his living by painting portraits
(done in pastels), which he regarded only as a commercial activity, and

made controlled experiments with drugs, painting and writing under their influence.

1925

Organized with friends an amateur experimental theatre in Zakopane, "The Formist Theatre," which presented several of his plays, including *The Madman and the Nun* and *The New Deliverance,* directed by the author. Theatre disbanded in 1927. Continued playwriting with *The Beelzebub Sonata, or What Really Happened in Mordovar* and *A Superfluous Man.* Despite an outstanding professional production of *Jan Maciej Karol Hellcat* and his own work with The Formist Theatre as director and scene designer, noisy controversies and hostile reviews continued. More and more disillusioned, turned to philosophical and social issues as well as to the novel, "a bag into which you can cram everything without paying any attention to Pure Form." Started writing *Farewell to Autumn,* a long anti-utopian novel showing the effects of three revolutions, each more drastic than the preceding one, on an alienated group of artists and intellectuals. Despite his lack of success in the theatre, never lost interest in playwriting in the years up to his death. Met and befriended the writer and graphic artist Bruno Schulz.

1926

Attempt to revive *Tumor Brainiowicz* in Warsaw canceled when the actors refused to appear in "such utter nonsense." Wrote two more dramas, *The Baleful Bastard of Verminston* and *The Vampire in the Flask or The Smell of the Bridal Veil.* Exhibited his portraits twice. Continued and finished *Farewell to Autumn.*

1927

Farewell to Autumn published. *Persy Bestialskaya* produced professionally in Łódź for two performances. Władysław Tatarkiewicz, professor of philosophy at Warsaw University, included Witkacy's *Aesthetic Sketches* in his seminar in aesthetics—the first recognition of the value of his work from a professional philosopher. Finished his third novel, *Insatiability,* which like the earlier *Farewell to Autumn,* presents a bewildered young hero whose sexual initiation and private pursuit of the mystery of existence are interrupted by vast social cataclysms and who is finally swallowed by a leveling Communist revolution. In *Insatiability* it is the Chinese Communists who, with their superior organization and discipline, take over the Soviet Union and all of Bolshevized Europe. Started writing his last surviving play and most ambitious work for the theatre, *The Shoemakers* (finished in 1934). Contributed many literary articles to magazines and journals. Began to feel discouraged in the face of opposition from various sources: "In the past I've been the sort of person the English call a 'fighting man'...and I felt there was something worth fighting for. The ideals for which I originally battled I still consider worthy ones, and I haven't abandoned my position. However, many things have changed in recent years."

1928

Wrote the drama, *The End of the World.* Established and published *The Rules of the Witkiewicz Portrait Painting Firm* in which he explained the conditions under which he would undertake the painting of portraits. "Any kind of criticism on the part of the customer is absolutely ruled out," was one of the principal clauses. "The client must be satisfied. All misunderstandings are automatically ruled out." The prominent Polish critic Tadeusz Boy-Żeleński, a close friend of Witkacy, wrote an article about the playwright for the French magazine *Pologne Littéraire* published in Poland. In the article he called Witkiewicz's theatre, "metaphysical buffoonery and supercabaret presenting the sadness, boredom, and despair of modern civilization with a spasmodic laugh." *Metaphysics of a Two-headed Calf* produced professionally in Poznan with inappropriate constructivist sets.

1929

Met Czesława Korzeniowska, the most important woman in the last years of his life.

1930

Insatiability published. Devoted his principal energies to philosophy. Published many articles and continued work on *The Shoemakers.* Delivered various lectures at philosophical and literary conferences and exhibited his portraits. He wrote at this time: "I'm temporarily in an uninteresting state; I'm worn out by a new series of portraits—and by quite strenuous work of correcting manuscripts." Wrote *Nicotine, Alcohol, Cocaine, Peyote, Morphine, and Ether.*

1931

Death of his mother, Maria, to whom he had always remained close. Published twenty articles on philosophy and literature.

1932

Nicotine, Alcohol, Cocaine, Peyote, Morphine, and Ether published—a treatise on drugs based on his own experiences since the mid-1920's. Singled out cigarettes and vodka as the most harmful; the drugs of the masses that destroy the ability of the brain to function clearly. Article, *On Pure Form* (written in 1921), published. Began work on a philosophical novel, *The Only Way Out,* about which he said: "I don't stop to describe slices of real life, but I try to create, perhaps unsuccessfully, a type of intellectual novel that is philosophical as well. The kind of novel I'd like to read myself, except it doesn't exist—therefore I'll write it myself, and not for cash or recognition, since I won't in any case ever have either one or the other." Exhibition of portraits in Cracow. Second edition of *The Rules of the Witkiewicz Portrait Painting Firm* published. Protested with growing bitterness against the incomprehension and hostility that had greeted all his work. "Is it possible that in any civilized country a person could have to fight for a higher level of literature and criticism of the arts and throughout the 12 years during which that struggle lasted be either ignored or kicked around with no holds barred by almost the entire world of literary men and critics?"

1933

The New Deliverance produced in Warsaw and *The Cuttlefish* performed as a forecast of Hitler and Fascism in Cracow at Cricot I, an avant-garde theatre formed by local artists and intellectuals.

1934

Finished work on *The Shoemakers*, wrote articles on philosophy and literature in which he called for a new type of literature and attacked the banality of contemporary Polish writing: "In a period in which the most infernal problems concerning the fate of all humanity are being decided, in a period in which this very humanity in unparalleled torments is being swept into fundamentally different dimensions of social existence, this literature of ours is practically speaking nothing but lukewarm water in which uncooked tripe is floating."

1935

Took a short trip to Lithuania with his wife. *The Concepts and Principles Implied by the Concept of Existence*, his major philosophical work, published in an edition of 650 copies of which 20 were sold. Witkacy commented, "Not a living soul has read it through, it's boring as all hell." *The Frightful Tutor* performed at the Bagatelle Theatre in Cracow by the experimental theatre group "Avant-scene." Given an award by the Polish Academy of Literature, but continued to feel a total outsider: "Every wise and honest man who has read my works and polemical discussions must admit one thing, that I'm not concerned with personal advantage, only with ideas. In this realm of ideas which have been my concern and which I considered would be beneficial for our art and society if put into effect—I am and have been completely isolated and alone." Published an article about Bruno Schulz and also an interview with him in order to bring Schulz's work to public attention.

1936

Attended a philosophical congress in Cracow; carried on polemical discussions with professional philosophers in Poland and in Germany. Fragments of his unpublished work on psychology and national character, *Unwashed Souls,* appeared in journals.

1937

Helped to organize and participated in a "Summer Vacation Program of Literary and Scholarly Lectures" in Zakopane. But even with the help of philosophy, his fits of depression became more frequent and suicide began to obsess him—a motif that had constantly appeared in his life and works over a long period. He wrote to a friend: "I often think about suicide—that it's going to be necessary to bring my life to an end a bit earlier that way, out of a sense of honor, so as not to live to see my own total downfall. Even philosophy, unfortunately, won't see me to the very end, despite the fact that without it life would have been too lousy."

1938

Attempted to revive the Formist Theatre in Zakopane and produce *Metaphysics of a Two-headed Calf* and *The Cuttlefish* under his own direction, but these plans never materialized. Participated again in a "Summer Vacation Program" in Zakopane and delivered three papers. Wrote feverishly and extensively on philosophy. "I'm in a fatal state and seriously think about suicide. I've a feeling that everything is as bad as it possibly can be. And at just such a moment I'm in good form as far as philosophy is concerned and could accomplish a lot." Inspired by his growing fear of the Nazis and the coming Apocalypse, began a new play, *So-called Humanity Gone Mad,* containing Ida Volpone, a Fascist. Published an article, "On the Artistic Theatre," a term which he preferred to "experimental theatre."

1939

Finished *So-called Humanity Gone Mad,* writing 90 pages in two weeks: "For two weeks I was an artist and I couldn't call it a 'positive' feeling. I feel nostalgia for dogs and Petersburg." Completed a social-economic essay 86 pages long. "I'm choosing death...an asphalt road in the sun with trees, ending in a yellow gate after which there is only total dimness and nothingness," he wrote to a friend in June. When the Nazis invaded Poland on September 1, he reported to the mobilization point, but was not accepted for service because of his age and poor health. On September 5, accompanied by Czesława Korzeniowska and several close friends, fled to the East along with thousands of other refugees. While in Brześć (formerly Brest-Litovsk, now Brest in Byelorussia) the city was bombed by the Germans; Witkacy's hearing, already failing, grew worse. With a bad heart and weak legs, he was in no condition to escape the onrushing Nazis. They stopped at the little village of Jeziora. On September 17, the Russians attacked from the East. On September 18, Witkiewicz committed suicide in the wooded countryside by cutting his throat. The following account is from Czesława's diary: "Staś began to slit his wrist with a razor, but the blood somehow didn't flow. He cut the varicose vein on his right leg, but there wasn't any blood there either. I felt weaker and weaker. I couldn't keep from drowsing off. 'Don't fall asleep!, Staś cried out. 'Don't leave me alone!' After a moment, he announced, 'Once you fall asleep, I'll cut my throat.'...I fell asleep again. When I woke up again, it was already morning. His jacket was under my head, he must have put it there. He was lying beside me on his back with his legs drawn up, he had his arms bent at the elbows and pulled up. His eyes and mouth were open...On his face there was a look of relief. A relaxing after great fatigue. I started to yell. To say something to Staś. We both were wet from the morning mist, acorns from the oak had fallen on top of us. I tried to bury him by raking dirt over him with my hands."

Francis Haar

THE BEELZEBUB SONATA (Kennedy Theatre, Honolulu, U.S.A., 1974)
Dir.: Bernard F. Dukore

THE
BEELZEBUB
SONATA

or

WHAT REALLY
HAPPENED IN
MORDOVAR

Motto:
*Musik ist höhere Offenbarung
als jede Religion und Philosophie.*

Beethoven

Dedicated to
Marceli Staroniewicz

1925

CHARACTERS

GRANDMOTHER JULIA—Sixty-seven years old. In a brown dress and glasses.

CHRISTINA CERES—Her granddaughter. Eighteen years old. Dark brunette, very pretty.

ISTVAN SAINT-MICHAEL—A composer. Twenty-one years old. Light chestnut hair.

HIERONYMUS BARON JACKALS—An elegant young man-about-town. Twenty-two years old. Brown hair, very fiery.

BARONESS JACKALS—His mother. Small, thin matron. Fifty eight years old.

TEOBALD RIO BAMBA—A bearded individual, dark hair. Fifty-seven years old.

JOACHIM BALTAZAR DE CAMPOS DE BALEASTADAR—Around fifty years old. Huge, broad-shouldered. Brown hair. Long black beard. Slightly graying hair around the temples. Bold. Planter.

HILDA PUREBRAY—Twenty-nine and a half years old. Red haired. Demonic. Opera singer in Budapest.

ISTVAN'S AUNT—A little old woman, rather commonish.

DON JOSÉ INTRIGUEZ DE ESTRADA—Forty-five years old. Van Dyck beard. Brown hair. Spanish ambassador to Brazil.

SIX FOOTMEN—Big strapping guys with Van Dyck beards, in red livery. Black stockings and braid.

BARONESS JACKALS' FIRST FOOTMAN—Navy-blue livery with red facings. Silver buttons.

(The action takes place in the XXth century in Mordovar, in Hungary.)

Act I

The drawing room in GRANDMOTHER JULIA's *apartment. Modest old-fashioned furnishings. Whitewashed walls. A dark-brown ceiling supported by cross beams. Pictures and miniatures on the walls. Wide French windows upstage open out onto a veranda overgrown with grape-vines turning red. In the distance, mountains covered with fresh snow are visible. A lamp with a green shade is burning.* GRAND-MOTHER JULIA, *in a white bonnet and a brown dress, is sitting at a round table. To the left on the other side of the table,* ISTVAN SAINT-MICHAEL, *dressed in a sports outfit, in a rocking-chair. A pause. Dusk is falling. Later on, a moonlight night.*

ISTVAN: Grandmother, couldn't you tell me a scary story before Christina gets back—waiting's such a bore. What I'd like most is to hear about the Beelzebub sonata that you've been promising me for such a long time now. You remember, grandmother, Christina wouldn't let you finish—she can't stand hearing the same story twice.

GRANDMOTHER: Well, all right then. Now here's what happened: once here in Mordovar there lived a young musician who was exactly like you, only for those times a bit more abnormal. Some people even considered him a moron, but that probably wasn't fair. When I was still a child, I knew people who had seen him. Now then, he was dreaming all the time, from when he was a little child, about writing the Beelzebub sonata, as he called it—he meant the kind of sonata which would outdo all others hands down. And not only Mozart's and Beethoven's sonatas, but absolutely everything that had ever been and could ever be created in music: the kind of sonata that Beelzebub himself would write if he were a composer. Then he went mad: he claimed that he knew

Beelzebub personally, that he traveled through hell with him. He was supposed to have been—Beelzebub that is—a perfectly ordinary gentleman with a black beard, dressed somewhat old-fashionedly, a little like our Brazilian-Portuguese hidalgo, de Campos de Baleastadar.

ISTVAN: Who's he, grandmother? And why did you have to compare him to someone real? I so like fantasy that's not contaminated by the slightest trace of real-life justifications.

GRANDMOTHER: You'd better not go in for things like that, Istvan, or you might go crazy too—the same way he did. I'm old, I'm going to speak to you frankly—it'll make things simpler. Remember, you're not to wrong my Christina—that I won't forgive; dead or alive—I'll avenge her.

ISTVAN: (*Shuddering*) Oh—not dead I hope. (*Seriously.*) Believe me, grandmother, it all just depends on money.

GRANDMOTHER: (*Severely*) I'd rather it depended solely on your conscience.

ISTVAN: Oh—let's not talk about that now; well then, what happened to this Beelzebub? And who is this hidalgo?

GRANDMOTHER: The foremost planter of vineyards in Mordovar. It's obvious you haven't been here very long if you don't know who de Campos is. Now then, the two of them kept on going around everywhere together looking for the entrance to hell which, according to an old Mordovar chronicle, was supposed to be in the vicinity of Mount Czikla. Supposedly that bearded fellow told the young man everything in great detail—he described what hell looks like just as though he'd been there himself any number of times or even lived there. Only he couldn't remember where the entrance was, poor fellow. Ha! ha! They both went mad—that is, no one actually knew who that fellow was. They said many different things about him. And then the young man was found hanging by his own belt at the entrance to an abandoned copper mine shaft on the slopes of Mount Czikla. They say he had the makings of a musical genius.

ISTVAN: That's not a very interesting story, and besides it's too short, grandmother dear—I expected something better. If no one knows who that gentleman was, where he came from and where he disappeared to—I must say I'm not at all taken by any of it. You can make up a dozen stories like that every hour.

GRANDMOTHER: You can make up quantities of them, and much more interesting ones at that. Mordovar's a place expressly created for extraordinary happenings. The mountains are strange and so are the people. And even the people who come here from the outside have to be the same way and not any other—strange too.

ISTVAN: I'm not at all strange. I'm an artist—I'm aware of that. Perhaps I don't fully realize what it means to be an artist—but there's nothing at all strange about being one. I compose because I have to—the same way another person is a bank clerk or a merchant. I write notes the same way I'd write figures in a ledger.

GRANDMOTHER: That's just what you think, Istvan. You're not strange to yourself, because you're totally immersed in the strangeness which you produce all around you—you swim in it like a fish in water; only the fish doesn't produce what it swims in. But others feel this strangeness: I do, Christina does, and even all those people on the other shore of the lake—I mean the permanent residents of course.

ISTVAN: I can't stand them. They sit in judgment on me. They think I'm a sponger, a loafer who's squandering his old aunt's fortune. If I were the piano player in some pub on the other side of the lake, they'd worship me. But since I'm studying in town, they're jealous of me and it's only for that reason that they turn up their noses at me. Our side of the lake is better.

GRANDMOTHER: Perhaps that's why it's so much the worse for you. Nowadays it's better to be from the other side.

ISTVAN: Oh—that's quite enough of that symbolism in the Norwegian style. Chance would have it that a bunch of disgusting parvenus live on that side whereas on this side there are a few individuals who have retained a trace of the old traditions. I'm not saying that out of snobbery—what matters to me is the tradition of truly important things.

GRANDMOTHER: Yes, yes—that's what they all say, but the fact is it's really something quite different. Only I don't know which group to put de Campos in. He's a person who doesn't fall into any known category.

ISTVAN: I'd like to meet him. Although . . . (*He waves his hand contemptuously.*)

GRANDMOTHER: Undoubtedly he'll he coming here to see us today—as he usually does on Saturday. I always tell his fortune for the entire week. But I wouldn't advise you to get overly friendly with him. They say that his relations with young people have not always been devoid of what could be called—if one wanted to—something in the nature of . . .

ISTVAN: (*Impatiently*) Oh—I'm absolutely sure nothing will happen to *me*. I'm completely immunized in that respect. Whatever isn't esthetically beautiful doesn't even exist for me at all.

GRANDMOTHER: Alas—human nature is so constructed that what fills us with disgust in our youth later on becomes a passion which drags us down as low as we can sink. It's calm here in Mordovar the way it is before a storm—and I'm afraid that future events are gathering like threatening banks of clouds on the horizon of our destiny.

ISTVAN: Grandmother, you're the one who always urged me to be coura-
geous and today you're saying that! Today when I so need peace and
quiet.

GRANDMOTHER: What for?

ISTVAN: I don't precisely know.

GRANDMOTHER: Then why are you saying it?

ISTVAN: Perhaps it's because of my undefined attitude towards Christina.
I feel within me a spatial-auditory vision of sounds which I cannot capture in duration. It's as if I held a closed fan in my powerless hands and
could not open it and discover the picture which is already present in
sections on each of its parts. I see the absurd shreds of something, as
though on a chaotically mixed-up puzzle made of blocks, but the whole
of it is hidden from me by some kind of mysterious shadow. Perhaps it's
the Beelzebub sonata that the piano player was dreaming about.
Because really that something that is within me seems to have the form
of a sonata and is somehow almost beyond the human. I'm no
megalomaniac, but ... (*From the right side enter, without knocking,*
BARON HIERONYMUS JACKALS *dressed in a riding outfit with a whip in
his hand.*)

JACKALS: Grandmother: your fortune-telling cards — and be quick about it.
(*Kisses* GRANDMOTHER *on the cheek and nods his head from a distance
to* ISTVAN *who bows without getting up.*) I am, as they say, in the clutches of a demonic woman. It's all so disgustingly trite — as in the
trashiest romantic novel. Well, what's new, Maestro? How are your
masterpieces coming?

ISTVAN: (*In an offended tone of voice*) First of all, I'm not a Maestro, and
secondly, I haven't created any masterpieces yet ...

JACKALS: (*Not at all taken aback*) Excessive modesty, Maestro. How about
dropping in on us for dinner sometime — my mother loves music with a
passion — even yours: futuristic as it is. (*Shuffles the cards while he is
talking.*) I wonder what our legendary Modovar Beelzebub sonata
would sound like in a futuristic transposition. All right, grandmother,
you can begin. (*He gives the cards to* GRANDMOTHER *who begins to lay
them out for a fortune telling. Behind the French windows to the veranda* RIO BAMBA *stands unnoticed, with a glowing cigar in his mouth. He is
dressed in a long black Spanish cape.*)

ISTVAN: (*Belatedly*) Thank you, Baron, but I always eat dinner at home ...

JACKALS: Oh, how depressing ... Well, what about it, grandmother? That
queen of spades is undoubtedly my demon, next to the nine of
hearts — for the sexual feelings. (*Hums and then recites.*):

A thousand loves I've had from different spheres,
A thousand loves — is that beyond your reach,
You guttersnipes with just one woman each?
A thousand loves — that's why there now appears
A heart forever when my fortune's told,
Surrounded always by those spades so bold.
Each one of them was a betrayal to be
Of her, the one and only, the true she,
Who's non-existent, but just the one for me.

ISTVAN: Aren't you ashamed to recite such a doggerel? No doubt it's your own handiwork.

GRANDMOTHER: Istvan, be polite. The Baron isn't accustomed to being treated that way. Anyhow, the thought behind that poem is quite nice.

ISTVAN: Poetry is not the expression of thoughts in rhyme, but the creation of a synthesis of images, sounds and semantic meanings in a certain form. But if the form is nauseating, then even the finest thought can make us sick.

GRANDMOTHER: (*Threateningly*) Istvan!

JACKALS: No cause for alarm — the Maestro's in a foul mood — that's why he's talking so pedantically, but in such bad taste.

ISTVAN: (*Rising*) If you call me Maestro once more . . .

JACKALS: Then tomorrow you'll probably be a corpse, Mr. Saint-Michael. I've hit an ace on a pendulum at a distance of thirty-five paces, and with a sabre I don't have an equal in the whole district. All right, grandmother, go ahead.

(ISTVAN *sits down. From the left side* CHRISTINA *runs in, in a green dress and an orange and black shawl.*)

GRANDMOTHER: Get these young men to make up, Chris. They were almost at each other's throats.

CHRISTINA: How can I get them to make up when I know that *I* am actually the cause of their quarrel?

GRANDMOTHER: Chris!

(CHRISTINA *becomes embarrassed.*)

JACKALS: You're mistaken, Christina, I'm in the power of a demonic woman. I came to ask your grandmother for advice.

CHRISTINA: (*Very embarrassed*) What's that? Oh — anyhow I don't believe it. It's revolting.

ISTVAN: (*Getting up precipitously*) I can't stand this any longer. I've got to leave. Baron, tomorrow we duel with pistols. The meeting place — the old mine shaft at the foot of Mount Czikla. Seconds are unnecessary.

JACKALS: At your service. However, I'll bring a second: my game keeper.

ISTVAN: As you wish — I don't care in the least. After all, I'm only doing this for my own personal artistic goals. You're nothing but a totally accidental pretext.

JACKALS: Superfluous confessions.

CHRISTINA: They've started to go mad! Hieronymus, how can a cipher like you, such a well-dressed, sharp-shooting and impeccably-mannered cipher, dare deprive Hungary of her future glory!

JACKALS: But Christina, I only came here to have my fortune told. I had no intention of offending the Maestro. I swear that I'm no rival of his for you. Still, I am compelled to duel with him.

CHRISTINA: You see, Istvan, you're the one who's making all the trouble. You've got to stay — we'll play the piano, we'll improvise four hands the way we did last Sunday at your aunt's.

ISTVAN: I was drunk that evening. All in all that was an unfortunate day for me, let's not say any more about it. That's when I fell in love with you. (*Suddenly in another tone of voice, with sudden decision.*) Well, all right — I'm staying. But on the condition that you don't ask Jackals to stay. It's not fitting for me to be seen with him socially.

JACKALS: Oh — what excessive tact. And in any event, it's unnecessary: I'm occupied this evening. Well, how about it, grandmother, am I ever going to find out what's going to happen to me and whether I'll succeed in subduing my demon?

GRANDMOTHER: Frightful things are in store for you, young man. Tonight you'll murder a woman with flaming red hair, at daybreak you'll shoot yourself, towards evening on the following day your mother will take her own life. Unless you stay with us — then perhaps you'll be able to save all these people and yourself as well. The fates are busy tonight.

CHRISTINA: I'll keep you company, Hieronymous — even till morning.

GRANDMOTHER: How can you . . .

CHRISTINA: To save this young man from certain death, I think I can sit up with him till eight in the morning — at eight-thirty I have to go to the Lycée. I see nothing wrong in that. As it is, I wouldn't be able to sleep tonight. I'm somehow abnormally excited. You won't hold it against me, Istvan.

ISTVAN: (*Gloomily*) I don't know about that.

JACKALS: I don't want any new misunderstandings to arise because of me. As a rule I am too frank with the wrong people. So be it. I must make clear to all of you that I am not in love with Christina and even if I were, I would never marry her — I am a snob who is conscious of his own snobbery.

CHRISTINA: Yes, but at any moment you might marry Miss Purebray, a a singer from the Budapest opera, since that would be scandalous enough for you.

JACKALS: Why mention names right away — it's so vulgar.

GRANDMOTHER: Unfortunately, all Mordovar knows about it.

CHRISTINA: Once you've divorced her and surrounded yourself with an aura of scandalous legend, you'll give your exhausted heart to some young lady from a good family for purposes of propagating the race and transmitting property.

JACKALS: Given the constant threat of revolution and the expropriation of property that will follow, those questions play less and less of a role in the marriages of our social sphere.

ISTVAN: All that's so boring.

JACKALS: Oh, yes — I can shoot myself at any moment: I'm distracted to the point of madness. (*Pulls out a revolver.*) No one understands me. Oh, if you only knew! (*He points the revolver at his temple.* ISTVAN *springs at him and tries to take it away from him. A struggle.*)

ISTVAN: Don't deprive me of the possibility of getting satisfaction. And don't twist my arm: I'm a musician. Anyhow, none of that will do any good.

(ISTVAN *wrests the revolver away from him and puts it in his pocket. At that same moment enter through the French window* RIO BAMBA, *wrapped up in a cape, with a cigar in his mouth.*)

RIO BAMBA: (*Without taking off his black hat with its gigantic brim; the cigar constantly clenched between his teeth*) It's agreeable to relax a bit in this Mordovar of yours after adventures on the south seas and in tropical jungles — but only then. Life here on a permanent basis must have a deadly effect: simply debilitating. Istvan, I must inform you that I am your uncle. Rio Bamba is my name now and anyone who calls me anything else will pay dearly for it. I count on the discretion of everyone here.

ISTVAN: Oh, uncle, I remember that night on board the "Sylvia" as though it were yesterday — it was an old war hulk converted into a merchant

ship; I was five years old then. We were going to Rio and you, the pro-
digal uncle, were puffing away on your everlasting cigar, just like now.

RIO BAMBA: I am a character from a forgotten dream. But Mordovar has
always been alive in me. I had to come back here. I owe this opportunity
to my partner, Joachim Baltazar de Campos, who'll be arriving at any
moment.

ISTVAN: Our poor Mordovar invaded by Brazilian planters. But what do
we care about the experiences of ordinary people? With artists experiences become transformed into something else and transported into
another dimension, and that's why every detail of an artist's life has such
a tremendous value and why their biographers are concerned with these
details to a ridiculous extent.

JACKALS: He's already dreaming about his future biographer who's going
to do research on the mystery of this evening as it relates to his musical
compositions. Art is a plaything no better or worse than any other. Putting artists on a pedestal in our times is a proof of our decadence.

ISTVAN: I'm not answering you since for the moment we are enemies, according to the silliest of social conventions that has ever existed. Honor
is a relic of the past — nowadays no one can give an exact definition of
that concept.

JACKALS: Yet you're still talking to me. And despite what you say about
honor, you're going to fight me.

ISTVAN: Solely and exclusively for my artistic goals. I need some kind of
shock to release from inside what I have to write. I'm a terrible
coward — that's why I choose fear which chance has sent me. If I were a
sex-fiend, I'd choose to give up my one and only love-affair.

JACKALS: And if you were a gourmet, you'd decide to go on a hunger-strike.
Fear, sex and hunger — these are the three causes to which materialistic
and pseudo-scientific bird-brains would like to reduce religion.

ISTVAN: They'll never succeed. Religion, just as much as philosophy, is an
intellectually inspired working out of certain feelings which I call
metaphysical.

RIO BAMBA: That's all very well and good — but, gentlemen, consider if you
will the fact that I have returned to Mordovar.

JACKALS: What has that got to do with what we're talking about?

RIO BAMBA: Perhaps more than you think. But I don't have any idiotic
notions about sticking to the subject. Now then: to all appearances, I
was better off in Brazil. Yet I couldn't stay there; I took advantage of
Joachim's mania for Hungarian wine and these local mountains and I

came here. Besides, I must tell you an important secret: the person who ruined my life was grandmother Julia. Even though she was older than me, I embezzled funds for her, and I am still doing penance for it.

GRANDMOTHER: Yes, alas—I was his mistress and he was the father of my late daughter. In my youth I was a moral monster, but I was so physically attractive that people slashed their wrists because of me.

RIO BAMBA: That's right—she's telling the truth.

GRANDMOTHER: Your father was one of them, Baron. (*Deep twilight; the snow-covered mountains shine in the evening's orange glow, and later in the cold moonlight.*) So now we live through this night of memories, leaning over a well from which we can draw forth whatever we wish: bane and gall, or nectar and ambrosia, or even a cure for the pain in our souls, for our longing and the torment of conscience.

ISTVAN: Yes—it's a typical Mordovar evening: the mountains are ablaze with the orange glow of twilight and the earth truly seems a strange planet, not a place of everyday triviality.

RIO BAMBA: That's it exactly: you expressed it wonderfully, my nephew. I wanted to interest all of you in a fact without general significance: to have you all share my personal sensations—by making you feel the magical enchantment of my own memories. But that can't be done. Each one of us lives enclosed in his own world as in a prison and thinks that the same evening cloud he sees *as he meditates on eternity* is also floating across someone else's sky—yet for that other person it may be a starless night filled with debauchery, or a revoltingly bright noon, in which a business deal has just been concluded.

JACKALS: Rio Bamba, old boy—you have expressed quite simply and somewhat imprecisely a very important but nonetheless banal fact: the absolute isolation of every single individual in the universe.

ISTVAN: Oh—if I could only capture that in musical sounds. But I jot down notes on the staves the way a book-keeper jots down figures in his ledgers, and my work is dead for me, despite the fact it pleases others. It's well-made music all right, but it's not art. Oh, now I understand that fellow who wanted to compose a sonata which Beelzebub himself might have written! I've suddenly grasped it in a flash. (*Enter through the French window upstage* BALEASTADAR *in a black cape and black pointed hat with a broad brim; following him, momentarily hidden from the others' view by his imposing figure, comes* HILDA PUREBRAY *in a black fur coat without a hat.*) I don't want life to be expressed by sounds, I want the musical notes themselves to live and fight among themselves over something unknown. Oh, that's something no one will ever understand!!

BALEASTADAR: But suppose I understand it already? Suppose what you're thinking of actually takes place because of me? (*They all turn towards him.*) Good evening. Please, don't disturb yourselves. I don't want to spoil this truly Mordovar atmosphere, possible only here in these mountains.

GRANDMOTHER: There's your Beelzebub, Istvan. (*Catches sight of* HILDA *whom no one had yet noticed.*) What sort of alien presence has found its way into our little gathering? Perhaps she will actually help fulfill my prophecies.

ISTVAN: Don't play innocent, grandmother. That's Jackals', demon. A marvelous woman — Miss Purebray — I only know her from the opera. She has a phenomenal voice.

JACKALS: Hilda! Why have you come here? The one place where I could stop thinking about you, and you poison it for me with your presence, reminding me of the whole reality of my downfall. I'd just begun to think I'd been successful in transposing it into an artistic Mordovar mood.

HILDA: Shut up — there are strangers here. No one's asking you what you feel. There are more important things.

ISTVAN: Her voice is so different when she's not singing . . .

HILDA: (*To* JACKALS, *pointing to* CHRISTINA) What do I see here — some innocent little lambikins that you're seducing with the poison I injected into you. Apparently you need women like that, you good-for-nothing. Oh — how unhappy I am! That's how this clown consoles himself instead of conquering my soul, which little men can never reach.

JACKALS: Hilda! You're forgetting yourself. Now it's my turn to tell you: there are strangers present.

HILDA: Not to be able to humble oneself before the man who arouses one's wildest passions — is there anything more abominable for a woman of my sort?

BALEASTADAR: (*Puts his hand on her shoulder*) But Hilda, you were already on the right track. Remember our first conversation in the vineyard by the light of the afternoon sun.

JACKALS: Have you already bought this bitch? (*Points to* HILDA.) Because, make no mistake about it, I'm the only one she finds attractive.

BALEASTADAR: No, I have not bought her and I don't intend to, although I could outbid you easily enough, Mr. Jackals. There's something far more interesting in the wind. Even the stupidest legend contains some particle of truth; it's based on some form of reality, no matter how symbolic.

ISTVAN: Tell us frankly, why did you come here all the way from Brazil?

CHRISTINA: (*Bursting out laughing*) Ha! ha! ha! In other words: who knows whether you're not Beelzebub—that's priceless!

BALEASTADAR: Don't laugh, my child: there are many, many strange things in the world which city dwellers have long since forgotten. Sometimes, in the depths of the mountains, or on the boundless prairies, something comes rolling by and, catching hold of something else, creates the tangled web of a new ultrasurreal possibility. To unwind such a web . . .

ISTVAN: (*Impatiently*) Then who are you, actually?

BALEASTADAR: I am Joachim Baltazar de Campos de Baleastadar, a breeder of bulls in Brazil, but here—in this country of yours—a planter of vineyards. I am also an unsuccessful pianist—unsuccessful because of a certain love-affair which has nevertheless created something within me that all the fame and concerts in the world could never have given me.

ISTVAN: Well—is that all?

BALEASTADAR: Don't think I want to mislead you. But I've been strengthened in my belief by meeting this woman here, today of all days, three days after your arrival, Mr. Saint-Michael. It's time to break off this Mordovar magic with its peaceful moods; otherwise until the end of your life you'll go on jotting down your little musical notations which others will admire, but you will never realize yourself as an artist.

ISTVAN: Could you really be the Beelzebub that grandmother has been promising? I don't believe in that dimension of strangeness. Art is the strangest thing.

BALEASTADAR: But not the kind you're creating. That's common, ordinary strangeness, the kind so many artists nowadays delude themselves with. They're successful—that goes without saying, but in two hundred years no one will want to play their music, or read their books or look at their pictures. They exist only to make people thoroughly sick of both art and life. Nothing will remain of them.

ISTVAN: I don't want to be one of them. I'd rather stop creating. Even though that would be frightful torture.

BALEASTADAR: You needn't give up anything yet. Rather risk everything —either-or . . .

ISTVAN: But how? Risk what? I'm totally helpless, I don't know where to begin. Should I climb a cliff somewhere on Mount Czikla and throw myself over the edge like an idiot or run out in front of the Kosice express when it's going at top speed or drink five litres of Czech brandy—

these are the available risks at my disposal.

BALEASTADAR: So you're a coward? Is that it?

ISTVAN: Yes, I am — so what? Stop trying to embarrass me.

JACKALS: I'm beginning to take a new interest in life. Even though I'm suffering atrociously on account of that copper-haired beast, for the moment I'm not thinking about it so virulently.

RIO BAMBA: Why not try beating her, Baron? That works in novels some-times — perhaps it will work in real life too.

JACKALS: I've tried it — a cold-blooded beating doesn't do any good. You don't understand me, my good Rio Bamba. She is mine and she refuses me nothing. And yet I still can't subdue her. I have no idea what her soul is like, I don't even know if she has one. And how can you subdue something that doesn't exist?

ISTVAN: Gentlemen, couldn't we talk about these matters later on? There are really far more interesting things right at hand which may indirectly affect you as well. *Everything* may be transformed in a way no one has ever seen before.

BALEASTADAR: Yes — I'm not lying, I'm not speaking symbolically, and I don't believe in anything, even though here in this world, I feel, hmm — how can I put it — quite strange — but not so much as to start believ-ing . . .

CHRISTINA: In what? That you're Beelzebub?

BALEASTADAR: Let's say that — for lack of something better.

CHRISTINA: These are the hopeless ravings of maniacs.

BALEASTADAR: Wait a minute, wait a minute! There's no need to be exces-sively realistic about life. When Rio Bamba, Istvan's uncle, first told me that whole supposed Mordovar legend of yours, I only laughed at it. But then I began to mull it over again and again, endlessly, until something finally snapped inside me, something I knew about unconsciously as though in a dream. My wife stopped existing for me even though — but that's another story . . .

GRANDMOTHER: That's it — exactly!

BALEASTADAR: Don't interrupt! I felt something strange inside me, a kind of conviction that somehow I had known all this from before, and that I had to see this part of the country. I immediately had my agents buy me a vineyard here, and for three weeks now I've been waiting here for Istvan.

CHRISTINA: Here's your Beelzebub, Istvan. There's no getting around it.

BALEASTADAR: (*Without paying any attention to her*) In the last analysis
it doesn't matter whether I'm Beelzebub or not, a question that so
preoccupies Christina. The only thing that matters is that sonata.
Actually, I am a pianist, only I missed my calling in life. But I always
dreamed about someone who would incarnate my ideas — which ones I
don't even know myself — I feel them inside me like a huge charge of
explosives for which there is no fuse or match.

CHRISTINA: Exactly, there's no match, and yet he comes here all the way
from Brazil!

ISTVAN: Just you wait, Christina.

CHRISTINA: A new candidate for going nuts . . .

BALEASTADAR: (*Finishing what he had to say*) And when I found out that
there was a musician in the neighborhood and that he was the nephew
of my old friend Rio Bamba to boot, I knew all there was to know.
Because why did his uncle become my steward, why did Istvan, a little
boy of seven, run away from Rio to Budapest right after he got there?
Eh? Those aren't accidents. You only have to have the courage to try.

CHRISTINA: To try whether you can't succeed in going crazy by accident —
for lack of anything better to do.

BALEASTADAR: We can call it that if we like. But if we all go crazy that way
and everything turns into something else, even though our relative posi-
tions remain the same, that is, if we simply change the center of coordinates . . .

CHRISTINA: I've just taken analytical geometry and your comparisons don't
impress me. Changing the center of coordinates used to be called simply
going nuts.

BALEASTADAR: (*Threateningly, irritated*) That's enough of that silly girlish
giggle-gaggle! This evening is no accident. I was waiting for all this
while I was still down there in Brazil. During the sweltering nights in
town, when the hot wind carried the sounds of the guitar from the
street, or in the quiet of the pampas when my family had long since
gone to bed, I dreamed about these wretched mountains of yours and
the caved-in mine and about you, Istvan.

ISTVAN: But if this comes true, I mean: if I write the real Beelzebub
sonata, perhaps we'll all come out in some other dimension.

BALEASTADAR: If I succeed in instilling in you the strangeness of the music
which is potentially within me, then perhaps you will create what you've
been dreaming about. I can't do it: I don't have the talent. That's why
in the legend they talk about the sonata that Beelzebub would [*the stress
on "would"*] have composed if and so on and so forth . . . It's not a lack

of belief in the possibility of his really existing, only in the possibility of his composing the sonata—even given the strongest inclinations in that direction.

CHRISTINA: It seems to me Beelzebub couldn't possibly be a person of real talent; he could do everything, but it would all be counterfeit.

BALEASTADAR: A person! But he was able to achieve the truth of evil through others, at the cost of destroying their lives. On the other hand, in art he should be able to create greatness—but only in our times, in an epoch of artistic perversity. *Up to now* there was no greatness in that dimension.

CHRISTINA: You talk about this Beelzebub so convincingly that at times I'm really starting to believe in his existence.

(*A violent gale suddenly starts to rage. A pause.*)

GRANDMOTHER: You've ruined the prediction, and the cards have never failed me before.

BALEASTADAR: You see, grandmother, whenever I've had my fortune told, it's never come true.

JACKALS: Part of it must come true. I won't stand for any more of this humiliation. If I don't do it, I'll die in a state of moral collapse a hundred times worse than anything that might happen later on.

(*He pulls the revolver out of* ISTVAN's *pocket, while* ISTVAN *is lost in thought, and shoots* MISS PUREBRAY, *who falls to the floor.* JACKALS *runs out through the door to the right in the midst of blasts of wind from the growing autumn mountain storm.*)

GRANDMOTHER: And the word became flesh! In the name of the Father, the Son, and the Holy Ghost—give grandmother a kummel toast.

CHRISTINA: My God—grandmother has gone crazy!

RIO BAMBA: Look after that person, Chris. I'll bring grandmother back to her senses with memories of the past.

(*He strokes* GRANDMOTHER's *hair and whispers something to her with his cigar between his teeth.*)

HILDA: (*Sitting on the floor*) My God, he'll kill himself. I love him so. What does he want from me? He's got it into his head that he doesn't know my soul. Who'll cure him of that obsession if I die?

(*She suddenly falls over backwards.* CHRISTINA *feels her pulse and checks to see whether she's still breathing.*)

CHRISTINA: I think she's dead—I don't hear her breathing. She's lovely as an angel! It can't be that what they say about her is true.

BALEASTADAR: And so the evening has begun. Come along, Istvan, let's go to the mine in Mount Czikla. And if we don't find hell there, we'll find quite enough of it within ourselves to outdo all the Beelzebubs in the world with our sonata. I don't believe in it myself, but some secret force superior to me and to everything else forces me to talk this way.

ISTVAN: Oh, what happiness it is to live and suffer in Mordovar! I feel something joining the previously isolated sounds into a theme which I still cannot hear. I'd like to plunge to the very bottom of moral wretchedness and from down below look at my work piling up on top of me like a gigantic tower in the rays of the spectral setting sun. Then dusk could fall in the valleys of my life.

BALEASTADAR: Come along—this is precisely the right moment. But remember: if we don't find hell either there or in ourselves, and it turns out that I'm purely and simply an ordinary Brazilian planter and would-be pianist, then neither of us will breathe a single word of complaint. We'll drink our morning coffee at the railroad station at Uj-Mordovar and go home to bed. And then ordinary life will resume again as though nothing had ever happened. Promise?

ISTVAN: Promise.

(*They go out into the midst of the gale through the center door.* ISTVAN *takes his black overcoat and gray sports cap from the coat-stand by the door.*)

CHRISTINA: Things have got off to a nice start. The only good thing about it is that Jackals has totally stopped appealing to me.

RIO BAMBA: (*Solemnly*) Let's not put a stop to this evening, this truly Mordovar evening in which the strange and the commonplace are intertwined in a marvelous garland of moments, eternal in their beauty. Oh, the commonplace be praised—without you there would be nothing strange in this world! Chris, pour some wine!

(*The wind blows more and more powerfully.* CHRISTINA *gets up and goes to the left.*)

Act II

A subterranean vault in an abandoned mine in Czikla, fixed up like a comparatively fantastic hell. Facing the audience, a recess between pillars. A door behind the left pillar on the left side. Bizarre chairs and sofas. Everything in black and red. The dominant tone is that of the demonic frippery found in public places of amusement, plus something really unpleasant in the highest degree and even menacing. A piano on a small platform in the recess between pillars. Through the door to the left, enter BALEASTADAR *and* ISTVAN. *The former dressed as in Act I, and the latter has on a black overcoat with the collar turned up and a gray sports cap.*

BALEASTADAR: Now you see, Istvan, even though it's not quite all we could ask for—there is *something* to all this. To be sure, this hell does suggest a bit too strongly some Parisian cabaret or even the latest refurbishings in the Salon di Gioja in Rio, but there is *something* to it—no doubt about that. As far as I can make out, we're in the chamber for psychological tortures.

ISTVAN: It reminds me of one of those so-called demonic chambers in Ös-Buda-Vár in Pest.

BALEASTADAR: Yes, that's right: it isn't a first-class establishment. But I think that the kind of hell we dreamed about is not only unattainable in reality, it's even unimaginable. But just think: to enter a buried mine shaft in the depths of Mount Czikla on the outskirts of Mordovar and to find a cabaret there in the Parisian and Budapest style—that too might be considered a certain kind of miracle. Don't you agree?

ISTVAN: (*Reluctantly, hiding his fear*) Yes, of course. Still, I do feel a bit different. That evening seems to me to be at least some five years ago. We left at eight, and now it's midnight — four hours: time has dragged terribly for me.

BALEASTADAR: For me too — but that's not it. Quite simply you're afraid, aren't you?

ISTVAN: (*Evasively*) Something is swirling around at the very bottom of my being. I've turned into a cave full of crooked passageways where ghosts lie in wait. But it still doesn't have any connection with music yet. Infinity separates my own form from what it's to be filled with ...

BALEASTADAR: Can't you keep your mouth shut for a while — we'll soon see what's going to happen next.

(*From behind the fantastic purple sofa to the right there appear two* FOOTMEN *in red livery, with Van Dyck beards. Mephistophelian appearance. They go over to* BALEASTADAR *and speak in unison, bowing.*)

FOOTMEN: Monseigneur!

(*They remain bowed over.*)

BALEASTADAR: (*To* ISTVAN) That's how the proprietors of some cabaret in Paris — "le Chat Noir" if I'm not mistaken — address each and every customer. Can it really be that hell, even one located inside the Mordovar mountains, is nothing but some stupid sort of fun-house? That would really be something too idiotic for words. Too bad we didn't go instead to the Magas Cafehaz on the other side of the lake for a quiet talk. I don't feel the slightest bit like Beelzebub.

FIRST FOOTMAN: Your Highness, look at yourself from behind. (*He places a mirror appropriately.* BALEASTADAR *twists about, feels himself from behind under his cape and looks at himself. The* SECOND FOOTMAN *removes his cape for him.* BALEASTADAR *is revealed to be holding his own thick devil's tail in his hand, a tail like a rat's, but ending in a triangular metal hook.*)

BALEASTADAR: What the devil! I never noticed that before. (*He looks at his tail carefully.*)

SECOND FOOTMAN: The Prince of Darkness has to have a tail. And that kind of swearing is considered bad form here.

BALEASTADAR: This is incredible! But this tail is dead, even though it's growing out of me. And you both have tails — are yours dead too?

FIRST FOOTMAN: Even with today's technical advances hell has to be shown as it really is. In the old days it was better. But we don't tolerate any trickery even though if we wanted to ...

BALEASTADAR: (*Suddenly in a completely different tone: imperious, Beelzebubian, and getting more and more so all the time*) Enough! Supper for nine—there'll be more of us any minute. But first of all: an ax and a chopping block! Look lively! Get a move on.

FOOTMEN: Yes, Your Highness! At your orders, Your Highness! (*They run behind the pillars to the left.*)

ISTVAN: (*Through his tears*) You're beginning to enter into your role, Mr. Baltazar.

BALEASTADAR: What else can I do—we shall see what will come of it. A wild strength is rearing up in my entrails. I'm swelling hard as steel. I'm bursting with a furious hatred totally without object. That, it would seem, is pure evil. (*The* FOOTMEN *bring in the chopping block and ax and place them in the middle of the stage.*) And now, Istvan, you're going to chop off my tail—I can't stand third-rate demonic effects, out of keeping with the general situation. Chop away—I wonder if it's going to hurt.

(ISTVAN *puts* BALEASTADAR's *tail on the chopping block and takes aim.*)

FIRST FOOTMAN: (*To the* SECOND) Chebnazel, there's something suspicious about this.

(ISTVAN *chops. The tail falls off.* BALEASTADAR *screams with pain. Blood pours out of the chopped-off part and the stump.* BALEASTADAR *sits down on the sofa side-ways.*)

SECOND FOOTMAN: (*To the first*) You know what I think, Azdrubot, it's the first sign of his authenticity. Who else but the Prince of Darkness himself would dare to do something like that? (*To* BALEASTADAR.) Sir, say those four words again: you know the ones?

BALEASTADAR: (*Getting up*) Banabiel, Abiel, Chamon, Azababrol!! I don't even know what I'm saying myself. But it's full of some sinister meaning. I am already *on the other side!*

SECOND FOOTMAN: (*To the* FIRST) Azdrubot, hadn't we better fall down on our faces. It's him. At last hell has its Beelzebub.

(*They both fall down on their faces in front of* BALEASTADAR.)

FIRST FOOTMAN: (*Lying on the ground*) It isn't always this way. Sometimes we have to wait a long time for such a one to be born among men. You alone, Sir, have had the courage to believe what others think is total nonsense. You are the one, you are the one! By that very fact you raise us, poor flunkeys in a cabaret, to the dignity of true devils.

BALEASTADAR: Azdrubot is right. Stand over here by the chopping block, boys, and put your tails on it, side by side. (*The* FOOTMEN *execute the order immediately.*) Chop away, Istvan: let's finish this disgusting comedy once and for all. Underground cabaret or modern hell—what's the difference—it's got to be in good taste. Down with ignorance, obscurantism, and superstition! Chop away! (ISTVAN *chops, the tails fall off. The* FOOTMEN *make terrible faces due to the pain, but remain in place.*) And now take away that ax and chopping block and if there's anyone else in your crew with a tail—chop it off immediately. Understand? And see that supper is ready in ten minutes. Forward, march!

FOOTMEN: Yes, Sir, Your Highness! At your orders! (*They run off with the chopping block and ax behind the pillar to the left.*)

ISTVAN: This hell is way behind the times: I don't know whether you'll be able to fit in here with your exuberant temperament.

BALEASTADAR: All that's going to change right now. We still have impenetrable sloughs of psychological horrors ahead of us. Naturally, we'll simplify because of lack of time.

(*Through the door on the left side four other* FOOTMEN *[without tails] carry in three dark red coffins and place them in a row along the left side. During this action,* BALEASTADAR *speaks.*)

BALEASTADAR: Most likely those are yesterday's corpses. You know, Istvan, it's already the next day. Everything's going faster and faster. At first you won't be able to keep up with events, but then you'll get used to it. Life here depends on constantly catching up with and then outdistancing oneself. (*To the* FOOTMEN.) Open the coffins!

(*The* FOOTMEN *begin to pry the coffins open.*)

ISTVAN: How I wish I could relive that last Mordovar evening! I wasn't ready for it then.

BALEASTADAR: You prematurely crossed over a certain dividing line which great politicians, artists or thinkers sometimes reach only in their sixties or seventies. But you're a musician—music makes its appearance in childhood and doesn't demand maturity.

ISTVAN: Oh—so many people react to music with what I'd call "the howling dog reaction." A dog howls exactly the same way whether you play him Beethoven or Richard Strauss—he howls because his feelings are stirred up by the sheer noise of the sounds, by their emotional and artistically irrelevant factor. I must go all the way to pure music.

BALEASTADAR: You'll get there, but first you have to give vent to all your feelings in musical form. It's by working them over, pursuing them relentlessly, that you'll acquire your own style and Pure Form. *Here* it can be done through an inner process, without having to put useless little notations on the staves so as to give adolescent girls and hysterical women thrills. Hell — even one like this — is a marvelous incubator for an unfledged musician.

ISTVAN: When will it happen, and how? Am I supposed to earn my living as a wretched piano player in this cabaret hell, throwing to the diabolical rabble what I hold most precious in life: my feelings?

BALEASTADAR: He doesn't understand a thing, the creature! What's happened to your ambition to create the Beelzebub sonata that would beat the world-wide record for musical monstrosity? Have you forgotten about that already? You'll understand it all once I show you. (*To the* FOOTMEN.) Hurry up there, you satans. (*The corpses of* HILDA *and the* BARON JACKALS *appear in the coffins. The* FOOTMEN *start to pry open the third coffin.*) Possibilities are all I can give you. I'll never write my sonata myself even though I know all there is to know about it. You will write it through my inspiration, but it will be your own. The evil spirit, barren in its essence, can never be satiated: it must have mediums — interpreters of its murky conceptions and that's why its work will never be what it ought to have been.

ISTVAN: Then must I choose between life and art? For the voluptuous pleasure of creating musical values must I give up the immediate experience of life? Will it all be dead for me even before it's born?

BALEASTADAR: That's what all great artists have always done, appearances sometimes quite to the contrary. That's why the madness of artists, so fascinating to ordinary people and arousing such envy, is nothing but the bitter aftertaste left by the true events which have taken place in their inner world of imaginary greatness — a pure construction for its own sake. In the past this happened within the sphere of good; now that art is coming to an end, it has to take place in the realm of evil and darkness.

ISTVAN: I'd still like to get my fill of happiness in the world of feelings.

BALEASTADAR: Too late. Unless you want to continue being a would-be artist, the vilest thing in the world. And what's more a would-be artist in your own eyes, not for the pack of howling dogs.

ISTVAN: I don't want that — not for anything. Let the sacrifice be made once and for all. The only thing that concerns me at this moment is how it's going to happen.

BALEASTADAR: Quite simply, like everything in hell. Here, we don't stand on ceremony with feelings. It will only be a kind of abridgement of life, not something qualitatively different from it. Not even Beelzebub himself can create that.

ISTVAN: Perhaps I won't miss that other world so much after all? Perhaps

I'm just pretending to myself? Why is it impossible to experience any feeling all the way, why are states of feeling so contradictory? Everything has always seemed the past even before it's taken shape as the present. And to suffer such remorse about those I've cheated vilely, repaying their truth with the falsehood of my defective — oh, they're not even feelings — but rather psychic states.

BALEASTADAR: (*All of a sudden threateningly*) Enough of that gushing! (*Claps his hands; two* FOOTMEN *come dashing in.*) Get those corpses out! Have them ready for me at once! (*The* FOOTMEN *have just pried open the coffin in which the* BARONESS JACKALS *is lying dressed in black and violet.*)

FOOTMEN: At your orders, Your Highness!

(*The six of them start to work taking out the corpses and placing them in chairs. The corpses are stiff and have their eyes closed.*)

ISTVAN: (*In a trembling voice*) Mr. Baltazar, I'm afraid of you. You're so strange and frightening — let me out of here.

BALEASTADAR: Shut up, you clown! Do you want to hang by your own suspenders at the entrance to the mine shaft, like that other musician? Even before creating the works which will justify your miserable existence? Afterwards you can hang yourself to your heart's content. If you run away now, you'll never be able to lead a normal existence again.

ISTVAN: I don't want anything, Mr. Baltazar. I only want to go home to my aunt. I just want one more nice Mordovar evening to come back again, with everything calm and peaceful . . . I want to play those old preludes of mine, read a novel, and fall asleep. And to dream of that beloved Mordovar of ours, heightened, the way it was in the past. I won't ever do it again. Forgive me, Sir.

BALEASTADAR: (*Glaring at* ISTVAN *with a devastating look*) I am not Sir, I am Beelzebub, Prince of Darkness. Address me as: Your Highness. Understand, you might-have-been?

ISTVAN: (*Falling to his knees*) It's frightening here . . . I don't want anything . . . Just to get out of here . . .

BALEASTADAR: (*In a terrifying voice*) In you I mortalize original sin by the artistic creativity which I kindle in you. Through art alone humanity remembers that everything in Existence is self-contradictory. Without art there'd be no life for me any more nowadays. I have no work to do among cattle reduced to mechanized pulp. But as long as art exists *I* exist, and by creating metaphysical evil I satiate myself with existence on this planet. On the moons of Jupiter they have their own Beelzebubs.

ISTVAN: Oh, God! Save me! Mercy, Your Highness! (*The corpses sit stiffly in their chairs. Standing up very straight, the* FOOTMEN *wait rigidly for orders.*)

BALEASTADAR: Don't you dare mention that Name here. For me it's only the symbol of Nothingness, *my own* Nothingness — but I want to live and I'm going to live. Yet I must live through someone else. Artists, they're the only material for me nowadays. To create by destroying! The last form of strength left capable of blowing things up, now that the various religions which once created the evil spirit's ghost have died. *I* personify all that — do you understand? What have you got a brain for? Think, but don't feel anything.

ISTVAN: (*Falling into a state of catalepsy*) Something monstrous is turning my blood to ice. I feel the evil fang of an amorphous ghost ploughing my brain into zigzags of an inexpressible, lightning thought.

BALEASTADAR: What do you see?

ISTVAN: I see Mordovar the way it used to be, as in a dream, heightened to the limits of inhuman, bestial beauty. Masks are falling from the trees, mountains and clouds. I see a merciless black sky and a small stray globe which you, the Prince of Darkness, envelop with your bat-like wings. And I am a worm, a little caterpillar, crawling along the leaves, irradiated by the sinister glow of suns bursting in the Milky Way.

BALEASTADAR: Come down lower, to the level of your own feelings. Dig deep into yourself one last time.

ISTVAN: My feelings are pills prepared by some hideous interplanetary pharmacist and hurled into nothingness to be devoured by frozen, starving space.

BALEASTADAR: Lower still . . .

ISTVAN: (*Suddenly waking up from his cataleptic state*) I want to go back to Mordovar, to my aunt! (*With a final attempt at labored irony.*) You've entered into the role of Beelzebub wonderfully well, but I've had enough of this comedy.

(BALEASTADAR *smacks him one on the head with his fist.* ISTVAN *stays on his feet and falls into the previous state all over again.*)

ISTVAN: This is the end. The very core of my being has gone numb in an icy blast from the center of Non-Being.

BALEASTADAR: Do you understand now? There's only one thing I can't do, just one: create art. And yet I am a born artist. In the past I was told to create life, now I am unemployed in a world growing ever more perfectly mechanized. Don't ask who told me to, don't think about it. Certain secrets must be kept. Know that I alone am the sole superreality, the sole evil. If it weren't for evil, nothing would exist, not even your aunt, even though she's a notoriously saintly person.

ISTVAN: (*With a final effort*) And yet I can see you, a cursed planter from Rio. Oh, look—horns are growing on your forehead—oh, that's very funny! I know how it's done. He had his tail cut off because having a tail is ridiculous. But he kept the horns for effect. Or perhaps those are the horns which your wife Clara di Formio y Santos bestowed on you . . .

(BALEASTADAR *smacks him another one on the head with his fist.* ISTVAN *falls down. While* ISTVAN *has been talking, small horns about 4 inches long have been growing on* BALEASTADAR'*s head. [On his wig he has two rubber fingers connected to a bifurcated tube with a bulb on the end in his pocket with which he can blow them up.] The* FOOTMEN *upstage burst out laughing.* BALEASTADAR *doesn't notice this.*)

BALEASTADAR: Well—that takes care of him. Put him with the corpses. That clown doesn't understand that in embryo he's the greatest musical genius in the world. What he'll do—no one will be able to accomplish. (*To* HILDA *who suddenly opens her eyes wide and stares at him, sitting stiffly in her chair; the other corpses sit with their eyes closed.*) What are you giving me the eye for, Hilda? He's your true lover. Through him we'll create the music of Pure Evil distilled into Pure Form. Oh—if only I could be an artist myself!—(*Sobs wildly for a moment, then gets control of himself and says.*) The Beelzebub sonata has *got* to be created. And you (*addresses* HILDA) will sing the songs of Beelzebub, and through my inspiration that clown will also write a string concerto—cello or violin—it doesn't matter—and some violinist will perform it without understanding the first thing about what he is playing; the piano works I'll perform myself, suffering the torments of the damned, because I didn't create them myself, and they'll all howl in ecstasy like jackals.

HILDA: But why do all this here tonight, instead of gradually out there on the surface of the earth?

BALEASTADAR: To condense evil—out there it would ooze away into a rotten jellyish mass of Mordovar or even Budapest moods. (*In a different tone.*) It's all so little: miserably squeezed out of the last recesses of the very depths. (*In the previous tone, passionately.*) But unique of its own kind—do you understand, Hilda? There's nothing else to start with in this grand *finale* of the world. Thus art must be the synthesis of evil and for the sake of art it's still worth attempting something, despite all the anguish and repulsion, because art is the only thing that has come down to us from the good old days, even though it's going to the devil too and quite rapidly at that. I'll begin with music, and then later on perhaps I'll work on the other arts in the same fashion, although I doubt

there's much that can be done with them. But first of all, the sonata, a
school exercise like the first sonata at the conservatory. All right — wake
up, you mannequin genius.

ISTVAN: (*Suddenly wakes up from his stupefaction and gets up; all at once
he becomes a completely different person; controlled, joyful and almost
demonically evil*) At your orders, Your Highness. Where do we begin?

BALEASTADAR: Here's a woman for you, Istvan. You must love her and lose
everything that you have treasured until this moment. You won't find
anything like her on this earth. She is the personification of woman's
strangeness in the wildest transformation of the center of coordinates for
pure evil.

ISTVAN: I understand. You're exaggerating a bit, Prince. Hilda, I never
really understood you until the present moment. I was a child.

HILDA: And you're still a child now, despite all your musical demonism.
Come to me — I'll teach you to be yourself. You'll be mine and you'll die
because of it, like all the others but in a different way: together we'll
create hellish works which lonely satans will long for during sleepless
nights as they dream of satanesses such as have never existed. The inner
hell of my unsatisfied desires will drag every love down into the mire of
destructive sensuality. But die you must in a frightful state of moral collapse such as you have never even suspected until this moment.

ISTVAN: I've heard of men destroying themselves like that over women, but
I never believed it. But I'll convince you. Beneath the mask I wear,
there's nothing real. I'm not afraid of anything. A whirling mass of
dark sounds conceals the mystery of your body from me. Dagger-like,
I'll rip it open with a kiss on your guilty lips. (*Kisses her.*) Now I know
who I am. My strength knows no limits. I'll enclose it all in a pyramid of
diabolical music, in a construction of pure metaphysical evil, of frozen
Dionysian frenzy.

HILDA: I am yours in the unattainable depths of my innermost being which
is insatiability in crime and lying. Nothing can satiate me. You're a
monstrous, horrid little boy. I love you. I can feel you transforming me
into those sounds of yours.

BALEASTADAR: And to think how low I've fallen! I, who centuries ago
battled against the holiness of art, now only dream of being able to compose as much as eight measures of good music. I'm being torn apart by
that contradiction. Oh — what hell to be Beelzebub and not be able,
even nowadays, to be an artist! (*To* ISTVAN.) But you, you idiot, without
me you wouldn't be anything either. That's the only thing that consoles
me. I can't express it in these cursed human concepts. But what's going
to happen will speak for itself. (*Through the door to the left enter* RIO

BAMBA, *leading in* ISTVAN's AUNT *and* GRANDMOTHER.) Rio Bamba —
bring those matrons over here closer. Let them watch and see. I'm glad
you've all come, you'll be the background for my ideas.

RIO BAMBA: So now we see clearly that this whole Mordovar legend was not
such nonsense as it might have seemed at first. (*Embraces* GRAND-
MOTHER.) You see, Julia, how old sins can become a splendid setting for
new monstrosities.

GRANDMOTHER: Oh, I feel so good with you, Teobald.

AUNT: (*To* BALEASTADAR) I'm grateful to you, Your Highness, for totally
transforming my nephew. The Prince of Darkness could not have acted
more graciously.

(*She kisses* BALEASTADAR's *hand.*)

BALEASTADAR: (*To the corpses*) Baroness, wake up, please. And you too,
Hieronymus.

(*The corpses of the* BARONESS *and* JACKALS *open their eyes.*)

BARONESS: But Your Highness, please arrange it all nicely, so that nothing
bad happens to my boy Ronnie. That murder's already worn him out so!
But I think a Jackals might be allowed to kill some little Budapest floozy
who has dared to treat him disrespectfully.

JACKALS: (*Suddenly getting up*) Hilda! What are you doing here with that
vile piano-player? How dare you in my presence?. . . Do you want me to
kill you all over again?

BALEASTADAR: Baron, you don't yet know that Istvan is a count. We found
out about it at the Bureau of Records here, by the entrance. I looked
over the papers when I first came. Everything's in order. They show that
Istvan is a descendant of the Count Palatine Clapary, the one who was
lord of the Orava castles. Istvan's grandfather was mixed up in the War
of 1848 in a not very commendable fashion — as an Austrian spy out of
conviction. He escaped to Mordovar, lived under an assumed name,
and had a son, who died, leaving Istvan in the world. Rio Bamba is a
Count too — but that doesn't matter.

JACKALS: Oh, this is disastrous! I've lost my last trump. What a tiresome
complication!! Since that's the case, Count, we're fighting.

ISTVAN: I could disqualify you, but I don't want to. If you'd known I was
some idiotic Count last night, you wouldn't have dared commit suicide
once you'd been challenged. Snobbery is killing all other feelings in you
except jealousy over her, and now she is mine.

(*He points to* HILDA. *The* FOOTMEN *provide them with swords.*)

BARONESS: Don't let that good-for-nothing get the better of you. Even though he has spared us from the question of marriage with that (*points to* HILDA) lady, still you must avenge yourself for his daring in the first place to take a woman away from you.

(*The young men fight.*)

JACKALS: My arm is going numb. I've forgotten all my best lunges. I, who defeated Count Sturz and Trampolini. Enough of this. It's frightful. Where did he ever learn to do all that?

(*He falls, hit. The* BARONESS *and the* FOOTMEN *rush over to him, give him first aid, and bandage his wound.*)

HILDA: Oh, Istvan, how I adore you! (*She throws her arms around* ISTVAN. CHRISTINA, *wrapped in a black shawl, runs in through the door to the left.*)

CHRISTINA: What's going on here? Oh, I'm so tired. A tremendous gale has blown down half the woods on the slopes of Czikla. I was barely able to get here. Oh, it's so frightening here! A strange person in an old Spanish costume brought me here. (*Enter* DON JOSÉ INTRIGUEZ DE ESTRADA *in the costume of a seventeenth-century Grandee.*) Don't be angry, grandmother, but he said that you sent him to get me.

DE ESTRADA: Greetings, Baltazar. I couldn't restrain myself from coming to see you. I arrived from Rio tonight. I'm on leave for two months.

BALEASTADAR: Ladies and gentlemen, may I present to you: my wife's lover, Don José Intriguez de Estrada, ambassador of the King of Spain to Rio.

DE ESTRADA: (*Disconcerted*) You must be joking, Baltazar.

BALEASTADAR: Don't Baltazar me, I am Beelzebub, Prince of Darkness! Can't you see these horns? (*Points to his head.*) You're the one who put them on me. But now they have become the symbol of my devilishness. Sit down. (DE ESTRADA *sits down, but it is obvious that he feels very ill-at-ease.*) The only thing that matters here is for this young musician to write a sonata worthy of Beelzebub himself—that is to say, worthy of me.

DE ESTRADA: I feel very uneasy in this whole affair. Very well, if you want to play the madman, I'm not going to stop you. I remember you once told me something like that when you were drunk. I'm in a strange situation; instead of returning to Madrid I came via Fiume-Budapest directly to Mordovar. Now I see that none of this makes any sense. Once in Mordovar I went straight to a totally unknown house as soon as I left the station, and then with this young lady here, whom I saw for the first time in my life, I came here to this cabaret in an abandoned mine. On the way, our horses dropped from under us and it was on foot, amidst falling trees — you have no idea what a gale . . .

BALEASTADER: Shut up! I'll give you some cabaret! (DE ESTRADA *faints and falls over backwards in a chair. His hat falls off his head.*)

CHRISTINA: Now I see it clearly for the first time. But it's too late already! I loved only Istvan.

GRANDMOTHER: And besides it's turned out that Istvan is a Count. With the help of the Prince of Darkness, he's going to be the greatest musician in the world.

CHRISTINA: Everything's collapsing. He can be whoever he wants — I don't care in the least! (*Cries.*) I love him so terribly, so hopelessly.

JACKALS: My last hope of salvation gone. Christina, I ran away from you because I was afraid of Mother and a misalliance.

HILDA: You all can see how vile he is!

ISTVAN: Don't interrupt me. Something is starting to be created within me. The first theme of the sonata . . . In F sharp minor . . . (*becomes absorbed in thought*) I have it all inside me like a big, murky bomb.

BALEASTADAR: Oh — at last! Sometimes I really feel like laughing when I think that the ultimate goal of all this is to be some idiotic sonata. In recent times the very idea of Beelzebub has, how shall I put it — *passez moi l'expression* — gone to the dogs. In order to truly experience his own existence, even Beelzebub himself has to become some cruddy patron of the arts and a virtuoso — because that's the only place where the individual can still assert himself in a tolerably perverse manner. Everything else is mechanized pulp, not worth a glance from even the vilest of devils. Isn't that right, Chebnazel? And you, block-head, Azdrubot, would you like to tinker around with the mechanism of our ideally run social systems?

SECOND FOOTMAN: (*Laughing*) Never, Your Highness. I prefer working in this cabaret.

FIRST FOOTMAN: At any rate it's better than the Enfer or the Cabaret du Néant at Place Pigalle.

BALEASTADAR: And now let's get to work! Get the piano ready. Bechstein or Steinway?

FIRST FOOTMAN: Bechstein, Your Highness.

(*They run to the back of the stage and open the magnificent Bechstein.*)

CHRISTINA: Istvan, you're the one I really . . . Drop that slut from Budapest. Remember how we played four hands together. Back there in our dear, peaceful Mordovar—those evenings of ours.

ISTVAN: There weren't so many of them, and they were all poisoned by my cursed unrequited love for you. I shudder in disgust at the very thought of it. If I had married you, I never would have become an artist. For me you're only the theme for a macabre minuet which will be the second part of my sonata, the true Beelzebub sonata. I can already see it published in a Universal-Edition, and it will be dedicated to the Prince of Darkness: *Dem Geiste der Finsterniss gewidmet* — just like on those sonatas of Beethoven which amused me when I was seven years old.

BALEASTADAR: Go on, go on—I hope something more is going to happen. All this is still not enough.

ISTVAN: Is that so? Then get away from me, my last miserable pang of conscience! May nothing furthur ever presume to remind me of those Mordovar trivialities. (*He pulls a knife out of his pocket and cuts* CHRISTINA'*s throat.*)

BARONESS: Serves her right—for having the nerve not to love my only son. Besides I never would have approved of that marriage.

HILDA: (*To* ISTVAN) Now you are truly mine. That young calf would never have been enough for you anyhow. (*They whisper together.* RIO BAMBA *starts to dance with* GRANDMOTHER.)

RIO BAMBA: I'll become a devil in my old age. Together that witch and I will create a terrific house of psychic ill-repute for the ruggedest individuals of our times.

BALEASTADAR: If only such people existed. I'm afraid it will be nothing but a cooperative society for the last remnants of lonely lost artists.

GRANDMOTHER: (*Hopping about*) Really—to be able to stop playing the matron and satiate myself on life once more—that was something I never expected. To be a sorceress for so long and have to play the respectable little matron on a small scale: that was torture.

(*She dances with* RIO BAMBA. *One of the* FOOTMEN *plays a shimmy very softly.*)

BALEASTADAR: It's all so hopelessly night club-cabaret, so tasteless. But without the setting nothing could be accomplished. And now—listen, Istvan, you shouldn't throw yourself into life so totally—our joint work—the initial sonata, the germ of all Beelzebubian music—will suffer for it. Give you a little foretaste and then totally cut off the possibility of satisfaction—that's what I had in mind.

ISTVAN: I don't understand—then what am I . . .?

BALEASTADAR: Leave that lady alone. She's my quarry. For you she's a momentary plaything, for me — the last love of an old man who has nothing more to look forward to, even if he is Beelzebub himself.

ISTVAN: And Your Highness dares say that to me? For the first time I've come to understand what existence really is, and Your Highness wants to take it away from me. No, I'd rather have life than every conceivable musical composition à la Beelzebub. In art I will be pure without any evil, even metaphysical evil.

(*They glare at one another, locked in a staring duel until instructions to the contrary.*)

BARONESS: That's all very well, but why does it have to happen just like this? There isn't the slightest necessity for it: *c'est contingent tout cela* — pure chance. Somewhere in Mordovar in Hungary — why not in Mexico? — a handful of people happened to meet by chance. But why precisely must *this* gentleman be Beelzebub and why must *that* fellow use him for his own artistic goals — that I do not understand and I never shall.

AUNT: It's so my nephew, who is like a son to me, can be a great musician.

BARONESS: That's not a sufficient reason for things as grand as the appearance of the true Beelzebub. And why here, and not somewhere else?

BALEASTADER: (*To* BARONESS) It had to happen somewhere, sometime. It doesn't matter where, does it, given the infinity of different worlds? There are scores of planets, Baroness. It's the same as with the speed of light: it has to be some speed, and a finite one at that — does it matter whether it's 186 or 386 thousand miles a second?

(ISTVAN *lowers his head and stands more dead than alive.*)

BARONESS: Yes, but I don't like that anthropocentric world view. I am an enlightened woman, *un bas bleu*, if you want, but *au fond* a pantheist.

BALEASTADAR: I can't, at a moment's notice, give a lecture on the necessity of chance for précieuseish matrons. Hilda, you are mine, come to my arms. This evening is in a class by itself.

HILDA: (*Falling on her knees in front of him*) Oh, my one and only! So it's true? I'm to have the inhuman happiness of being mistress to the true Beelzebub? I think I'll go mad, I shan't live through it! (*She crawls at* BALEASTADAR's *feet.*)

ISTVAN: Ha — I'm not going to live through it so calmly either. He takes my only love away from me. He only gave her to me in order to rob me cruelly.

(*He throws himself at* BALEASTADAR, *but stops as though hypnotized.*)

GRANDMOTHER: Quiet, for Satan's sake! The Ambassador will wake up and be an unwanted witness. He's not one of ours yet.

DE ESTRADA: (*Getting up*) Oh, but I am, grandmother dear. I'm one of yours. I regret that all this isn't taking place in Spain. I'd be proud if it were. You can all count on my discretion. Baltazar, old boy, I believe that you are the true Prince of Darkness. To be on a first name basis with Beelzebub, that's a great honor even for a Grandee of Spain and ambassador of His Royal Highness.

ISTVAN: I'll kill that scoundrel.

(*He throws himself at* BALEASTADAR *who purposely falls over backwards to the ground just as* ISTVAN *is about to reach him, spreading out his arms, and laughing demonically.*)

BALEASTADAR: (*Falling*) Hit me, shoot me, cut my throat, stab me. You'll never kill me . . . I am eternal. Here's a revolver! (BALEASTADAR *offers him a revolver.* ISTVAN *stabs him several times with a knife in a wild fury.* BALEASTADAR *keeps on laughing.* ISTVAN, *driven mad with hopeless rage, grabs the revolver and shoots him six times.* BEELZEBUB *gets up laughing, and raises* HILDA *up, taking her in his arms.*) And now to the piano, you non-entity! Now at last life will be transformed within you into that hellish melange of form and content called art. Enough of this perversity in life. It's miserable, miserable, indeed, like all art, but unique and evil—that is what's most important.

ISTVAN: (*Awakening from his reverie*) Come to me, Hieronymus. You'll find consolation with me after those women. I still need something more myself, some little monstrosity to tip me over to that other side, the dark side of my destiny. The mystery of this transformation is unfathomable, no matter how commonplace its manifestations may be in real life. (*The Baron gets up,* ISTVAN *embraces him and they both go upstage.*)

BARONESS: Ronnie, don't get into that demon's power. I've been keeping something else for you in reserve: the heiress of Keszmereth castle—a ravishing little fifteen-year-old. I've dreamed about it all my life, but didn't want to tell you prematurely.

BALEASTADAR: That's enough out of you, you old puff-ball. Can't you see that he's going over to play my sonata, the Beelzebub sonata—and for that he must have the final setting. Oh, happiness without limits! Now at last I am something of an artist. Through him a frightful mass is being celebrated to the unknown, unknowable evil of which you are all separate particles within me.

BARONESS: Then it's a kind of pantheism, even though transposed into Beelzebubian concepts.

BALEASTADAR: (*Crossing to the piano with his arms around* HILDA) Quiet there! Here's an apparatus to record the notes you play – you can start by improvising.

(*He points out the device on the right side of the piano.*)

ISTVAN: (*Sitting down at the piano*) Now at last I know what is meant by the formal spatial conception in music. The entire Beelzebub sonata exists within me beyond time. I shall unfold it like a fan—the greatest work since the beginning of the world.

(*The* BARON *stands behind him, leaning on him in a state of ecstasy.* BALEASTADAR *and* HILDA *stand by the end of the piano.* ISTVAN *strikes the first chords of wild music.* RIO BAMBA *dances a fantastic dance with* GRANDMOTHER. *Seated in her chair, the* BARONESS *falls into a trance as she listens intently. Meanwhile the curtain falls slowly.*)

Act III

The BARONESS JACKALS' *salon in her castle on the outskirts of Mordovar.
The whole thing is a rather narrow strip (about ten feet in width) along
the footlights. The rest of the stage is separated from this visible part by
a black-cherry colored curtain which can be pulled open on both sides.
Rococo furniture. Doors to the left and to the right. To the left the*
BARONESS *and* ISTVAN's AUNT *are seated—they are knitting. Near them*
DE ESTRADA, *dressed as in Act Two. A fire is burning in the fireplace to
the left. A pinkish twilight is slowly falling.*

AUNT: I'm so grateful to you, Baroness, for letting me spend the night here.
I'm terribly worried about Istvan.

BARONESS: But, dear Madam, ever since they found the papers proving
he's a count, a career beyond reproach has opened up for him. The
misalliance which Istvan's father, Mr. Saint-Michael—I mean, Count
Clapery—made when he married your sister—you'll forgive me for
speaking so frankly—is in no way an insurmountable obstacle. We'll
marry Istvan to one of those innumerable rich Americans who keep
coming here to Mordovar for the summer.

AUNT: Oh, let's not worry about that now. I'm afraid that old madman will
drag him into some scandalous affair with that Beelzebub sonata.

BARONESS: Oh, I'm sure they'll come back—nothing will happen to him.
It's only what they call artistic experiences. I'm more worried about my
son.

DE ESTRADA: But look here, Madam, that ridiculous shot he took at that
Budapest courtesan—I can't describe that woman in any other

way—can be hushed up completely. And the suicide wound is, if I may express myself in the Spanish manner, light as a feather. A slight scratch on the skull and temporary paralysis of half the body due to cerebral hemorrhage. I came across countless such cases during the war—the symptoms went away without leaving a trace.

(*A* FOOTMAN *enters from the left side.*)

FOOTMAN: Countess Clapary, Your Ladyship.

BARONESS: Countess who? I don't understand at all.

DE ESTRADA: You're forgetting that Istvan's father's brother—alias Rio Bamba—has also turned out to be a count—altogether automatically. And immediately, as befits a gentleman, he married the person known as grandmother Julia, née Ceres. Petty nobility, but it doesn't really matter. We'll use our influence there too to hush up his youthful escapades, and everything will be all right. In our times there are a good many things that must be overlooked.

BARONESS: Oh, so that's it—then ask her to come in.

AUNT: How nice—everyone's so well-born—and such titles—I'm so glad!

BARONESS: Yes—though not altogether—not everyone, of course. Let's hope for the best.

(*Enter* GRANDMOTHER JULIA.)

GRANDMOTHER: Isn't Istvan here, Baroness? (*The* BARONESS *shakes her head negatively.*) I couldn't wait at home any longer. Something simply pulled me out of the house. Like a cork from a bottle.

BARONESS: He hasn't come back yet, Countess.

GRANDMOTHER: I left word that I'd be here.

AUNT: So did I. The Baroness was kind enough to take us in at this difficult moment.

BARONESS: But *I* think tonight will have a wonderful effect on his creativity. He's a strong boy. Surely he won't let himself get into that *marchand-de-vin's* power. A young person must experience everything. Please sit down—we'll wait for the news together.

GRANDMOTHER: (*Sitting down*) Yes, quite so—it's not worth a second thought. But I upset him needlessly with that Mordovar legend. An absolutely ridiculous story, and it had such an effect on his imagination.

BARONESS: He's an artistic soul in every inch of his spiritual being. But I've forgotten to congratulate you on your elevation up the social ladder. My heart-felt felicitations.

GRANDMOTHER: Oh — a mere trifle. If only nothing bad comes of it. I won't ever tell fortunes again. I'm giving up palmistry too, and even astrology, forever.

BARONESS: Yes — in your present position, it's hardly the thing to do.

DE ESTRADA: That's absolutely right, Baroness.

BARONESS: You see, fortune telling comes true because people unconciously push events so as to fulfill the predictions. Even if a person's forebodings all came true every five minutes, I'd still consider it pure chance, given the infinity of this world and the infinity of events and premonitions. *C'est tout à fait contingent,* isn't it, Don José?

DE ESTRADA Certainly: the law of Large Numbers, a simple calculation of probabilities. Statistics play an increasingly important role in everything. Even the laws of physics, so they say, are only statistically true, that is, approximate, although. . .
(*From the left side enter the* BARON, *half paralyzed, led in by the* FOOTMAN.)

BARONESS: Oh, what happiness! So you can walk already, Ronnie? We'll go South and everything will be just fine, as Don José says. My son, Hieronymus, Mr. Ambassador.

(*They greet one another. The* BARON *kisses* GRANDMOTHER'*s hand with profound respect and shakes hands with the* AUNT.)

JACKALS: (*Sits down in a chair; exit the* FOOTMAN) I have such a desire to live, Mother. I feel as though I'd been reborn. The world has never seemed more beautiful to me. I remember I had the same feeling when I was recovering from typhus. Today, the delicate little leaves, which can be seen through the window against a cloudy sky, looked more beautiful to me than the African wilds as I hacked my way through the underbrush hunting big game. I'll never kill another living creature again — except perhaps flies — sometimes they're so frightfully infuriating. And you know what? I've stopped being a snob; snobbery is an ugly thing — not worth ruining one's life for. I know I love Christina even though I tried to free myself from her by debauchery — but only to avoid making a misalliance. That's why I got involved in that other love-affair. Now Miss Purebray has totally stopped existing for me.

BARONESS: (*Embracing him*) My darling child! Just don't torture yourself with thoughts like that. There'll be time for everything. Don't make any decisions now — things may not be quite normal yet.

JACKALS: (*Pushes his mother away, slightly let down*) Oh, mother, I wish you were completely on my side at this moment. This is the great turning point in my life. I know what you're thinking about — Miss

Keszmereth—she's a very nice young lady—but I love Christina.

DE ESTRADA: (*Who has been listening with certain uneasiness and furrowed eyebrows*) Baron, in our youth we sometimes like to make great decisions, apparently great decisions which subsequently seem small and petty to us, and sometimes we suffer for it our whole lives. Tradition is a beautiful thing—one shouldn't treat it lightly . . .

JACKALS: You don't understand me. Mr. Ambassador. I can't tell you all how beautiful everything is. But will Christina still want me after all this scandal? Will my paralysis go away?

DE ESTRADA: (*Insincerely*) Certainly—after the hemorrhage has cleared up. In two months you'll be well and then everything will seem different to you.

BARONESS: (*To* DE ESTRADA) Why are you acting so strange, Don José? Do you suppose . . .

JACKALS: Mother, stop worrying about trifles. I'm happy for the first time in my life. Even if I remain paralyzed and Christina refuses to give me her hand—even then I'll be happy; I have found a strange peace within myself . . .

BARONESS: (*In despair*) My God, My God, My God! . . .

(*She covers her face with her hands.*)

DE ESTRADA: Come now, Baroness, it may disappear completely after the operation.

JACKALS: Mother suspects I've gone crazy in a benign sort of way as a result of the hemorrhage.

(*Enter* RIO BAMBA *without being announced.*)

DE ESTRADA: Here he is, our Count Clapary, I congratulate you with all my heart.

RIO BAMBA: I am and I will continue to be Rio Bamba. I have wiped out a sin of my youth, and I trust all of you will save me from any other bad consequences of my past so that I can mend my ways in my old age.

DE ESTRADA: But of course, Mr. Rio Bamba—I'll call you by your pseudonym if you like. The devil always looks for the ways to do the maximum amount of evil in that one point in the universe where he meets the least resistance. Nowadays that point—or rather the plurality of them—is found in art. Where new forms are coming into being, that's where *he* is, make no doubt about it. I am convinced of it.

JACKALS: (*Vehemently*) Don't talk that way, Don José! (*Gently.*) There's something dreadful in those words that terrifies me. I don't want anything bad to happen—after all, I still am very weak.

BARONESS: Calm down, my child. Sit here next to me. I'll rock you to sleep the way I used to when you were little. (*She sits down next to him, he puts his head on her shoulder. She rocks him to sleep.*)

RIO BAMBA: (*To* GRANDMOTHER) Well, what do you say, old girl? Aren't you touched by this scene? The world is marvelous! But we must be good. There's no way of getting around that—it's straight as any line in Euclid.

GRANDMOTHER: Yes, that's right, Teobald. Our old age will be mild like an autumn morning in the mountains. And the old Mordovar evenings on this side of the lake will return once more.

RIO BAMBA: (*Laughing*) But just don't call up spirits anymore from the depths of Mount Czikla. Down with ridiculous legends. Mordovar! My God—what a world of miracles lies stored in that idiotic word! It's good that at least now we can finally appreciate all the sweetness of life. Once those two maniacs come back, we'll make them forget all that revolting musical demonism.

JACKALS: Oh, yes—you're right. Only I'd like to get rid of my evil forebodings. Istvan seems to love Christina too. But if she chooses me, Istvan and I will get along. We'll listen to Bach and Mozart, he'll compose in a new way. All that art is madness.

AUNT: I too believe he can be great without those artistic eccentricities. That takes its toll on one's life. If it were only possible nowadays to create that Pure Form of theirs without evil. I believe it is—don't you?

BARONESS: Oh, Madam, that insatiability for form; that constant acceleration of the fever for life! Even in total seclusion, even reading only the Bible and drinking milk, one cannot isolate oneself from the spirit of the times.

AUNT: You're well-educated. I don't know these things that well, but I believe . . .

(CHRISTINA *runs in.*)

CHRISTINA: Has Istvan come back?

DE ESTRADA: They haven't come back yet, but I believe this evening everything will end perfectly.

JACKALS: Mother, you know what you must do to assure my happiness—not only mine: to increase happiness in the entire universe.

BARONESS: (*To* GRANDMOTHER, *stiffly*) Countess, I have the honor of asking your granddaughter's hand for my son.

GRANDMOTHER: (*Embarrassed*) Yes, of course — it's a great honor — although . . . But, if she loves him, naturally — only I have to tell you all that only my first daughter is Rio Bamba's daughter . . . The other one, Christina's mother — but that's enough on that subject; Chris, what do you think, my child?

CHRISTINA: (*Falling on her knees in front of the* BARONESS) Madam, it's too much happiness for me!

BARONESS: (*Brutally*) But he's paralyzed and he seems not quite right in the head since his suicide.

CHRISTINA: Madam, even if he were the most horrible cripple, for the rest of his life — I would always love him.

JACKALS: Come here to me, Chris. I still can't move about. Kiss me. I've always loved you so.

CHRISTINA: (*Gets up, laughing*) And what about your snobbery? Have you stopped being a snob now, Hieronymus?

JACKALS: Yes — and I'm ashamed I ever was one.

BARONESS: Stop joking, I beg you. (DE ESTRADA *hems very loudly to show his dissatisfaction.*)

CHRISTINA: (*Chilled*) Oh, yes, I . . . I'm awfully sorry. And Miss Pure -
bray . . .

JACKALS: (*Jumping up awkwardly*) Oh, wait! I forgot! I'm a criminal! I shot her yesterday! Tell me whether she's alive. Quickly — where is she?

DE ESTRADA: I was afraid of this. He's forgotten as a result of nervous shock.

JACKALS: I beg you, Don José . . .

DE ESTRADA: But she's alive, healthy as a Murcia bull. Calm down, boy, for God's sake, or you could do yourself some harm. She fainted — you put a bullet through her wing — she'll be all right soon.

(*Deeper and deeper twilight falls.*)

JACKALS: (*Sinks back into his chair again*) What luck! But I could have been a murderer and not lived to see *this* happiness. All the same, they'll drag me through the courts — and suppose I get several years? Christina, will you wait for me?

CHRISTINA: Yes, yes — but that won't happen.

DE ESTRADA: Why of course not — with our connections? It'll be totally hushed up . . . Oh, what the devil!

(*The curtain parts in the middle and* HILDA PUREBRAY *enters from behind it. Black ball dress, hat. Her left arm bandaged. They all turn around in her direction.*)

BARONESS: Where did you come from? In there? Without being announced?

HILDA: Calm down or you'll cause still worse misfortune. Please don't yell that way. The atmosphere is steeped in explosive matter. Hochexplosiv! There's absolutely no telling what will happen next; the problem of the Beelzebub sonata still isn't . . .

BARONESS: Don't talk about it, please. Peace and quiet for the invalid before everything . . .

HILDA: Who gets excited during an earthquake if someone has a stomachache? The way it seems to me, those Mordovar moods won't come back anymore. They'll all talk about it, as a piece of interesting gossip, on the other side of the lake: at the Kurhauz and the Magas Cafehaz and at the train station in Uj-Mordovar and perhaps even in Budapest. But believe me, I came here for the good of all of you, to warn you. Perhaps it's not the appropriate moment, Baroness, and a bit unexpected — but it can't be helped . . .

BARONESS: (*Has recovered her composure*) Oh, Miss, since yesterday a great many things have changed. We're gradually getting used to it all . . .

JACKALS: (*Reproachfully*) Mother!

BARONESS: No need to call "Mother," that's the way it is. My son . . .

AUNT: (*Trying to change the subject*) But, that's right, we were just saying that art can be great even without perversionalism, as the Baroness calls it . . .

(*Suddenly the curtain upstage is drawn and the entire hell from Act II is visible, but without the forestage which is taken up by the drawing room. Total dusk on the forestage. Hell is lighted deep red. In the middle stands* BALEASTADAR *in a frock-coat. A fantastic diabolical coat thrown over his frock-coat. Horns on his head. Next to him stands* ISTVAN, *likewise in a frock-coat. He is very pale. Upstage the infernal* FOOTMEN. *From the left side, enter the* BARONESS's FOOTMAN.)

BALEASTADAR: (*As the curtain is being drawn*) And I tell you all, no. (*Claps* ISTVAN *on the shoulder.*) I have the proof in Istvan. He is a genius such as the world has never seen. Evil — metaphysical, personal, hairy, fanged, bloody evil — he has heaped it up and puffed it out shamelessly in the crystal form of pure music, malevolent as a sudden attack by the Huns. These are the final death throes, but they have the savor of former greatness, even if it is only in art.

DE ESTRADA: (*Forcedly*) Well — here they are at last, those Beelzebub sonata maniacs. That cursed going around in circles is about to begin all over again. But this setting I don't like in the least. There's some kind of extremely unpleasant demonic "truc" in the way it's got up. They're very nasty things, these Mordovar legends of yours. I'm no coward, but I'm beginning to get a bit frightened. Brrr!... Baltazar, don't make silly jokes! He got all dressed up like the real Beelzebub! Don't play the fool!

BALEASTADAR: (*Roars in sudden fury*) I've had enough of your familiarities, you court jester! I am Beelzebub, Prince of Darkness! Address me as: "Your Highness!" Understand?

(*Silence. In the midst of the silence the* BARONESS's FOOTMAN *suddenly starts guffawing.*)

FOOTMAN: (*In a peasant accent*) Maybe for all you noble folks, this is some kinda comedy. I ain't scared of no Beelzebub.

(*He chokes with laughter.*)

BARONESS: What a way to talk! I don't even recognize you, Francis!

BALEASTADAR: (*Yells*) Stop laughing, you representative of future humanity!

(*The* FOOTMAN *keeps on laughing. Baleastadar shoots him on the spot with a revolver. The* FOOTMAN *falls.*)

HILDA: Oho — this is no joking matter. That was a Beelzebub shot which the grand masters at *tir-aux-pigeons* can dream of, the way Istvan dreams of his sonata. He knows how to shoot, but he can't compose anything himself. So you see, my friends: I'm a plebeian, like Istvan's aunt, if I'm not mistaken. But I belong to the quote, "aristocracy of the soul" — the latest swindle of our times. Ronnie, do you...?

DE ESTRADA: (*Interrupts her*) What insolent nonsense! That's all very well, but where in this Hungary of yours are the police at times like these? I mean, this is a perfectly organized gang, these three!

BALEASTADAR: At times like these, whether here or in Spain, the police don't know the first thing about diabolical metaphysics — they find out what's happened afterwards when it's too late. Go on, Hilda! I don't have any idea what you're going to say and I'm curious.

HILDA: Now listen, Ronnie: do you think it's going to be enough for you, that turtledove and all this goodness of yours, and being infatuated with the pretty little leaves against the gray sky, and that mawkish self-satisfaction which fills me with disgust? You love only me and you are mine. You know how I keep hold of you — remember? Keep that in mind — no one else will give you that — come! Let's go to that hell of theirs. There true life and enjoyment are bubbling over to the sounds of the Beelzebub sonata, the last farewell fanfare of that dying swarm of insects once called humanity. You're healthy, you're not paralyzed. Stand up and come with me.

JACKALS: (*Gets up, suddenly healthy as a bull*) You're right, Hilda. All that's an illusion. I'm yours. Let's go.

BARONESS: I prefer even this to that misalliance. Ronnie, I'm so happy you've recovered! And when you've enjoyed life, you'll marry Miss Keszmereth. I know after you've passed through that school, your wife will never be bored with you. That was the chief shortcoming of husbands in my generation, they. . .

JACKALS: I know, I know — good-by, mother, for now.

(*He enters hell with* HILDA *in a circle of red light.*)

BALEASTADAR: Bravo, Ronnie! All right, Hilda, go on!

HILDA: (*To the* BARON) And did you think I had really fallen that low? I only wanted to get you away from that goose . . .

CHRISTINA: I'm going with you! I love Istvan. I made a mistake too. Forgive me, infernal people. I won't ever do it again. Take me with you!

HILDA: You miserable little lap-dog bitch. You go to hell? No — that's a place for tigers and hyenas only. Stay in your cosy drawing room and keep on enjoying Mordovar evenings. Away!

JACKALS: (*Pulls out a revolver*) This time you won't get away from me, you stinking female! (*He shoots* HILDA, *who falls to the ground.*)

BALEASTADAR: Fine — now he's bumped her off for good. But Istvan and I don't need women. Pure Art will suffice us. Ha, ha, ha, ha, ha! (*He laughs demonically.*)

JACKALS: Oh — so even this hasn't been spared me! Istvan, I implore you, be my only friend. Now I'm completely alone. You're a count — we can be on an equal footing. I'm giving you everything. Women don't exist for me anymore.

ISTVAN: You've forgotten that we were supposed to fight, Baron. You insulted me. I love no one but my Master, the Prince of Darkness!

JACKALS: No — I won't fight. Too much misfortune. I've had enough of all this. This is the end. (*He shoots himself in the temple. A scream in the drawing room. The* BARONESS *falls.*)

DE ESTRADA: *Me cago en la barba del Belzebubo.* I smell almonds. The Baroness has taken cyanide. Let's try to save her. But after all, what does it matter! I'm going over to hell too.

BALEASTADAR: Oh, no! I'm no specialist in matrimonial triangles. You won't get away with that a second time, Joe. Seducing a man's wife is something even Beelzebub himself won't forgive.

(*He shoots* DON JOSÉ *who collapses on the threshold of hell, his face towards the audience.*)

RIO BAMBA: Too many corpses, by Beelzebub! They're toppling over like at a shooting-gallery. Old Mordovarians, let's get out of here, while there's still time. This way. Come along, Julia, and you, old aunt. We're completely superfluous here.

(*They run off to the left.*)

AUNT: (*Running off*) Be great to the end, Istvan dear. I can't watch this any longer. I'm too old for these new directions of yours.

(*They disappear to the left.* CHRISTINA, *as though beside herself, goes over to* ISTVAN.)

CHRISTINA: I won't ever leave you. On the highest summits — in life or in art — I will be yours. I only want to serve you. I don't care about myself.

BALEASTADAR: Istvan doesn't need women anymore, or anything else at all. He is finished. But you can get to work sorting the manuscripts — that is actually — the typescripts. All the compositions which he was to create, he has already created — starting with the sonata opus one and going up to the homo...how can I put it: the hyperhomogeneous, in their boundless complication, and almost hypnogogic ultramadrigals and interlubrics — it's all here. Look, this heap of papers here, it's all his posthumous works ... *oeuvres posthumes* — written on the machine for noting down improvisations. But these weren't improvisations — these are works born out of spatial conceptions in another dimension.

CHRISTINA: What did you say? Posthumous?

BALEASTADAR: Can't you see he's a corpse? Now we'll go on tour and I'll perform it all. Because, although I'm not a creator, as a pianist I surpass Paderewski and Arthur Rubinstein and all the others by one thousand degrees on the scale of greatness. No one will be able to play these pieces but me. He couldn't do it himself with his technique. He only played enough for it to be noted down in the rough. But now we must "*le mettre à point*," you understand, polish it up rhythmically. I believe you're rather musical, aren't you?

(ISTVAN *stays where he is without moving.*)

CHRISTINA: Yes — I studied a bit.

BALEASTADAR: Good. You'll be able to help me. These are mountains of explosive matter, the last glimmers of individual diabolicalness. For a moment more, if only in the dimensions of art, it's possible to disturb the slumber of mankind as it drowses off into social well-being. Because crimes committed in the name of the working classes are not my speciality. They aren't even actually crimes — the devil knows what they are. I loathe and despise them. All right — you can get down to work. (CHRISTINA *digs into the piles of papers, totally unconscious.*) And now I'll try out the famous Beelzebub sonata. Thus the most idiotic Mordovar legend has come true. (*He goes to the piano and begins to play what* ISTVAN *was playing at the end of Act II; he plays magnificently with gestures typical of a frenetic pianist: during the pianissimo he speaks.*) The height of irony, possible only in our vile times — Beelzebub, Prince of Darkness, ends up as a pianist!

(ISTVAN *turns around like an automaton, goes upstage and out to the left.*)

CHRISTINA: (*Uneasily*) Why did he leave? Where did he go?

BALEASTADAR: (*Playing softly*) He can't stand the fact that I play it better than he does. And then too, he's tormented because he knows that without me he wouldn't have created anything. (*Frightful scream offstage.* BALEASTADAR *plays furiously. The purple curtain at the back of the stage is drawn apart. Red dusk falls in hell. At the back of the stage Mount Czikla is visible: a rocky peak with streaks of snow as in Act I — but by the light of the rising sun. Woods at the foot of the mountain. In the foreground a black opening in the midst of whitish stone debris. Against the opening,* ISTVAN *can be seen hanging by his suspenders from a pine tree. The* AUNT, RIO BAMBA *and* GRANDMOTHER *approach the corpse cautiously from the side and take it down.* BALEASTADAR, *getting up from the piano.*) Now you see why I said these works are posthumous. We don't have to lament for him. He couldn't have gone on living anyhow. He'd lived himself out completely, and what's most important, he'd composed himself out through and through — there was nothing left of him. When he hanged himself, he was already a corpse. We can leave the other arts in peace. We won't squeeze anything more demonic out of them than this. (*Points at the heap of papers — to the* FOOTMEN.) And now, clowns, look lively! Bring in a chest. We can still make the Budapest express which stops at Mordovar at six fifteen. We're going on a final world-wide tour, and then it's the end of Beelzebub.

(*With mad speed, the* FOOTMEN *bring him the chest into which* BALEASTADAR *and* CHRISTINA *begin to throw the papers.*)

CHRISTINA: Oh, my Prince of Darkness! You're the only one I love. You won't drive me away now. There's some kind of rondo here for two pianos — we'll play it together.

BALEASTADAR: All right — we'll see. Tonight you'll take an examination with me. And as for love — that still remains to be seen. For the moment, sexual matters leave me cold.

CHRISTINA: Oh! Yes, yes — I agree to everything. But I couldn't stand any more of these Mordovar moods. I've got to get out of here and really start to live.

BALEASTADAR: All right, agreed — what are you complaining about! We're going together, aren't we? (*To the group of Mordovarians at the back of the stage who are standing over* ISTVAN's *corpse.*) Good-bye! And don't go creating any new legend. The next time it won't come true quite so easily.

(*He goes to the left, followed by* CHRISTINA *and then the six* FOOTMEN *dragging the chest. The Mordovarians wave their handkerchiefs. A far-off train whistle. Ringing of distant bells.* BALEASTADAR, CHRISTINA *and the* FOOTMEN *leave by the door to hell on the left.*)

END

TUMOR BRAINIOWICZ (Jaracz Theatre, Olsztyn, Poland, 1974)
Dir.: Wanda Laskowska

TUMOR BRAINIOWICZ

Dedicated to
Zofia and Tadeusz Żeleński

A Drama in Three Acts with a Prologue

1920

CHARACTERS

TUMOR BRAINIOWICZ — Very famous mathematician, of humble origins. Forty years old.

GAMBOLINE BASILIUS — From the princely house of the Transcaspian Trun-Duhl-Bhed's. *Primo voto:* Madam Roman Countess Kretchborski; *secundo voto:* Madam Tumor Brainiowicz. Thirty-six years old.
He: a giant built like a wild ox. Low buffalo forehead with a huge head of rumpled blond hair falling. down over his face. Magnificently dressed. A red decoration in his buttonhole. Across his shirt front there can be seen the green ribbon of some Eastern order. A gray suit of the best cord and yellow shoes. Clear blue eyes. Close-clipped flaxen moustache. Otherwise clean-shaven.
She: magnificently developed brunette with light down on her upper lip. Fiery black eyes. Somewhat Oriental. A wildly exciting thoroughbred.

BALLANTINE FERMOR — Spinster. (The Right Honorable Miss Fermor.) Daughter of Henry Fermor, VIth Earl of Ballantrae. Thirty-two years old. Beautiful, majestic blonde; healthy, very exciting, a thoroughbred.

PROFESSOR ALFRED GREEN of the MCGO — (The Mathematical Central and General Office.) Blond hair, pince-nez. A thoroughly English type. Forty-two years old. Completely clean-shaven.

JOSEPH BRAINIOWICZ — A crafty peasant, seventy-five years old. Fit as a fiddle. Nothing like Tumor. (Tumor takes after his mother.) Peasant overcoat, glossy high boots. Brown hair going gray. Aquiline nose.

IBISA (IZA) — Countess Kretchborski. Daughter of Gamboline and Roman Kretchborski. Eighteen years old. Red hair, blue eyes. An utterly wildly exciting, demonic young girl, a real thoroughbred. As like her father as two peas in a pod.

ALFRED BRAINIOWICZ — Sixteen years old. Tumor's first son from his third marriage with Gamboline. The very image of his father. Dressed in a pinkish-gray sports outfit.

MAURICE BRAINIOWICZ — Fourteen years old. The next item in the collection of young Brainiowiczes. Very like his mother. Dressed in a gray-dun sports outfit. Turned-down collar. Raspberry "La Valière" tie.

IRENE BRAINIOWICZ—Twenty-three years old. Tumor's daughter from his second marriage. Plain, very intelligent brunette of a slightly Semitic type.

LORD ARTHUR PERSVILLE—Fourth son of the Duke Osmond (future Duke of Osmond, Marquess of Broken Hill, Viscount of Durisdeer, Master of Takoomba-Falls), the greatest demon at the Mathematical Central and General Office and the greatest of unpunished criminals; so-called "King of Hells"; king of enfers and gambling dens (amphibology of the plural of Hell). Thirty-three years old. Sharpest geometrician on the planet earth. Student of Hilibert. Leader of fashion. Dressed in a tail coat and striped trousers and a top-hat, with a cane in his hand. A youthful face of unusual beauty. Clean-shaven; black eyes. Brown hair, strong build, something between a true lord and a criminal type from the penal colonies. Distinguished gestures. His eyes never laugh but his beautifully drawn full lips, fixed in delicate, yet monstrously powerful jaws, have the smile of a three-year-old baby girl. Moreover, he is a man (if he can be called a man) who arouses the most diabolic jealousy and envy throughout the entire globe.

PRINCE TENGAH—A very beautiful Malay, son of the Rajah Patakulo of Timor. Twenty-three years old. Blue turban, red sarong. Kris at his side.

OLD RAJAH PATAKULO—Old Malay with a gray beard; sixty years old. Loin-cloth around his hips.

CAPTAIN FITZ-GERALD—Clean-shaven sea-wolf. Commander of the cruiser "Prince Arthur."

MALAYS—(from the guard)—Dressed like Tengah, with lances.

TWO OTHER MALAYS: In red turbans with lances.

A CROWD OF MALAYS

TWO WHITE MEN—In khaki outfits and pith-helmets.

SIX MEN (from the crew of the cruiser)—Dressed in white sailor suits.

TWO OF GREEN'S AGENTS—Impersonal beings.

FOUR PORTERS—In blue aprons. Completely impersonal characters with beards.

ISIDORE BRAINIOWICZ—In diapers.

Prologue

Living salamanders' branded mugs
Cackle in a nameless planet's red expanse.
Serrated in the anguish of surexistences,
Denticulated into baby puckers,
Enfolded into old, senile dentures,
Living murderers' funereal stilettoes,
Driven by the desire of their swollen hearts,
Draw near the goal:
A hyperbolic comet's nodal point.
Into senile dentures' clavichords
I shove squashed words, by fervor exacerbated.
A monster's carcass, battered at the crossroads,
Eats out its belly-button and drills holes into little birdies' rainbow
    wings.
I know that well.
And find it good that it is so.
The gesture of a ghost along the world's steep cliffs
Allays the anguish of the cretinized masses.
Youthful prophets decoy one another
Amidst fragrant shrubs and shady shrines.
Beyond the wall she (who?) cries out for "more!!"
At a fatally irreversible lecherade.
Her body crushing against bones, her jaw turned back,
She shows her fiery teeth from behind sharp corners
And poking with a pelican's beak,
In a cave conquered by their shadows,
Shadows of the masses gutted by superbestial anguish,
Bisects the watery abyss with a faience cup.
I know that I am lying and above laughter higher only is the
    construction of truth,

Etching itself into darkness like a spiral Babylonian tower.
Babel, Jezebel, and English Mabel,
Who reads the Bible at insipid five o'clock tea,
While the thundering photosphere of our star
Snorts in an explosion of flaming gas.
Hydrogen burns and helium drifts aimlessly.
Illumining the expanses of intermediary dusk.
An old man without beard measures evening and dawn
And at the edge of ultimate concepts
Puts the world's manometer on Nothingness.
To be him or to stay oneself,
In metabestial, rococo dress,
And keep on rutting in uproarious pastures.
Dilemma worthy of great Caesar's lies.
Worn-out teeth still munch the food
Ruminated long ago by the double pouch
Which proud Pasiphaë now glories in.
An electron in a magnetic field fosters
The blind sight of a specter stopped in its tracks.
The relativity of space incurves all lines,
And a blind man licks objects that are colorless.
Pure as a tear, the spirit ceaselessly vomits a nondescript fluid . . .
Mankind, that loathsome machine of former dieties,
Heaps up on ancient Tiber's banks the pukings of desire,
Into tigers' pleats, into anthers of corn cockles.
(Somewhere a marabout is standing on one leg.)
It's all worn out, the pulp of words no longer flows
And fails to swathe the dread of ancient devils.
They abase themselves before a spit-out pip,
Tybalt fears the Cains and Abels.
In centipedes' embraces a panther bewitched,
Its mottles shining pink and proud.
Through the grass there crawls a splendid courtesan,
Her belly mashing far too lucid words.
Draw the curtain, enter upon the scene
Tumor Brainiowicz, with a tumor in his brain.
For us what does all of it really mean?
That flail-macerated flaneur with a lion's mane.

Act I

Scene 1

The children's room on the second floor of GAMBOLINE's *house.* TUMOR
BRAINIOWICZ *sits alone in an armchair. Children's toys on the rug. A
huge cylinder full of gas stands in the corner to the right. The furnishings of the room are the height of modern hygiene. Everything
white as snow. The sun streams through large windows to the right and
left. It is bright and warm. Upstage a blackboard for school work. To
the left of it a door facing the audience. Another door to the left.*

BRAINIOWICZ: I'm banging away full steam ahead. Grips coming to grips,
grips sinking into grips, and in the fiery splutter, stirring up a little dust
in a storm beyond the grave. Cursed civilization! (*Bangs his fist on the
back of the chair.*) Who's forcing me to pretend? Yesterday I read their
entire new program. It simply makes one sick to one's stomach. Vomito
negro. (*Enter* IZA. *Short black dress. Azure stockings. Shoes with red
pom-poms.*)

IZA: Mother wants to know if there's anything you need.

BRAINIOWICZ: I need a bull, a chariot, boundless fields and your blue eyes,
Iza. Tell your mother she is like Pasiphaë. She'll turn green with envy.
She's so frightfully complicated, I'll probably burst in this whole whirl-
wind you're all creating.

IZA: Please calm down. I know a great deal — a great deal more than
Mother or even you.

(*Exit.* BRAINIOWICZ *gets up and winds his watch.*)

BRAINIOWICZ: Cursed civilization. I don't have an ounce of the artist in
me, not even that much! (*Indicates by holding his thumb and forefinger
very close together*.) Still they all keep trying to make me believe that I
am an artist: Oh, what a great talent! oh, what a genius! If only she
wouldn't think that! All my children look so much like me that I am
simply terrified there hasn't been a single woman with the strength to be
unfaithful to me.

(*Enter* BRAINIOWICZ's *father in a peasant overcoat and high boots.*)

JOSEPH BRAINIOWICZ: (*Old but still spry peasant; broad-shouldered like his
son; speaks with a peasant drawl*) You're invincible, sonny boy.

BRAINIOWICZ: Always full of bright ideas, aren't you, Father? So old and
yet so foolish. (*Recites.*)
>In the depths of my soul
>Primordial vengefulness,
>My coat of arms
>A juicy maggot.
>Hordes of horses all aghast
>And officers with looks downcast
>Over the fate of harlots long, long this life departed.

(*Speaks.*) Besides being myself, I could be a waiter, an officer or a
harlot. If I were a woman, I'd be a terribly depraved one.

JOSEPH BRAINIOWICZ: How fantastically beautiful you are, sonny boy.
(*Picks up a doll from the floor and kisses it.*) That's what your little sister
Anselma looked like.

BRAINIOWICZ: (*Recites*)
>Worms are wriggling through my eyes
>In dark, dissolving images,
>Like a sharp-edged knife
>I'd like to use myself to slice
>Clean through speed-jealous space.
>Weights I bear and balance, the likes of which
>None of the Caesars of this world could weigh,
>And yet away it all flies like wisps of hay.
>And everything seems light to me,
>Like the spider's insubstantial pelf,
>Like some unobtrusive little elf,
>Or his other, interplanetary self.
>My face I've powdered with my greatness
>And I am a loathesome puppet.
>Such fine disgust as I feel for myself
>No one has ever known since worlds began.

JOSEPH BRAINIOWICZ: (*Staggering*) Oh, how lovely you are, sonny boy!

Come on, let's go to the corner pub.

BRAINIOWICZ: (*In despair*) Oh, go by yourself, Father. I have to finish writing the rules and regulations for the new Academy of Sciences today. And besides they just sent me the proofs for my treatise on transfinite functions. But you don't even know the first thing about algebra, Father. It's like drawing water with a sieve. (*He hands his father a piece of paper which he pulls out of his pocket.*)

JOSEPH BRAINIOWICZ: (*Puts on round-rimmed glasses and reads*) "Über transfinite Funktionen im alef-dimensionalen* Raume, Professor Tumor von Brainiowicz." Oh, how clever you are, sonny boy! And just for that they nobilified you that way. (*Sorrowfully.*) I had a dream. I saw you as a divinity in some kind of Oriental temple. You didn't recognize me and you were laughing at something I couldn't see. And the guard—a puny little old man, trembling like a leaf, threw me out. He had a face like our Fido, only human.

BRAINIOWICZ: (*Putting the proofs away in his pocket*) I never had time for anything, not even love. But what is love for me? My children are growing up. My son will soon graduate from high-school; my daughter already integrates differential equations not half bad at all, but I can't even get a little rest. At least if I were religious. "Aber mir, keine Marter ist erspart," as Franz Joseph used to say.

(JOSEPH BRAINIOWICZ *nods and heads for the exit. At the door he meets* GAMBOLINE *dressed in a light balachan, a Russian peasant overcoat.*)

GAMBOLINE: Joseph, I told you to take care of yourself. And here he's walking about again!

JOSEPH BRAINIOWICZ: Oh, may I breathe my last in the society of people who really are people. And how is Your Ladyship feeling?

GAMBOLINE: Like a steam bull. (*She laughs. Exit* JOSEPH. GAMBOLINE *suddenly grows sad and goes over to* BRAINIOWICZ.) What's the matter with you? Tumor! Don't you love me?

BRAINIOWICZ: (*Picks up the doll and looks at it*) But you know all about it. I'm a low-born slob, an utter beast. I remember, I can't forget. I smashed your cupboard into smithereens and made you ashamed of me in front of them all. But I couldn't help getting drunk.

GAMBOLINE: Don't think about that. It's all been made up for. I wish I could have a baby every month so there'd be more like you. I'd like to own one of those islands in the Pacific Ocean and have you there and our children, the whole lot big strong strapping boys like you, the whole lot math wizards, each one an exact copy of the others. The Academy would be right in the middle and you, the one and only, lord of all suns, king of numbers, prince of Infinity, shah of the world of absolute ideas,

---

*Alef: Cantor's first transfinite number. [Author's note.]

leaning back in the entire universe like in your armchair, you'd sit there mighty as . . .

BRAINIOWICZ: Stop—I'm choking on my power as if it were a pill too big for even the jaws of a whale.

GAMBOLINE: You don't love me. Do you want Isidore to come into the world with crooked legs and eyes on the side of his head?

BRAINIOWICZ: (*Hugging her impetuously*) No! No! Don't talk like that! I love you, I love you desperately. (*Suddenly goes limp.*) But I can't forget that you're a princess. There's something absolute about that. One only has to take a look at your legs. (GAMBOLINE *looks at her legs, then studies him carefully.*) If your father, Prince Basilius, could see you in the arms of a low-born slob like me, he'd die a second death from shame. I tell you there's something absolute about that, about the whole question of birth. What good does all my knowledge do me? (*Flings the proofs against the wall.*) I can't be born again.

GAMBOLINE: (*Hugging him*) My one and only, my dearest darling Tumor-kins—that you don't even understand that. That's exactly the whole point, where the whole devilish charm lies. That's why I left Kretchborski. I can't stand those demi-aristos. The cursed snobs. You're a monstrous low-born slob and when I feel my blood, of a devilish blue indeed, mingling with your scarlet, low-born slobbish gore, how together we're creating a race of violet demi-gods, when I think about that, I have the urge to spurt into molten lava from some other world out of sheer happiness. (BRAINIOWICZ's *face lights up in wild triumph. Enter* ALFRED BRAINIOWICZ.) Look! There he is, my fetish. Fred—come here, let me give you a hug . . .

BRAINIOWICZ: (*To* ALFRED) Did you solve the problems?

ALFRED: (*Kissing his mother, speaks in a quiet voice*) Yes, papa. I made the solution more difficult for myself by using Whitehead's method. That atrocious old man knows how to make the simplest question impossibly difficult.

BRAINIOWICZ: Show some respect for that wise man. Remember, I was his student.

GAMBOLINE: (*Looking at them admiringly*) I'm not sure I'll survive this happiness. Oh, why, why can't I be a rabbit!

BRAINIOWICZ: (*Gloomily*) Remember the white rabbit who gave birth to brindled cats for the rest of her life. She was unfaithful to her husband only once. Alfred reminds me of Kretchborski a bit too much.

GAMBOLINE: (*Laughs, stroking* BRAINIOWICZ's *head*) Poor brain-pan! Numbers have eaten up all your gray matter, Tumor!

BRAINIOWICZ: (*Roars*) Don't make fun of my name! It's rather well known throughout the entire world.

(*He stamps his feet and rolls his eyes in a mad fit.* ALFRED *goes over to the blackboard and starts writing on it with a piece of chalk. Gigantic integrals and complicated symbols appear.* GAMBOLINE *gets down on her knees and starts building something with the blocks.* BRAINIOWICZ *remains where he is. He calms down and sinks into deep thought.* IZA *runs in with the youngest Brainiowicz,* MAURICE.)

MAURICE: (*Pronouncing his words aristocratically and saying his "r's" very gutturally in the Parisian way*) But papa only writes poetry to keep his mental balance when the numbers have gone clean through all of his pores right into his soul. Iza is a true poet. Her poem has been published in our futuristic children's magazine. Iza, recite it.

IZA: (*Recites*)
Once there was a little foetus in the dusky by-and-by's,
Someone gave a shove by chance, someone stole a secret glance,
And out came pretty toes.
First of all they had to christen, find a name and then baptize,
Then baptize it Moogle-wise.
Once there was a little kitten, once there was a soft green mitten
Ate its breakfast in the by-and-by's.
Someone gave a secret glance, someone stole a shove by chance,
They all cried out their eyes.
In the children's picture book, in the cosy girlish nook,
A new tableau arose.
In the dusky by-and-by's someone stole a secret glance,
The cat devoured Moogle-wise.
Whether it was only dreamed or really happened as it seemed,
In vain they would surmise.
Did the illustration by itself arise,
Did the dream out of the drawing spring alive,
Not a guess from even soft green mitten,
Not a guess from even Moogle-wise.

BRAINIOWICZ: (*Glumly, tersely*) Makes too much sense.

ALFRED: (*Coming back from the blackboard*) What a waste of time. Father's a two-timer. Father's in love with Iza. Mama keeps whining about it all night long. I want no part of it.

BRAINIOWICZ: (*Screams*) Have you gone crazy?

MAURICE: (*Pointing at his father*) Yes, I know. He paces up and down all night and howls. He's a madman.

(GAMBOLINE *jumps up.*)

GAMBOLINE: Tumor!

IZA: (*Claps her hands with delight and jumps up and down*) The avalanche has started coming down!

BRAINIOWICZ: (*Beside himself*) I'll go stark raving mad! How dare they?

ALFRED: A perfectly ordinary story. There'll be a little article in the papers tomorrow under the heading "Imposter Unmasked!"

GAMBOLINE: (*Suddenly bursts out laughing*) The old brainpan is coming unscrewed, completely unscrewed!

BRAINIOWICZ: (*Sorrowfully*) It was so great and it's all gone completely to pieces. (*To* IZA.) Because of you, you aristocratic little demon! I always said it's exterminate the Kretchborskis or else we won't get anywhere.

GAMBOLINE: (*To the children*) Quiet! Calm down, all of you. There's still time to straighten this all out. (*Threateningly to* ALFRED, *hypnotizing him.*) That's not the way it is at all. Understand? (*Through the center door enter* JOSEPH *with an unknown gentleman wearing pince-nez.*) Too late!!

IZA: Good afternoon, Joseph. Who is that you've dragged in here with you?

JOSEPH: Well, you see, he was looking for Her Ladyship. He says to me, he says, he's first-class company.

STRANGER: Indeed, I am company and it seems I have come just in time.

(ALFRED *comes over to the* STRANGER.)

ALFRED: (*To the* STRANGER) Don't you dare butt into our private business.

GAMBOLINE: (*Uneasily*) Quiet, children! It's my private business, and only mine. I'm so worried about Isidore. Leave, all of you. I must be alone with him.

BRAINIOWICZ: (*Dolefully*) With whom? With Isidore? (*To* IZA.) I told you, all this makes too much sense. (*Exit to the left.* MAURICE *and* ALFRED *try to hold him. He breaks away from them and gets away.*)

STRANGER: One moment more and it will be too late. I have found the last possible means of salvation.

MAURICE: I don't believe you. We've already been through all that. We keep going around in circles until our heads are literally spinning. We can't take any more.

ALFRED: That's right! It's all a masked ball for them, for the members of the Academy, but we're in very bad shape.

IZA: (*Falls on her knees in front of her mother*) Send that man away. Mother, send him away!

GAMBOLINE: (*Gently but firmly*) No, Iza. We must reach a decision now. The tainted blood of the Kretchborskis is speaking through you.

STRANGER: (*Harshly, to* GAMBOLINE) You've got to choose between him and your daughter. The entire universe is watching you and you alone. He can't change the binding laws of mathematics just for the whims of that callow brat! He can do anything. I already know the proof he'll use to convince even the great Whitehead himself. It all started with the alephs; where intrinsic infinity comes into play, his omnipotence is absolute. But for the whole of civilization, in the name of all the ideals which humanity has ever held until now, we have to stop this.

ALFRED: (*Begins to get the picture*) Moritz, guard the door. (MAURICE *stands in the center door.* GAMBOLINE *doesn't know what to do. In her face and movements she displays signs of a monstrous struggle with herself.*)

GAMBOLINE: (*Screams with sudden resolution*) Tumor! Help!!

STRANGER: (*Pulling a card out of his wallet*) That won't do any good. I am Professor Green from the M.C.G.O., the Mathematical Central and General Office. Green, Alfred Green.

(*In one jump* IZA *is by the door.* GAMBOLINE *faints, screaming "Green."* MAURICE *grabs* IZA. ALFRED *whispers something in* GREEN's *ear.*)

GREEN: (*Loudly*) My agents are out there. (IZA *breaks away from* MAURICE *and dashes to the door. The two agents rush in and grab* IZA. *All the while* JOSEPH *splits his sides laughing and coughing senilely at the same time, spitting phlegm, and choking, until he simply squeals with delight. At this point* TUMOR BRAINIOWICZ *rushes in from the left and stops, absolutely petrified.* GREEN *yells to his agents.*) Off to the automobile with her and away you go in fifth gear! (*With mad speed the agents wrap a red scarf around* IZA's *head and run out through the center door holding her in their arms.* TUMOR *leaps over* GAMBOLINE's *prone body and dashes to the door.* GREEN *blocks his way threateningly, but with respect.*) Professor! Not another step. (ALFRED *and* MAURICE *close in on their father from both sides, stalking him like cats.*)

JOSEPH: (*Yells, setting them on*) Zoop!

(*Both boys hurl themselves at their father, trying to pin his arms behind him.* GREEN *hurls himself at him from the front, seizes him by the throat and tries to hold him. A motionless and mute scene like Ursus with the bull in Sienkiewicz's* Quo Vadis. *It lasts a very long time. The silence is broken by the loud panting of the combatants.* JOSEPH *makes his decision and like a predatory, wingless vulture creeps up to* BRAINIOWICZ, *grabs him by the legs around the knees and throws him to the ground. In silence they all tie* BRAINIOWICZ *up with scarfs and watch-chains.*)

GREEN *uses the rope which he had ready.* BRAINIOWICZ *roars briefly, then gives in passively.* BRAINIOWICZ *lies bound. They all are seated on the floor breathing heavily.*)

GREEN: (*Calmly*) I have done my duty.

JOSEPH: (*With pity*) You see, sonny boy, what you've come to. I always told you: don't pull too hard on the thread or it will break.

ALFRED: (*Getting up*) That was no thread, it was a rubber band.

MAURICE: (*Very aristocratically*) I have the impression that infinity is steaming out of every single one of papa's hairs. (*He draws near his mother.* GAMBOLINE *comes out of her faint.*)

GAMBOLINE: This is a terrible dream.

(GREEN *gets up and looks at his watch.*)

BRAINIOWICZ: (*Lying without moving*) Who will ever beat my last idea? I am invincible. You can put me in jail. I'll keep quiet, just leave me a pencil and paper. My last poem has to be completed.

GAMBOLINE: (*To* GREEN) Where is Iza?

(*She gets up, brushing herself off.*)

GREEN: Sacred blue, as the French say. I wish I knew myself. It happened so quickly, I didn't have time to give them orders.

GAMBOLINE: (*All at once joyfully, as if everything has become clear in her mind*) But perhaps this is the only possible solution! Perhaps this is exactly how it ought to be.

BRAINIOWICZ: (*Indifferently*) Perhaps it is. Who can say?

(*Enter* BALANTINE FERMOR *dressed in a golfing costume.* GAMBOLINE *rushes over to meet her.*)

GAMBOLINE: Thank goodness you've come. Do you see what a terrible thing has happened? It's so wild and unlikely I can hardly keep from laughing.

BRAINIOWICZ: (*Recites. They all listen dumbfounded*)
   Above the planet's shell
   Amidst the starry night,
   The alephs creep out one by one into Infinity.
   And Infinity infinitized
   Itself dies off, self-victimized.
   Coils of Titans, hornéd ghosts
   Pour galaxies of stars
   Into the ragged abysses.

Thought sunk its claws in its own gizzard
And bites itself within its own abyss,
But whose thought this? Can thought think itself?
As thunder thunders all alone and lightning too.
The point expanded into space's nth-dimensions
And space went plop
Like a punctured balloon.
All air shot out of it. So nothingness draws breath
From its own emptiness
And each thing crushes something else in time that stopped.

Hey! A glass of beer!

GREEN: Coming right up, Professor. I'm glad they didn't hear that poem at the M.C.G.O. I can just imagine the looks on their faces.

BRAINIOWICZ: Pure nonsense, my dear Alfred. Am I going to get that beer of mine one of these days? What a shame Iza didn't hear that poem. (*To* MAURICE.) Well, blockhead, still think I'm not a poet?

ALFRED: (*To* MAURICE) Don't say anything to papa.

BALANTINE: (*To* GREEN.) Send for more of your people, Professor. We've got to take him off to jail immediately. (*Exit* GREEN.) And you, children, go for a walk. It's a glorious day. There's spring in the air. The buds are turning green on the trees. I even saw two butterfiles, two brimstones, which awakened by the warmth, left their larvae and made broken circles in the air so drenched in aromas. The poor unfortunate creatures, they don't know there are no flowers yet and that what awaits them is death from starvation.

(*The boys' faces brighten up.* GAMBOLINE *kisses them on the foreheads.*)

GAMBOLINE: Yes, go for a walk. You're right, Balantine. You and I are like those butterflies you were talking about.

BRAINIOWICZ: (*Ironically*) And I'm a flower that hasn't bloomed yet. But I'll bloom yet. Never fear.

(*Exit the boys.*)

JOSEPH: I'll see them out, if you please, Your Ladyship.

GAMBOLINE: Yes, all right. Go now, Joseph, and then come back and have dinner with us. There'll be your beloved mush.

(*Exit* JOSEPH, *bowing low. Enter* GREEN *with four porters in blue smocks who take* BRAINIOWICZ *and go out.* GREEN *goes out after them.* GAMBOLINE *rushes over to* BALANTINE FERMOR *suddenly very anxious.*)

GAMBOLINE: (*Imploringly*) Tell me, what does it mean? I beg you, don't torture me anymore. By all you hold dear, tell me.

BALANTINE: (*Reassuringly*) Quite simply, you've all grown restive and intractable when it comes to certain ideas. Of all of you, Iza has the truest intuition about the future.

GAMBOLINE: (*In despair*) Poor, poor Iza!

(*She stares straight ahead of her with a pained look.*)

Act II

The action takes place on the island of Timor (the Sunda Archipelago). The seashore. In the distance the red cliff of the island of Amak Ganong. To the left, palm trees and bushes covered with gigantic purple flowers. To the right, a stockade with loopholes for rifles, and an entrance to the Malay Campong. Five-thirty in the morning. Black night. Canopus is in the ascendant. The crescent of the moon, like a canoe, with its points turned upwards, barely gives off any light. At the gates of the stockade there are two MALAYS *in red sarongs and blue turbans with spears. They stand guard without moving. In the middle of the stage there are two Ceylonese deckchairs (Colombo style), the feet to the audience. Enter* TUMOR BRAINIOWICZ *from the Campong in a white tropical outfit, almost carrying in his arms the fainting* IZA KRETCHBORSKI, *also dressed in white. The* MALAYS *prostrate themselves in front of them, then get up.*

BRAINIOWICZ: So that's how it was, that animal Green fell in love with you. They've always been like that at the M.C.G.O. In the morning abstract theory and pure multiplicity for its own sake. After dinner, when they've had their whisky and soda, they have time until the next morning to do the wildest things. How I loathe Europe. I'm a low-born slob, a totally primitive animal, but I can't stand that mealy-mouthed democracy anymore.

IZA: I love you. Now you're a true prince out of a fairy tale. (BRAINIOWICZ *puts her in one of the Ceylonese deckchairs; he collapses in the other one which creaks under his weight. He sticks his feet over the back of the chair.*)

BRAINIOWICZ: This is all a comedy. I don't have any feeling for reality, I don't have it in my blood. Pretend to be the ruler of these animals! That Anak Agong, Son of the Heavens, whom I defeated, he was a true ruler! Oh! I'll make mincemeat out of him! Potted viande! That animal is better born than I am. His great great grandfather's father is sitting on that volcano, look, Iza, over there where Ganong Malapa rises up.

(*He points to the audience. For a moment red lightning floods the stage from the direction of the audience and distant rumbling can be heard. Ganong Malapa is erupting.*)

IZA: You came out of that volcano yourself. The mystery is unfathomable. Today I'd like to beat Malays with rattan rods. I'd like you to beat me like a true ruler. Yet at the same time I'd like to keep you in a cage, feed you raw meat and use you the way only various domestic animals are used. Keep you for a moment of the highest, bestial, cruel sensual pleasure.

(BRAINIOWICZ *thrashes up and down furiously on the deckchair, gnashes his teeth and bellows.*)

BRAINIOWICZ: Shut up! The very demon of infinity is tearing apart my skull of steel. Don't drive me to do something frightful. I can't satiate myself with you. You are flimsy as kapok and insubstantial as a spider's web, but you torture me atrociously. Remember, I now have power greater than all the Greens in the world.

IZA: I like the way the hippopotamus in you gets aroused. Who is better born: you or the first hippo who happens to come along?

BRAINIOWICZ: (*Rolls about on the deckchair and roars*) Oh! Just let Green fall into my hands. I'll fix him all right—in the Malay fashion, in cold blood.

IZA: You won't be able to. To do that you have to be a thoroughbred. You won't even manage to annoy him, Professor. In another moment you'll fly into an ordinary blustering fit of temper, the kind I so love, the kind I'm so frightened of, the kind I so despise. And that gives me that invincible pleasure of subjugating myself, you and the whole world. I'd like to be even smaller; to be a mosquito and drink your blood through a tiny little tube that was part of my body, and have you roar with rage.

BRAINIOWICZ: (*Gets up from the deckchair and, his fists clenched, goes over to* IZA) Oh! If I could first differentiate you, examine every infinite tidbit of your cursed, red-head blood, each element of your steaming-hot whiteness and then take it, mash it, integrate it and finally comprehend where the infernal strength of your elusiveness lies which burns and consumes me to the very last tissue of my low-born, slobbish meat.

IZA: Remember, if I hadn't seduced Green, you'd be rotting in jail now.

BRAINIOWICZ: (*With a superhuman effort gets control of himself and sits up in the deckchair with his profile to the audience, his face turned towards* IZA. *He speaks calmly, in a hissing voice*) What took place between the two of you? How could you give him what was my property alone?

IZA: Property!! That from the great Brainiowicz, Tumor the First, Anak Agong, ruler of Timor and adopted son of the fire-breathing mountain. A vulgar display of jealousy! (BRAINIOWICZ *roars and beats his fists on his knees.*) You're old. A boring professor. What do I care about those stupid alephs of yours? Your property? How dare you? If you were a poet at least, I'd forgive you half your wild strength. What Moritz is able to do with one word, you have to use whole mountains of your ordinary, animal energy. One's property is what one takes and holds oneself, not refuse snatched by chance from the Mathematical Office. My infinity is no symbol. I am like a true Astarte. If I had come into the world earlier, I'd have truly been a queen, not a cheap actress on some stupid island. You're the one who gave me to Green. That mathematical instrument was my first lover; since I can't consider your six sons as lovers. You acted like a pimp! Too bad I couldn't have Isidore in my collection, there's been so much talk about him in your household recently.

(BRAINIOWICZ *gets up and yells for the* MALAYS. *Dawn suddenly breaks, red clouds drift across the sky. The palms sway in the morning breeze. In the distance the volcano erupts. Blood-red flashes of lightning illuminate the landscape, and muffled rumblings can be heard.* MALAYS *run up with spears poised aloft.* IZA *lies motionless with her eyes closed.*)

BRAINIOWICZ: (*Roars*) Get her! Run her through! Kaffirs, sons of dogs!

(*The* MALAYS *prepare to strike, waiting for the final command. Unable to take his eyes of* IZA, BRAINIOWICZ *freezes in motionless rapture. Bright sunlight suddenly floods the stage and the shrieking of a thousand parrots can be heard.* BRAINIOWICZ *falls on his knees in front of* IZA *who stretches voluptuously in the deckchair, half-opening her lips. She raises herself up slowly, looking with bright eyes into the sunny expanses of the sky. The* MALAYS *fall on their knees.*)

IZA: If only you believed in yourself. If only your cursed brain, which is stretching that buffalo-noggin of yours right out of shape, didn't prevent you from believing you're really the son of the fiery mountain, if only you were just a little bit of a poet, I'd be yours forever. Now I don't know. Who invited that atrocious expression: the metaphysical navel?

Oh, yes, that's right, it was Alfred, your first-born half-breed, the blue-gray blooded. That says it all. You and your kind have killed the true beauty of life, and you have made death no less hideous. You can even kill me. I prefer the spears of those animals to the knife of a famous surgeon. But I won't let you and your clever paws touch my body ever again. (*The parrots scream as though possessed. A Malay boat with a rectangular orange sail sails by.* BRAINIOWICZ *runs his hand through his hair.*) Bring the white rajah a pith-helmet, you sons of dogs. You'll overheat your brainpan, Professor.

(*The* MALAYS *run to the Campong.*)

BRAINIOWICZ: Now I'm really mad. I feel such monstrous insatiability my brain is turning to hot mush. The kind I used to eat years ago in my little thatched cottage. That's what's so frightful; the abyss that separates me, a civilized peasant, from these savages. The pettiness of this whole comedy. I'm an ordinary adventurer and, when you come right down to it, a mealy-mouthed liberal—and that's all. All Tumor's problems, all transfinite functions are absolutely nothing. (*The* MALAYS *bring his white tropical pith-helmet and* IZA's *hat and, with signs of the deepest reverence, put the pith-helmet on* BRAINIOWICZ's *head.*) But I'll play my role to the very end. (*To the* MALAYS.) Send for Anak Agong. (*The* MALAYS *run to the left.*) Now I'll rise above mealy-mouthed democracy once and for all. First I'll be a cruel and awe-inspiring ruler, and then I'll establish total socialism. Let those animals stew in their own juice.

(*Throngs of* MALAYS *gather to the left in the midst of the bushes. Only the first rows are visible. In the distance, thunder can be heard and the sun takes on a reddish color.* IZA *is lost in reverie. A pause. Two whites in pith-helmets and khaki uniforms lead in the old* RAJAH PATAKULO *from the left. Two* MALAYS *in red sarongs and red turbans follow them. The gray-bearded* RAJAH *wears only a loin-cloth around his hips. The* MALAYS *set up a deckchair to the right.* BRAINIOWICZ *sits down on the deckchair. A* YOUNG MALAY *of unusual beauty approaches* IZA *and whispers something in her ear.*)

BRAINIOWICZ: (*To the* RAJAH) Patakulo: I, Tumor the First, ruler of Timor, son of the Heavens and the Fiery Mountain (*the volcano flashes blood-red against the darkening, stormy sky*), I am he who has the right to dissolve you all into a pulp, to dry up the sea and extinguish that mountain which gave birth to me. (*The stormy darkness keeps increasing. It thunders and lightnings more and more violently. He points to the* RAJAH.) Compared to my white power, your former ruler is only the shadow of a shadow.

IZA: (*Interrupting her conversation with the* YOUNG MALAY) You don't recite that well, Professor!

(*The* MALAYS *whisper among themselves.* BRAINIOWICZ *becomes flustered.*)

ONE OF TWO MALAYS FROM THE GUARD AT THE CAMPONG: (*In a blue turban*) I saw it. He humbled himself in front of her. Our enchanted spears could not strike her body.

SECOND MALAY: She is the new divinity of the whites. The hand I held my spear in turned to stone when I tried to strike her. The white Rajah worshipped her as a celestial being.

(BRAINIOWICZ *gets up; with one last effort he tries to gain control of himself. He pulls out a revolver and shoots the old* RAJAH *who topples to the ground.* BRAINIOWICZ *yells.*)

BRAINIOWICZ: Boy! Lemon squash!! (*A pause; he goes on speaking calmly.*) I, Tumor the First, ruler of Timor, am the one and only lord of this earth. There are no other divinities. (*Another* YOUNG MALAY, *who has raced out of the Campong, serves him lemonade on a tray; to the whites in khaki uniforms.*) Bring her over here!

(*He points at* IZA. *She comes to him, and for a moment they look one another in the eyes. A frightful flash of lightning illuminates the landscape and thunder crashes from the clouds down onto the earth.*)

IZA: (*Bursts into uncontrollable laughter*) Tumie! You old ham. Did you really think I'd fall for a trick like that? You, you old lazy ox of a minx!

BRAINIOWICZ: (*Resignedly, looking at her with complete submission*) I'm helpless! Iza, Iza, what is all of mathematics and absolute knowledge compared to one square centimeter of your skin. Oh! If I could only be an artist!

(*The* YOUNG MALAY *comes over to them with a reptilian smile.*)

YOUNG MALAY: Oh, white Rajah! Give me your divinity. The volcano has fallen in love with her. Since she came to our island Ganong Malapa has been trembling all over and breathing fire. He hasn't been this angry for centuries. I am the son of Patakulo and the rightful ruler, and the great grandson of the underground fire. I'll marry her like a sister, and honor her as I have always honored our gods in the Unity of Being beyond the grave.

BRAINIOWICZ: (*Furious*) They understood one another right away. Cursed aristocrats. The sole art lies in rising above the problem of birth. Iza, don't think I don't love your mother. But for you alone I committed this hideous crime. (*To the* YOUNG MALAY.) You don't know her, Prince Tengah. She isn't a divinity. She's an ordinary young white she-goat, bored and frisky. If you take her as your wife, a frightful punishment awaits you for defiling the fire of the mountains.

PRINCE TENGAH: You're the one who doesn't know her, white Rajah. You look at everything through your horrible cleverness which has concealed from you the true beauty of the soul, the sea and the mountains. You killed my father without even being his enemy. Could anything be more hideous!

BRAINIOWICZ: How does that colored whipper-snapper know about that?

IZA: You killed that old man to make an impression on me. On me! Oh, how I despise you, schoolmaster of present-day infinity. Go on begetting your degenerate brood on my poor mother whom you have deceived, but don't you dare enter my sanctuary.

(*The storm passes them by. The darkness slowly dissipates. Bored by the spectacle, the* MALAYS *go off in different directions carrying away* PATAKULO's *body.*)

BRAINIOWICZ: (*In despair*) Oh, how drab and petty everything is! I don't know whether I'm a supercivilized human or only an ordinary animal pretending to be a featherless biped. Oh! What a shame Green isn't here. Up there at the M.C.G.O., I could still make an impression. Up there I could show them that class of numbers which I designated with Persian numerals. But the number of alphabets is limited. Those numbers, my own numbers, I call them tumors. Tumor The First will not be the ruler of a petty little island, he'll be the first number in that monstrous series which will turn their brains inside out like an old glove.

IZA: (*To* TUMOR BRAINIOWICZ) Still in a certain sense you do have something great in you. (*Embraces* PRINCE TENGAH.) But I love only him, true offspring of the fiery mountain.

PRINCE TENGAH: (*In wild rapture*) If I have gained possession of the love of a divinity through the death of my father, be blessed, Oh, white Rajah!

(*He kisses her on the lips.* BRAINIOWICZ *pulls off his tropical pith-helmet and wipes his sweaty hair.*)

BRAINIOWICZ: (*In greater and greater despair*) What should I do, what should I do now? There's no place in the world for me. I exist and I don't exist. Infinity has devoured my entrails. If I could at least write, write one poem. Oh, what inhuman torture! (*To* IZA.) Do you think that that savage loves you? He sees only the poetess in you. You turned his head with your silly poetry.

IZA: (*Recites*)
In the dark and soul-less fire,
Sweaty flesh chokes out my light.
Thus I feel a strange god's ire
For the deeds of pigeons bright.

Pigeons white, and young girls dreaming
On wet grass the pigs are preening.
You are one, and they are thousands.
Would I had bodies as many as thoughts,
And each body lovers as many
As, say, numbers in the aleph-null.
Little words: if only—oh, chasm fearful,
Lumbering ox necks that bow and scrape.
Would I had passions burned black as crepe
Fastened in the months of sky-blue ore.
Fastened forever the lock on the prison door,
Builded on the world's wide wilderness
By some triumphant god, titanic, bold:
For devils sick and perverse angels
The madman's ward, beyond whose threshold
Goes no sage or prince of numbers.
There forever to the black one sue,
Whom the fiery mountain brought to light,
And continue there to dwell—worm white,
To the strange god ever true.
Writhe in some resplendent ape's embrace,
Hearing silence echo midst the stars,
Guzzle blackest blood, watch torture's hard grimace,
Icy laughter breathe on guts' raw scars,
Squeal with rapture, then kick rapture's face,
Till the final croak comes through the bars.
Be a girl pure, innocent and little,
Moisten my red tongue with sweetish spittle.

BRAINIOWICZ: (*Has gained complete control of himself*) You can put that in the futuristic children's magazine Maurice edits. But, unfortunately, it doesn't impress me.

IZA: (*Pouts contemptuously, drawing away from* PRINCE TENGAH *who keeps on trying to kiss her*) I'll show you something better yet. This black has a strange smell. Not musty laundry, not dried mushrooms. Oh, how horrible life is! Why is it that real people are nothing but wild animals, why is it that their smell is repulsive to our corrupted nostrils?

BRAINIOWICZ: (*Laughs savagely, triumphantly*) You see, you silly little European goose: civilization is winning out.

IZA: It's a triumph for you. That black idiot is simply repulsive. I've run out of steam.

PRINCE TENGAH: (*Does not understand very clearly what is going on; to* IZA) What are you saying, daughter of the moon?

BRAINIOWICZ: (*Ironically*) She's opening wide the treasure chest of her civilization for you. Now you're going to find out everything, son of a father I bumped off, why, I don't know myself.

IZA: (*Sadly*) Unfortunately, you know quite well. Everything has come to an end. I don't know who to give the rest of my days to. That black prince was my last hope.

BRAINIOWICZ: (*With anxiety*) What about me?

IZA: Oh, Professor, you'll go on being the prince of numbers, alephs, tumors of the nth-class and other such creations. I've lost what gave me strength over you, Professor. Your daughter will take my place for you in every respect. Such an able, young girl!

(TENGAH *looks at them with growing astonishment, not understanding a single thing.*)

BRAINIOWICZ: You know, I've run out of steam too. At least I've got the feeling I have. It's a good thing I haven't gone crazy. I wonder what Alfred would say if he could see my most recent ordeals. Not Alfred Green, of course, I mean my first-born reprobate of a son.

PRINCE TENGAH: (*To* IZA) My one and only, my divinity. Why don't you notice me, why do you push me away? Doesn't your white body want to be sacrificed to the underground fire? I am like the fiery mountain myself. If you want, I'll burn you up with one single breath of mine.

IZA: Prince, your breath doesn't smell of sulphur, only raw meat. No one ever burned up anyone yet with raw meat.

BRAINIOWICZ: (*To* PRINCE TENGAH) I told you, black-yellow beast, she is an ordinary silly little white goose. Now you have the truth from those lips you kissed a moment ago with the highest love.

(PRINCE TENGAH *staggers.*)

PRINCE TENGAH: (*In despair*) I have betrayed myself. Frightful are the lies of white people, frightful the venom in their souls poisoned by cleverness. Their words are more killing than our swords, their weapons stronger than the relics of our divinities. Oh, white Rajah! I shall not defile my sword destined for enemies worthy of me. (*Pulls his kris out of its scabbard and runs himself through.*) May you be cursed, white worm for whom I betrayed everything that was sacred to me. (*He dies.*)

IZA: At last I finally got rid of that colored Casanova.

BRAINIOWICZ: (*Looks at her with cold admiration*) Iza! You're marvelous. If it weren't for this insane heat and my new idea about an nth-class of tumors, I don't know if I wouldn't fall in love with you all over again. Actually you're the only woman who . . .

(*Two* MALAYS *in blue turbans rush in. They fall down on their faces in front of* IZA. BRAINIOWICZ *shows his displeasure.*)

MALAY I: Queen! A boat has come into Bangay bay. The white chief is coming here. They have brought a new divinity.

MALAY II: She is bigger and fatter than you are. (*Notices the prone body of* PRINCE TENGAH.) But what is this? Our chief dead, run through with his own kris.

MALAY I: He put himself to death according to the commands of his ancestors.

(*They both humble themselves in front of the corpse; it becomes completely light and the sun floods the entire landscape.*)

MALAY II: We have run out of rulers. Perhaps the new goddess has brought us someone from beyond the far seas.

(*They get up and remain in an expectant attitude.* BRAINIOWICZ *pulls binoculars out of his pocket and looks over between the bushes to the left.*)

BRAINIOWICZ: (*Looking through the binoculars*) I recognize her. The "Prince Arthur," a cruiser first class. They've just come ashore. Sacred blue! Green is getting off the ship. Balantine Fermor, Captain Fitz Gerald and . . .

(*He lowers the binoculars.* IZA *grabs them and looks.*)

IZA: (*Stamping her feet with excitement*) Green is on his way! Green, Green has come! Balantine! She'll be a consolation for you, Professor. She adored you so.

BRAINIOWICZ: But the fact is I'm a criminal. I killed an innocent man.

IZA: (*Lowers the binoculars*) Really! To have scruples about some Malay or other. Spit on that! Long live the alephs and the tumors! What is death in the face of present-day infinity?

BRAINIOWICZ: Perhaps you're right. There's no such thing as crime. Just look at all the people nowadays who, just because they walk about on two legs, claim the rights of human beings. What is the criterion for distinguishing a human being from an animal? Once that was clearly known: nowadays, in the era of mealy-mouthed demo . . .

(*The roar of cannons from the cruiser prevents him from saying more.*)

IZA: That's Green banging out a greeting on the twelve-inchers aboard the cruiser. It's what we agreed on before.

(*Enter from the bushes:* GREEN, FITZ-GERALD, BALANTINE FERMOR *and five members of the crew, armed from head to foot.*)

GREEN: Hip! Hip! Hurrah! Brainiowicz is alive! Seize him, boys! Give the order, captain. We're taking possession of this country. (*The members of the crew throw themselves at* BRAINIOWICZ *and bind him with ropes.* IZA *laughs very embarrassedly. To* IZA.) Iza! You're a marvelous woman. We mathematicians are able to appreciate the strangeness of life. What happened before doesn't matter. Your past doesn't exist. The only thing that exists is science, for which everything can be sacrificed, even male honor. (*To* BALANTINE.) Miss Fermor, right honorable Miss Fermor, please vouch for my truthfulness. I love Miss Kretchborski; I renounce all the secret doings at the M.C.G.O. Miss Fermor, please repeat these words to the sole woman who is worthy to bear my name and perhaps even my title, if merciful God — mathematics and religion are two totally different aspects of the same thing — allows me to live longer than my cousins.

BALANTINE: Iza! I am here on behalf of your mother. (*To* BRAINIOWICZ, *who lies tied up on the ground.*) A propos! Gamboline finally begat Isidore. Marvelous boy. His eyes are so close together you can hardly see his nose, like all the Trun-Dhul-Bhed's. A born mathematician.

BRAINIOWICZ: (*Joyfully*) Oh, I'm grateful to you all for taking away my will power. I'm being poisoned by my own strength. I simply have too much will power and that's why I can't make any decisions. Infinity becomes reality in total freedom of choice. Oh, what a pleasure it is to be imprisoned. Iza! On behalf of your mother, and speaking as your stepfather, I give you full authority to exercise your free will. Green! You old scoundrel! You've got the prettiest girl in the world. She loves you . . .

BALANTINE: (*Interrupts him*) And besides, it will be no misalliance. Alfred is Green of Greenfield. He is the fifth son of the Fifth Marquess of Maske-Tower. I certainly hope his brothers live forever, but when they do die, he'll be a peer and the richest man in England.

BRAINIOWICZ: (*Furiously*) Dogs' blood! I didn't know that. Sangua del carno! Why aren't I something like that. From that vantage point you can look your nose down at everything.

GREEN: You are Brainiowicz. Tout simplement, Brainiowicz. Master, I'd give you ten titles for that devilish name, which I can't even pronounce.

BALANTINE: Oh, how true! There's something in that name that conjures up the smell of protoslavonic forests, of hives of wild bees stirred to life by the heat of the sun in flowering glades, and of rivers and lakes full of golden fish and water sprites. Oh, how beautiful it is. Carry him off to the ship. Isidore is waiting for him. Isidore is waving his fat little fists and in his own mute language calling for the father he already adores. (*She notices the bodies of the Anak Agongs.*) Great heavens! Brainiowicz has been chopping up Malays here like cabbages.

IZA: (*In* GREEN's *arms*) What has happened here has happened purely by accident. That young black died out of love for me. The old one tried to kill the Professor. I shot him down like a dog. What else could I do? It's every man for himself.

GREEN: (*Losing control of himself*) How I love you, Iza! How could we ... such a short time, so little opportunity ... And then a separation like that. Oh, how I love you ...

BALANTINE: (*To the Sailors*) Seize him, boys! And hold him tight. You see, he's the greatest brain in the civilized world. A bit perverted, since everything that's great has to be perverse, and perversion nowadays is simply synonymous with greatness.

(*The Sailors take* BRAINIOWICZ *and exit with* FITZ-GERALD *and* BALANTINE. GREEN *plants a pole with the British flag.*)

IZA: And yet I have regrets about something. But I don't even know what it is myself. Only the dream will remain. A memory of events that never took place. (*Making a sudden decision.*) Green—I've got to tell you everything—I was unfaithful to you with Tumor.

(GREEN *curls up into a ball from pain and jealousy and at the very same moment expands with wild desire.*)

GREEN: (*Throwing himself helplessly at* IZA) I love you, I love you! Quiet! There are only these moments, and everything else is an illusion in the infinite infinities of being.

IZA: (*Submitting to him indifferently*) But it was so lovely, so strange! What a pity, what a pity ...

(GREEN *carries her off fainting to the left, into the flowering bushes.*)

Act III

The same room as in Act One. GAMBOLINE KRETCHBORSKI, secundo voto BRAINIOWICZ, *dressed as in Act One, walks up and down with a young child in her arms humming, to the tune of a Slavic lullaby.*

GAMBOLINE:
Oh, ho, pussy cats two,
Both of them black and both of them blue,
Oh, ho, pussy cats three,
Ate the gray brains of a flea.
Oh, ho, pussy cats four,
Papa went to see a whore.
Oh, ho, pussy cats five,
Mother's caprice came alive.
Oh, ho, pussy cats six,
Tie infinity to sticks.
Oh, ho, pussy cats seven,
Papa said: Avec vous it's heaven.
Oh, ho, panthers eight,
Mother said . . .

(*Enter* BRAINIOWICZ.)

BRAINIOWICZ: How's Isidore doing?

GAMBOLINE: Isidore is doing quite nicely; and you, pater Brainiowicz, how do you feel in this ordinary everyday life of ours?

BRAINIOWICZ: I don't know how to stray from the path of virtue. What's more important, what do you think of Iza's marrying Green?

GAMBOLINE: You know I'm free from prejudices about family. Once his three brothers all die, it will be a wonderful match for Iza.

BRAINIOWICZ: You don't have any idea what it means to me. (*Points at* ISIDORE.) That is my last child with you. There's something about Isidore's face that completely takes away any desire I might have to beget any more Brainiowiczes on you. (*Making a sudden decision.*) I've applied for a divorce today and I'm going to ask for Miss Fermor's hand before the day is out.

GAMBOLINE: (*Indifferently*) I don't want anything anymore. Seven sons are quite enough. Everything is behind me now. Slobbish, low-born love, and all forms of spiritual perversion. I ennobled the house of Brainiowicz. Alfred can propose to a lord's daughter. No one will turn him down.

BRAINIOWICZ: You forget that *I* can propose to a lord's daughter, and even be accepted. I've been living all alone, totally wrapped up in my figures. I begat a new world. Cantor, Georg Cantor, is a pure infant compared to my definitions of infinity, and Frege and Russell are but the paltry decanting of a Greek void into the void of our own times with their definition of number, compared to what I thought up this morning . . .

GAMBOLINE: (*Keeps on dandling the little sniveller*) A hideous compromise. Alfred told me about it . . .

BRAINIOWICZ: I'll kill that first-born stinker of mine! He doesn't know anything. He's trying to denounce what he hasn't even been able to grasp. Can't you understand that certain brains are not capable of grasping certain things. My logic is not capable of being refuted. But to reduce the whole series of arguments to a single system, you've got to have a truly pre-eminent head on your shoulders. The only one who has the strength for that is me, me. They sense that and that's why they're afraid.

(*Enter* GREEN *with* IZA.)

GREEN: Professor! Your theory is winning out. Today I received the latest bulletin from the M.C.G.O. Even Whitehead has been shaken.

BRAINIOWICZ: They can only accept what falls into categories that have already been created. We, Brainiowicz, have given a different meaning to the very concept of logic. Those halfwits can't tolerate that.

GREEN: But what if you do win, Professor? What then? What's going to happen to the whole science of mechanics? What's going to take the place of the law of gravity? The first case in our times of pure deduction overturning a world view with several hundred years behind it.

BRAINIOWICZ: Do you think that these ideas that I am presenting are final? Can you really believe that *I* could speak the truth in the presence of halfwits like you and your cohorts from the M.C.G.O.?

IZA: Oh, how happy I am that such a genius was in love with me for two whole months.

GREEN: (*To* IZA) Stop it, you silly goose! (*To* BRAINIOWICZ.) Professor! Tell me, only me. Tell me how you arrived at the formula for the nth-class of numbers. Tell me, what is tumor-one?

BRAINIOWICZ: You're a stupid jackass. I'll tell you and the next minute you'll forget it. You've got to have the brains of a titan for something like that. Do you think that everything really is curved; that everything really is simultaneous? Those are elementary questions in transcendental dynamics, whose childish application quite simply constitutes my theory.

GREEN: Just tell me the definition of that one little word, "really," Professor. That's all I ask. Tell me how you define "or" and "except"—just those two words.

(*He falls to his knees in front of* BRAINIOWICZ.)

BRAINIOWICZ: (*Dolefully*) The posthumous edition of my works will contain an analysis of that problem too. For now I can only tell you this: it's either you or me. Iza is the exponent of my latest idea, that poor Iza whose slave you are and who is unfaithful to you during official excursions with the ship's stewards, not to mention the members of the M.C.G.O. Get to know her well, future Fifth Marquess of Maske-Tower. She embodies the mystery of the identity of those two little words: "or" and "except." I discovered that when I killed old Patakulo.

GREEN: (*On his knees*) Go on! I think I'm beginning to understand.

BRAINIOWICZ: Do you think *I* understand it? My last thoughts will be as hard to decipher as Egyptian hieroglyphics. But where will they find another Champollion of logic, someone with sufficient brain power to decipher these thoughts and turn them into symbols intelligible to all?

GREEN: I'll be that one person.

BRAINIOWICZ: You, you simple-minded idiot? (*Laughs savagely.*) You haven't any desire for the truth, you only dream of cosmic mathematical blackmail!

(GAMBOLINE *dandles* ISIDORE *more and more passionately.*)

GAMBOLINE: They'll resolve it. Our children will. The entire future lies with them.

BRAINIOWICZ: You're wrong, my child. The next generation must forego that. It's only us, the civilized slobs, who have that savage strength. We low-born slobs with the brains of buffaloes, but razor-sharp like a hysterical princess's emotional reactions—in twenty years time there won't be any more of us. This is the end of the line—our whole western democracy is heading in that direction. That's what's being opposed by the wonderful movement of destruction the East is now indulging in.

GREEN: (*Getting up*) Tumor Brainiowicz—an ordinary universal maniac for state socialism. What a come-down!

BRAINIOWICZ: You're wrong there, you idiot! Turning the clock back on civilization. That's what ruling the island of Timor has taught me. You know I murdered a man there, and another one killed himself because of me. Do you know what that did to me?

(IZA *falls on her knees in front of him.*)

IZA: Tumor! You're the only great man I've ever known.

GAMBOLINE: Shame on you, Iza! In front of your mother.

BRAINIOWICZ: (*To his wife*) Your dearest, darling Isidore is going to be a monstrosity all his ancestors will be ashamed of: the beastly tribe of Brainiowiczes no less than the Mongolian Khans, headed by the Great Ghengis himself. Out of my sight, you cursed bitch! *I* am lord of the world!!

GAMBOLINE: Oh, so that's how it is? So everything I've done amounts to nothing? So *I'm* to be kicked too for lowering myself? You dare insult what is most sacred within me? I'll show you! You double-dealing comedian!

(*She dashes over to the window to the right and throws the still-diapered* ISIDORE BRAINIOWICZ *out of it; then she stands still, her face turned towards the audience, with a look of total madness. The frightful look of tension on her face, expressing animal pain, lasts for a moment. Then she falls to the ground and howls wildly like a she-wolf.*)

GREEN: See here, Mrs. Brainiowicz! People don't do things like that. This is sheer barbarity.

IZA: Mother! I like monstrous things, but that's too much even for me.

(*She dissolves in tears.*)

BRAINIOWICZ: It leaves *me* completely indifferent. The umbilical cord which tied me to my children has been cut. One more crime takes place because of me.

GREEN: I worship you, Professor. You are a titan. A splendid deed done unintentionally!! Could there be anything more thrilling!

IZA: (*To* GREEN) Oh, so you're that weak, Alfred? You can humble yourself in front of that old puppet? I have been a witness to his crimes. Merciful God! Unintentional crimes committed by a bungler unfit for life. The inner recesses of his soul shown up in the light of transfinite ethics. He has a conscience, that lily-livered monster. He is suffering as well. Can't you see that, Alfred? Is there anything more vile than pangs of conscience?

GREEN: I must confess, that's something I've never been bothered with. After the most frightful orgies at the M.C.G.O., I felt perfectly wonderful. We used to kill little girls from the plebeian class in an incredibly cruel way . . .

GAMBOLINE: (*Covering his mouth with her hands*) You horrid rotter! You're the one who got this hideous conversation started. It's your fault that I killed poor Isidore . . .

(*Enter* JOSEPH BRAINIOWICZ *with a newspaper in his hand. He is followed by two porters in blue aprons who carry in the bloodstained diapers containing the mashed remains of* ISIDORE BRAINIOWICZ.)

JOSEPH BRAINIOWICZ: Begging your humble pardon. What I mean is they've written up my boy so nice here in the papers. A hero! A thinker! A genius at ideas and a genius at deeds. But where is that island? And is it true he claimed to be the son of a fiery mountain? Oh, my boy, that wasn't nice of you to disown your legitimate father and you'll be punished.

BRAINIOWICZ: (*Very ashamed*) But papa, but father (*stammers*), but damn it all to hell, get rid of that trashpaper!

(*He grabs the newspaper away from him and flings it at the wall. Enter* IRENE BRAINIOWICZ *in a black dress.*)

IRENE: Father! *I'll* free you from these last bonds. I don't want any love. I have everything.

BRAINIOWICZ: (*Deeply moved*) I forgot I had another daughter. Dearest Rena! You're the only one who'll stay with me.

IRENE: (*Embraces him tightly and kisses him on the forehead with infinite tenderness*) Yes, father! Give up that horrible work. You can have it published after your death. I know. Alfred doesn't understand a thing. He's just spying on you. He's very clever, but only up to a certain point. I know what he's like. I gave him the basis for the theory of pure plurality. (*To* GREEN.) Green! How dare you keep this great mind occupied with all that nonsense? Have you all gone mad at that cursed M.C.G.O. of yours?

GREEN: (*Bows humbly*) I know quite a bit too. You're very clever, Miss Irene, but what you don't know is that he has created a class of numbers designated by Persian symbols, and that he's now about to formulate the proof that the number of a certain plurality is higher than all the pluralities known to him and to Satan alone. He's even had the presumption to name it — he's calling it tumor-one.

(IRENE *looks at her father in horror; then she takes the bloodstained diapers away from the porters and presses them to her breast.*)

IRENE: Poor, poor Isidore!

JOSEPH BRAINIOWICZ: They didn't even spare the poor child, son of a gun.

IRENE: (*To* JOSEPH) Grandfather! Let's get out of here. It's simply impossible to breath here. I envy Leibniz so frightfully. He was a child just like this poor little corpse.

(*She takes* JOSEPH *by the arm and goes out, clutching the diapers under her left arm; the porters follow them out.* GAMBOLINE *regains her composure and smoothes out her dress. She gradually stops being a mother and a she-wolf, and once again becomes a woman in love.*)

GAMBOLINE: They've overpowered you now, pater Brainiowicz, and you'll probably never get back on your feet again. Even Rena has left you and your own Papa-Anthropoid has evaporated into thin air.

GREEN: I'm still here. I'll stay with him.

BRAINIOWICZ: You miserable crab; you eavesdropper on unthinkable thoughts; you psychic kept-man of a degenerate adolescent! I'd rather go into exile and fall prey to the Dyaks on the island of Timor than confide even one single thought to you. He thinks he knows something because he can pronounce the words: tumor-one. It's not a secret spell for discovering treasure; to understand it you've got to have a head on your shoulders, not a birdcage full of colored feathers. You blockheaded intellectual rag-picker! You powder puff, you lackey of strumpeted infinity!

(*He suddenly goes weak in the knees and sits down on the ground. Enter* BALANTINE FERMOR *in a pink dress and gigantic hat with colossal black feathers.* GAMBOLINE *rushes over to her.*)

GAMBOLINE: Oh, Balantine! I killed Isidore! Can you understand what's happened? Poor little Isidore smashed to pieces on the cobble-stones, and I did it. But *he* forced me to! That monster, that low-born slob, Brainiowicz.

BALANTINE: (*Calmly*) In the first place, he didn't force you to, and in the second place, you didn't kill Isidore. A long time ago, almost from his very birth, I saw frightful tendencies in the boy. And most of all, a tendency to hideous diseases. Joseph told me about it. Decent old chap. He's so very taken up with his role.

IZA: (*Who has been diligently putting away toys all this time*) That person has to spoil every last monstrosity, even the most modest and unassuming. Everything is clear and simple to her, like integral equations. That's fine for Irene. I tell you, she'll be back here in no time.

GREEN: Stop, oh, stop. I have the feeling a whirlwind of spirits is flying through my head. Those drowning in the sea of death while they are still alive are not denied their final wishes. Iza! I feel you slipping away from me. Your adorable little soul is as slippery as a school of slithering sardines.

IZA: I must ask you not to make me the subject of what is a pure play on words. I have created an entire little world from the scraps of the various words you have inadvertently let drop. Such a tiny little world, but for all that, mine, all mine.

BALANTINE: (*Ironically*) Oh, how touching. Don't go on that way; I feel the tears coming to my eyes.

(*Enter* ALFRED *and* MAURICE BRAINIOWICZ. BRAINIOWICZ *gets up off the floor.*)

ALFRED: (*Pulling a newspaper out of his pocket*) Listen! You too, mother! Only I beg you, be brave, don't let this news upset you . . .

GAMBOLINE: (*Imploringly to* ALFRED) Spare me . . . I can't stand anymore.

IZA: (*Tries to calm her down*) There, Mother dear! Nothing more can possibly happen. It was a dream. Alfred and I will have you come live with us. Green! Isn't that right? You wouldn't deny me that.

GREEN: (*Coldly*) On certain conditions.

ALFRED: (*Reads*) The heading is: "Monstrous compromise. Well-known pillar of present-day mathematical knowledge, Sir Tumor Brainiowicz, recently made hereditary baronet of Queensland, conqueror of the island of Timor and creator of a new constitution for the Malays in the IIIrd marine district, has fallen victim to his own weakness . . ."

BRAINIOWICZ: (*Dolefully*) Green wrote that. Remember what he said right here just a moment ago. He was lying flat on his face in front of me as though he were praying to the statue of Isis. Now isn't that just hideous swinishness?

MAURICE: Papa! Papa! Listen to the rest of it.

ALFRED: (*Reads*) " . . . weakness, which can be seen in his latest theory, published in the organ of the M.C.G.O., 'Unity and Diversity.' This theory is concerned with the now celebrated creation of a free class of numbers . . ."

GAMBOLINE: Green! How could you do something like that! (IRENE *runs in.*)

IRENE: It's a lie, a monstrous lie! Green's trying to test father. He put Alfred up to it. I know everything. Joe just gave you away. He's got a fever and told me everything. Green is vile. He used Iza just to have an influence over Alfred.

BRAINIOWICZ: But it appears in print. I know what will happen next. To make it impossible for me to carry on my work, I'm being presented as a person who's given up on the infinite series of numerical classes. I want to put a limit to these classes. I still don't have an over-all proof. But the number of the so-called tumor-one is the highest number that can exist. No one, not even the transfinite mind of God himself, is going to create a series of tumors.

IRENE: (*Falls on her knees in front of her father*) Papa! I don't want to hear about it. What have you done to Infinity!

BRAINIOWICZ: So you're against me too. There are no more Brains left in the world. I thought my daughter, at least my poor Renakins, would accept me for what I am. No — apparently I've got to go through all possible torments right to the very end.

(*He sits down on the floor. For a moment he plays with the blocks, then he begins to cry horribly, despairingly. He virtually howls, sobbing hysterically. They are all petrified with terror and anguish.*)

IZA: (*Embraces* BRAINIOWICZ. *Green wrings his hands in despair*) Now I really love you. I wanted to see your weakness just once. The days are past when you could tame demonic women by brute force. I am a demon! (*Leaps up and, with a fiery glance, transfixes those present, and even those not present.*) I am a priestess of Isis. *I* danced naked with a sunflower on my forehead. *I* humbled Lord Persville, the greatest demon at the M.C.G.O. Green! You miserable wet noodle, deceived and betrayed forty-five times over: Lord Persville, the creator of a geometry which can be presented analytically only in intermittent, transfinite functions, writhed at my feet like a stepped-on worm. I didn't sleep nights. I worked like forty steam oxen! Tumor! I feigned ignorance to get a glimpse of your weakness once. I know everything! I know the theory of numbers that are variable in a constant fashion! (GREEN *writhes in terrible sufferings.* IZA *embraces* BRAINIOWICZ *again.*) I really love him and only him. You don't know what I've been through.

IRENE: Wretch!

GREEN: (*Roars wildly*) Oh, the viper!!!

ALFRED: What about me?! Father, the mathematics you taught me was false. That futuristic adolescent knows more than I do.

MAURICE: Iza! So your poetry is fraudulent! Oh, I won't live through this.

(BALANTINE *looks on with icy calm, holding the sobbing* GAMBOLINE *in her arms.* MAURICE *falls on the floor and cries uncontrollably.*)

BRAINIOWICZ: (*Pushes* IZA *away with a sudden gesture; she collapses on the floor next to the weeping* MAURICE; *getting up, he speaks to* IZA) Out of my sight! I don't know you. I hate you. You thought you could degrade me that way; Brainiowicz, father of seven sons and an incredible number of daughters? Get out, you slut!

GAMBOLINE: (*Stops crying and suddenly bursts into a savage laugh of triumph*) Serves her right. Let the cursed house of Kretchborski die out.

BRAINIOWICZ: (*Stands like a wounded wild ox whose pride alone keeps him from falling*) I am completely alone. Where I get my strength, none of you will ever find out, and even I myself know little more about it than you.

GAMBOLINE: If you won't be mine, don't be anyone's. Pater Brainiowicz: you are truly great.

ALFRED: (*In despair*) And I spent all that time learning a pack of lies! My whole examination in transcendental dynamics was a cheap farce. Just who are these criminals at the Academy? Who are they (*points at* GREEN), who are the scum from the M.C.G.O.? There haven't been monsters like that since the world was born. Oh, if only I could rip my brains right out of my skull, if only I could start all over again to comprehend it!

(MAURICE *calms* IZA *down. She gets up with a smile.*)

MAURICE: (*Getting up with her*) We'll write poetry together. It's still not too late for all that.

IZA: Moritz, save me. Only you can. But won't it just be a repetition of everything that's already happened once before?

MAURICE: No, Iza. Remember our conversation on the green sofa yesterday? Do you remember what you told me?

IZA: That Infinity is individuality turned upside down. That was your father's idea. I've got to create it in pure form.

MAURICE: (*Embracing her*) We'll create it together. It's an antidote against intellectual insanity. We'll create a lovely gray bird who'll fly off into Nothingness. Without any rainbows or colors. Understand? I know how to do it.

BRAINIOWICZ: (*Coldly*) By simplifying things artificially.

IZA: That's not true! You have no right to talk about art. I believe in Moritz's genius.

BRAINIOWICZ: (*Pulls out a notebook and writes something down*) I can stop talking altogether. Oh, when I remember that I once used to write poetry, I go cold all over from shame. Tomorrow, without any further delay, I shall marry Balantine Fermor and we'll go off to Australia.

(GREEN, *who has been observing* IZA *and* MAURICE *with daggers in his eyes, suddenly goes over to* GAMBOLINE.)

GREEN: Madam! I have a strange premonition that the ship carrying my brothers off to war will sink this very night. If you wish to become the Fifth Marchioness of Maske-Tower right away — very well. If not — we can wait a while longer.

GAMBOLINE: See here, Alfred. People don't do things like that.

GREEN: Very well, we'll wait. But the matter is settled. (*To* BRAINIOWICZ.) Professor! Let's forget about all this. I could have you put in jail right away. But I believe you're going to be reasonable after all this. Only the posthumous edition of your works will contain the ultimate proofs. Through prolonged exposure, ordinary mortals will eventually familiarize themselves with the problem. (*Sadly.*) And me too, I hope.

BRAINIOWICZ: Stop this nonsense, Alfred. You're an intelligent fellow. So why not tell me when the "Euripides" of the Green Star Line sails and reserve a cabin for two. I promised the Maharajah of Penjar a game of poker once we're aboard.

GREEN: I see that time has really stood still for you, Professor. The "Euripides" sailed two weeks ago. The "Eurigone" sails today, but Penjar leaves on the "Euripontes" in two weeks' time. That's the fact of the matter. I'm glad that Europe will have a chance to catch its breath. Reserve a cabin then, shall I?

BRAINIOWICZ: (*To* BALANTINE) Two weeks all right with you?

BALANTINE: (*She expands in anticipation of unknown sensual delights*) Of course. With you, Tumor, even these two weeks in Europe will be superhuman bliss. But if you have no objection, I shan't give myself to you definitively until we're aboard the ship. I want the old moods to come back. After all, Fitz-Gerald courted me, didn't he? I saw the Southern Cross for the first time with him, and the hypersun of dreadful Canopus. When Canopus is in the ascendant for the first time, I shall be yours. How long I've been tormented by my virginity! Only sport saved me from Persville! Do you realize that demon begged me for mercy like a small child?

(GREEN *and* GAMBOLINE *whisper together.*)

BRAINIOWICZ: (*To* BALANTINE) That no longer concerns me. Fortunately, you don't know the first thing about mathematics. You'll be the last cold compress on my head, on this poor old brainpan. But I'll love you like a young man, like a raving boy.

(BALANTINE *presses against him with a smile; they both stand like statues.*)

GREEN: We'll bring your sons up for you to be healthy mathematicians with real heads on their shoulders. Only Moritz didn't work out too well. But that's a form of expiation.

IZA: I'm taking full responsibility for Moritz. The likes of that decadent have yet to be seen on this or any planet. Given the contingency of art, he'll reduce all absolute values to sameness in a tiny circle closed in upon itself.

ALFRED: Father, I forgive you everything. And I wish you well. I'll find some decent young lady and start a new life.

(BRAINIOWICZ *suddenly clutches at his heart.*)

BRAINIOWICZ: (*Uneasily*) I have such a strange empty feeling in my heart. (*Cries out.*) Patakulo! Don't look at me like that! (*He falls as though struck by lightning.* BALANTINE *lets out a wild cry of panic. They all dash over to him.* GREEN *feels his pulse. He gets up. They all wait in a state of frightful anticipation.*)

GREEN: He's dead. So the ultimate proof will never be known to anyone.

BALANTINE: (*Throws herself on* BRAINIOWICZ's *corpse with a wild laugh. The others remain where they are, rooted to the spot.*) See how my virgin dream has been fulfilled. Go for a walk, children. The spring is the same as it was then. The buds are growing green upon the young branches and warmth pervades the faded azure and the spidery clouds in the sky. Go, leave me alone with him. (*She laughs gently and quietly.* GREEN *offers his arm to* GAMBOLINE; MAURICE, *his arm to* IZA. ALFRED *puts his arms around* IRENE, *who is half-dead with pain, and one after the other they file out in silence through the center door.* BALANTINE *suddenly gets up and stretches her body voluptuously.*) No one knows that I, too, devoted my life exclusively to mathematics and am intimately acquainted with all Tumor's theorems.

(*The door to the left opens and* PERSVILLE *enters. He goes over to* BALANTINE.)

BALANTINE: Arthur! Arthur! My happiness, my life, my everything! (BALANTINE *throws her arms around him with wild passion.*)

PERSVILLE: (*Coldly*) Now you are mine. We're going to Australia. I was on the telephone just a moment ago. I've been appointed visiting-professor at Port Peery. Now we'll apply Tumor's theory to my geometry and create true transcendental dynamics. Not what they're studying at the Academy, which Alfred failed twice. True transcendental dynamics, my love, true transcendental dynamics.

(BALANTINE *laughs voluptuously, almost completely unconscious.*)

CURTAIN
THE END OF THE THIRD AND LAST ACT

DAINTY SHAPES AND HAIRY APES

(Virginia Commonwealth University, Richmond, U.S.A., 1978)
Dir.: James Parker

DAINTY SHAPES
AND
HAIRY APES

or

THE GREEN PILL

A Comedy with Corpses
in Two Acts and Three Scenes

1922

CHARACTERS

SOPHIA OF THE ABENCÉRAGES KREMLINSKA — Thin, rather short, very pretty and demonic, reddish blonde. Twenty-eight years old.

NINA — Blonde, seventeen years old. Pretty and very fickle. Daughter of the late Duke of Passmore St. Edwards.

LIZA — Pretty brunette, seventeen years old, eminently a Semitic type.

TARQUINIUS FLIRTIUS-UMBILICUS — Very beautiful young man, eighteen years old. Dark chestnut hair, soulful and at the same time passionate. Rather long hair. Aquiline nose.

PANDEUS CLAVERCOURSE — His friend. Very beautiful and blasé young person, twenty-eight years old. Dark hair. Straight nose. Completely clean-shaven.

SIR THOMAS BLAZO DE LIZA — English Baronet. Thirty-eight years old. Nina's uncle. Dark hair, clean-shaven. Tall.

SIR GRANT BLAGUEWELL-PADLOCK — Eminent biochemist, knighted for his discoveries, fifty years old. Rather fat and tall, balding on the crown of his head. Gray-haired. Aquiline nose.

OLIPHANT BEEDLE — American billionaire. Heavy-set, sixty years old. Short gray hair. Tremendous power in his every movement.

GOLDMANN BARUCH TEERBROOM — Semite, forty years old. Liza's father Dark-haired, graying at the temples, fat, but nonetheless, very sure of himself and of his people.

DR. DON NINO DE GEVACH — Cardinal. Dressed in red, in a cardinal's hat, fifty-two years old. Gray-haired, completely clean-shaven. Doctor of Theology. Absolute insatiability makes itself felt in his every movement.

GRAF ANDRE VLADIMIROVICH TCHURNIN-KOKETAYEV — Thirty-eight years old, Captain of the Horse in His Imperial Excellency's Life Guard of the Cuirassiers Regiment. Azure blue uniform, cuirass. White trousers, long cuirassier's boots. A helmet with an eagle in his hand. Moustache.

FORTY MANDELBAUMS — Small, large, old and young. Very large aquiline noses. Large moustaches and small beards. Long hair. Dark-haired and gray-haired. Dressed in normal suits, quite varied as far as color goes. *In the event of a lack of supernumeraries the number of Mandelbaums may be reduced to fifteen. However, it must never fall below this limit.*

YOUNG FOOTMAN — In a red frock coat.

OLD FOOTMAN — In a normal black frock coat.

Act I

Salon in PANDEUS CLAVERCOURSE's *Palace. Extremely fantastic furnishings in dark blue colors. An occasion for the most uninhibited scene designer to show what he can do. Facing the audience, a fireplace projecting out very far. A door in a recess to the right. Facing the stage, to the right and the left,* CLAVERCOURSE *and* UMBILICUS *in white tropical outfits sit sprawled in Ceylonese deck chairs in front of the fireplace and smoke gigantic red "cheroots."* NINA *sits in an armchair to the left, dressed in a red light dress and red stockings. Her shoes are a Veronese green. She is completely indifferent. The gentlemen do not pay the slightest attention to her. It is a white hot day. Nevertheless a green fire is burning in the fireplace. Offstage every so often there can be heard the singing of canaries, the cackling of hens, and the crowing of roosters. In designated places the glare becomes simply blinding. No windows. It is out of the question to have any modernistic paintings whatsoever hanging on stage, my own, for example, unless it is specifically called for in the stage directions. It is likewise out of the question to use a stage setting made out of old properties, for example, some "cosy little nook" from a Bałucki comedy, and so is the combination of this possibility with the preceding one. These last requirements apply not only to this play, but to all those that I have written up until now and that I still may write.*

PANDEUS: (*Speaks with growing grandiloquence*) I tell you, Quinnie, there aren't any problems any more in the real sense of the word, in the old sense of the word. In philosophy there are only so-called "Scheinprobleme," make-believe problems, and in life everything is defined, clarified, resolved. We are just one step away from complete social inertia, worse than what will take place after the sun has become extinct. Death during one's lifetime, almost unattainable for individuals, is actually becoming a reality in our present-day social systems. I say: "almost unattainable," since we do have creeping paralysis and drugs. But I cannot consider that the full equivalent of humanity's devouring itself in the form of growing specialization. Even belief in a catastrophic ending to this entire story is the last illusion on the part of degenerates from the old order. Catastrophe is something too beautiful to have happen to our species of Individual Beings. Everything that was more or less known is over now. And yet it seems to me that I have discovered something totally new, something that can be tested only by the two of us...

TARQUINIUS: There's always love. (*Points to* NINA *who does not bat an eyelash.*) That, Pandy, is the dilemma from which you isolated me by a wall of premature doubt.

PANDEUS: I want to shield you from all those monstrosities that I have lived through; I have loved innocent young ladies and demonic ones, going from the highest class down to the very lowest. I have been a victim, a tiny little fly in the clutches of frightful spiders, I have been a demon myself and crushed hearts like strawberries, and then I have gulped them down like jam made of pure anguish. I have experienced both sadism and masochism, not to mention love affairs exalted and harrowing — harrowing to the point of madness through their inability to satisfy even the simplest expectations. I am young and beautiful, and yet I am closing my life as casually and nonchalantly as if I were slamming the lid of my strong box after removing all the items of essential value. (*Emphatically.*) We must return to Greek times: revive friendship which is in the process of dying out. Nowadays friendship has become something revolting, since the feeling of fundamental enmity has disappeared. But we won't go astray in the wilds of hideous sexuality: our friendship will be a renunciation of all sensual shocks and tremors. Sublimation of homogeneous feelings in the highest sphere of life's knowledge. I will lead you along a steep path towards the absolute unity of male souls...

TARQUINIUS: (*Leaping up*) That's perversion in disguise. I beg you: at least once allow me to fall in love really and truly. A man is beautiful only when he is all alone or when he attains his highest dream in the form of a woman who is more than a casual encounter. When homogeneously united, the male elements are — I should say — too psychically hairy. Strength must be solitary, and the prey cannot be one with its conqueror.

PANDEUS: (*Striking the arm of his chair with the palm of his hand*) No, no, no. I won't allow you to defile yourself. Oh, what I wouldn't give at this moment to be able to rid myself of everything I have been through. You are pure, nature has given you what I must try to attain by plowing through the frightful deserts of the past, overcoming phantoms and ghosts at every turn. I love you and I cannot allow you to destroy what is most beautiful in you: your lack of memories. And besides, you won't have all the women in the world in any case. That is the most atrocious thing about this whole problem.

TARQUINIUS: (*Sitting down*) Yes, that's right. Oh, God, God. How frightfully I am suffering! At least permit me to take some drugs, Pandy. Otherwise I won't be able to endure your training.

PANDEUS: At the very most, you may smoke. I have triumphed over morphine, C_2H_5OH, et tu dois savoir, mon cher, alcoholism is the hardest to cure, since the majority of drunkards "ne cesseront pas de boire" — they do not want to stop drinking. I went on to conquer hashish and cocaine, to say nothing of all Sir Grant's latest discoveries, his invincible cerebro-spinaline and infernal aphrodisiacs of the family trinitrobenzoamidophends. You are familiar with his epoch-making experiments on Brazilian guans. I have been to all the institutes in the world where they are fighting poisons. I too have been fighting them, in the deserts of Australia and the jungles of Peru and Borneo. No — I won't give you one single drop of anything. I am the personification of will power in its most frightful, deluxe edition. You, as someone pure and innocent, will infinitely surpass me.

TARQUINIUS: But, I say, Pandy. Aren't you so powerful precisely because you already have all that behind you? Will I ever be able to achieve that perfection without first having known the dangers: both my own and those that are called external. Now isn't it renunciation that produces the most essential desire? And then it all attacks the brain and gains control of more and more of its areas.

PANDEUS: *Der Mensch ist ein sich selbst betrügendes Tier.* Man is a self-deceiving animal. I forgive you for it, but you must promise me that this is the last time. Promise?

TARQUINIUS: (*Getting up*) I promise. I feel I'm going to explode from this constant insatiability, but I'll hold out, even if I have to go mad, or just plain batty, I'll hold out.

PANDEUS: That won't happen. I know your nature better than you yourself can. On the basis of my own experience, I see you as a tiny little transparent piece of crystal under the deadliest Rutherford and Bohr rays. With my methods I shall make you into an athlete of those most essential unsatisfied longings, which only then will open for you the gates of the highest mystery: the principle of INTRINSIC INDIVIDUAL IDENTITY. This mystery has two levels, mutually inpenetrable, like Einstein's two possible Worlds. Even the most half-witted moron knows that a thing is what it is and not something else. And yet in a higher understanding of this principle, we can resolve the most hellish dilemma facing all potential and actually existing Beings. (*An old servant in a frock coat runs in from the right.*)

OLD FOOTMAN: Pandy! Sophia of the Abencérages Kremlinska is about to descend upon us in six autos with her whole staff. Forty Mandelbaums! God knows who else! I got the news by telephone from the station at the grange on Antares. They have already passed the embankment at Honed Fish River. (*He runs out.*)

TARQUINIUS: (*Uncertainly*) Well, what now?

PANDEUS: (*Slightly dampened in his former grandiloquence*) Don't worry —we'll hold out.

TARQUINIUS: But when will you introduce me to the higher sphere of your thoughts?

PANDEUS: Tonight—perhaps tomorrow—I don't know. The presence here of that whole disreputable mob will be just the perfect test for you. You'll see the negative side of life in its most deluxe edition. I'm going to the tower to watch the show when that band of metaphysical snobs arrives. (*He starts to leave to the right.*)

TARQUINIUS: Do you know this Kremlinska personally?

PANDEUS: (*Stopping*) I did once. But she was a bit different then than she is now.

(*He goes out to the right.*)

NINA: (*Raising her head for the first time*) Aren't you bored by all that high-flown talk in which our host indulges so freely? (TARQUINIUS *remains silent.*) Look here, Mr. Quinnie, you can be as frank and open with me as with anyone—including even your own master.

TARQUINIUS: Yes—I'm bored. You see, I know a great deal, but only theoretically. I've read far more than he suspects. I know the Kamasutra and Weininger, Freud and the Babylonian sexologists. I know all the first-rate novels that were ever written and almost the entire body of world poetry. Taken all together, I am already bored by all that in advance. Still, what Pandy sketched out for me in its general outlines does contain something new and unknown.

NINA: (*Getting up*) Do you believe in those final initiations? (TARQUINIUS *keeps obstinately quiet.*) I have the impression that it won't ever happen, that at the bottom of it all there's only an artistic cliché about creating reality. Why can't Mr. Clavercourse accomplish it himself? Why are you so absolutely necessary to him, why you precisely, and not any one else?

TARQUINIUS: I don't know. (*In a different tone.*) Do you know, I'm not even really so innocent? (*Mysteriously.*) Just imagine, I once kissed Lisa here — behind the ear.

(*With his finger he points to his neck behind the ear.*)

NINA: (*Sharply*) Oh — only no intimate confessions, please. Liza never said anything to me about it and I don't in the least wish to pry into her secrets quite by accident. (*In a different tone.*) Do you know what the arrival of that whole entourage means for me? My uncle, Sir Thomas Blazo de Lizo, is one of Madame Sophia's closest friends. He's sure to be coming here with her. That means: the end of my freedom.

TARQUINIUS: Oh, pish-posh — your freedom indeed! You'll get married, have lovers, do whatever you want. But what about me! I am the slave of the tumor which that infernal Pandy has planted in my brain. I'm a complete automaton in his hands. (*Suddenly.*) Tell me, was there ever anything between the two of you?

NINA: Nothing, I give you my word. In his relations with me he never over-stepped the bounds of the most proper guardian.

TARQUINIUS: (*Clenching his fists*) Actually, I'm not jealous of his past — I've already gotten over that, but, you know, if I were to find out that he's doing something now which he shouldn't, believe me, I would kill him like a dog.

NINA: (*Looking him in the eye*) You are jealous of him. You love him . . .

TARQUINIUS: (*In a daze*) I don't know. I don't know if it is love. (*Force-fully.*) I only know that if it's going to go on like this, if he really isn't going to introduce me into another world which can take the place of life for me, I'll become a monster such as has never been seen before un-til now.

NINA: Come, come — don't get carried away. You're a poor child, not a monster.

(*She strokes his head.*)

TARQUINIUS (*Pulling away from her angrily*) Don't pity me! That's in-sulting to me. I'd prefer to have you tell me what you think of him.

NINA: I'll tell you quite frankly: I love him too.

TARQUINIUS: (*Fearfully*) What? . . .

NINA: (*Laughing*) Calm down, nothing can ever come of it. (*Seriously.*) When he was your age, he was my late mother's lover. My mother was a bad woman. I read her diary. I cannot think about it without feelings of revulsion.

TARQUINIUS: (*Threateningly*) About what, about what?

NINA: (*Laughing*) About his kisses, only about his kisses. And besides he is finished, destroyed forever. (*With irony.*) Oh—he's invincible, he was threatened with atrophy of the front horns because of his love for Madame Kremlinska—she is invincible too. Perhaps you'll conquer him, Mr. Quinnie. You're so adorable.

TARQUINIUS: So you do love him then! You hope to provoke him up by feigning indifference. What perfidy!

NINA: (*With irony*) Oh, there's theoretical experience of life. Oh, there's loftiness of soul. (*In a different tone.*) And anyhow I love you too. You're a lovely, innocent little boy. You're like a tiny little star in the Milky Way. (*She kisses him suddenly on the mouth and runs out to the left.* TARQUINIUS *remains motionless for a moment.*)

TARQUINIUS: Oh, the mouth *is* a devilish thing. Now I don't know anything anymore. (*Through the center door, at the back of the stage, to the right of the fireplace, enter* SOPHIA *of the Abencérages Kremlinska, dressed in a motoring outfit, with a horsewhip in her hand. After her, come* SIR THOMAS, TEERBROOM, *and* OLIPHANT BEEDLE, *likewise dressed in motoring outfits. Next come* DR. DON NINO DE GEVACH *in a cardinal's robes and* GRAF TCHURNIN-KOKETAYEV *in the full dress uniform of the cuirassiers guard. 40 [unequivocally forty]* MANDELBAUMS *come crowding in last.* TARQUINIUS *becomes dumbfounded at the sight of* SOPHIA.)

SOPHIA: What are you so dumbfounded at, my good man? What's your name? Where is the proprietor of the chateau?

TARQUINIUS: He went to change his clothes. My name is Umbilicus.

SOPHIA: A lovely name. I am Sophia of the Abencérages and so forth. And why didn't you go change your clothes for my arrival?

TARQUINIUS: I was engaged in an important conversation with the Duchess Passmore St. Edwards. My head is in an indescribable fog, and for some time now . . .

SIR THOMAS: Hullo! So she is here, just as I thought. Don't you know. . . .

TARQUINIUS: You can rest quite easy, Sir Thomas. My friend loves me and only me. He has created a new order of absolute, purely spiritual friendship. Tomorrow or even tonight I am to be admitted into the ultimate mysteries.

SOPHIA: Then I came in time. (*Points to* TARQUINIUS.) Look how lovely he is. I shall have a hard battle with such a rival. (*A threatening murmur in the crowd of* MANDELBAUMS *and several voices from the general staff.*) Quiet, Mandelbaums, and you too, first-class worshippers.

TARQUINIUS: You are insulting my friend. With that tiny little female brain of yours, you cannot grasp the greatness of his soul. You seem to think that you have some rights to him. You'd better get over any such illusions once and for all.

SOPHIA: (*To the staff*) Did you hear that? It's quite unheard of! How did such a delicate little flower ever survive in this monster's house? And he still believes in him. (*To* TARQUINIUS.) Terrible moments await you, sad youth. You don't yet know what psychic crimes are like. Look at me; I am young and beautiful, am I not? And yet there is nothing inside me. I am a mummy, I am thousands of years old, and my cruelty is boundless. It is that Pandeus of yours who made a spider woman out of me — I devour souls after eating my fill of bodies. Look at that mob. (*Points to the staff and the* MANDELBAUMS.) Nothing but the sheaths of chrysalises from which the butterflies have flown away. And those butterflies, their souls, I hold in my net and I play with them when I wish and as I wish, you young idiot. Would you too like to be a specimen in my collection?

(*The crowd is silent.*)

TARQUINIUS: You are a banal, stupid hen. Those gentlemen have already condemned themselves, if what you say about them is true. I am superior to the vulgar appetite for life thanks to him, the one man on this earth who exists for me and whom you insult here in his own home.

SOPHIA: Stupid braggart. You will be talking differently in a few days. I shall reveal his intentions to you in all their horror. You don't know . . .

TARQUINIUS: I know all I need to know. Please leave me alone. (*He goes quickly towards the door to the right.*)

TEERBROOM: Young man! Young man! Is my Liza here?

TARQUINIUS: Yes, she is. Yesterday I kissed her on the ear. I'll atone for it however you wish — not only out of respect for your age and for her sake, but for myself. (*To* SIR THOMAS.) And today your niece kissed me on the mouth, thereby defiling the most sacred love which Pandeus and I have for each other. (*To* SOPHIA.) I detest all you women and I will never be yours. Your posthumous memoirs and stupid little poems will let the world know how thoroughly I could have enjoyed your quote "love," if only I had wanted to. (*Pulls a bundle of papers out of his pocket and gives it to* TEERBROOM.) Here are the poems your daughter wrote to me. (TEERBROOM *puts the poems in his pocket.*) I am sacrificing all that in order to achieve the ultimate truths of existence, far from your vile snares and machinations. Good-bye. (*He goes out to the right impetuously.*)

SOPHIA: That boy's a real gem, I'll make bloody mincemeat out of him. I'll eat his nerves sautéed over a slow flame. I feel the blood of all the Abencérages boiling inside me.

TEERBROOM: But I say, Madame Sophia! This very day I shall give you the automobile that belonged to the last czar of Illizia.

SIR THOMAS: I'll buy Saint Patrick's abbey for you. Whatever the consequences. Only not that, not that, or I'll go mad.

OLIPHANT BEEDLE: (*To* SIR THOMAS) Only not what? You've already gone mad, Sir Thomas. (*To* SOPHIA.) Madame: from today on the Duke of York's yacht is your own personal property.

SIR GRANT: The pills! The green pills! Today I'll write out for you on vellum my most closely guarded secret formula.

KOKETAYEV: I'll put all the platinum in the Ural mountains into your sweet predatory little hands, madame Sophia. (*Accented on the second syllable.*) We'll "blow up a tornado," as we say in Russian.

CARDINAL NINO: Madame, you do not know what sensual pleasure and satisfaction of the ambition seducing the Church's highest dignitaries invariably brings. In the old days that wasn't worth a straw, but nowadays! What's more, the villa Calafoutrini with all its priceless collections is yours. May God watch over me. (*He prays.*)

THE MANDELBAUMS: What about us? What about us? What about us?

SOPHIA: (*Silences the commotion with a twist of her hand and a stamp of her foot*) Don't speak to me as if I were a girl of the streets. I can't be had that way any more.

SIR GRANT: Since when, since when?

SOPHIA: Since right now, since right now (*looking at the watch which she wears on her ankle*), since two o'clock this afternoon when I became sacred. I can be had only by a very complicated psyche combined with a maximum of strength.

SIR THOMAS: Someone must have displayed such qualities for you to dare talk about them that way, as if they were actually to be found in someone. Who is that degenerate?

SOPHIA: That little boy who was here a moment ago, that young Umbilicus. (*The* MANDELBAUMS' *roar grows with each moment.*)

THE OLDEST OF THE MANDELBAUMS: We have those qualities — we, Mandelbaums. I protest on behalf of all of us . . . .

SOPHIA: (*Threatening to strike him with the whip*) Silence!! (*The roar sub sides. The* OLDEST MANDELBAUM *draws back.*) Service!! Service!! (*A* YOUNG FOOTMAN *in red livery runs in from the right.*)

YOUNG FOOTMAN: Yes, Your Ladyship.

SOPHIA: (*Indicating the crowd of* MANDELBAUMS *with her whip*) Show that horde of riff-raff out, give them something to feed their faces, and assign them rooms.

YOUNG FOOTMAN: Yes, Your Ladyship. (*To the* MANDELBAUMS.) This way, gentlemen. This way. (*He pushes them towards the center door.*)

SOPHIA: Mark my words well, Mandelbaums, for me you are nothing but a confused "background" of impersonal and intermittent masculinity, "un fond de masculinité impersonnelle et intermittente." Get out!! (*They leave.* SOPHIA *flings herself into a chair*) Out of that big baby I'll make an antidote to Pandy. Now I feel strong, this is *my* day.

(*From the left side enter* PANDEUS. *The two young girls hold onto him, one on each side:* NINA, *to the right,* LIZA, *to the left.* NINA *wears a black dress,* LIZA *the dress that* NINA *wore previously.* PANDEUS *in a black frock coat.*)

PANDEUS: Excuse me for having kept you all waiting so long. I had to change my clothes and prepare Liza for what awaits her. (*To* TEER-BROOM) Mr. Teerbroom, you do not know how to bring up your daughter. She will stay with me as long as necessary, until I deem it fit to return her to you a superior and accomplished woman.

TEERBROOM: Out of snobbery I am ready even for that. But what you do not know is that your friend and my Liza have already been kissing. I have here in my pocket a whole bundle of poems which she wrote to that Umbilicus. In you I have complete confidence, but in those..uh... wards of yours...

PANDEUS: That is impossible! How dare you!

TEERBROOM: He said so himself a moment ago. Isn't that so, gentlemen?

SOPHIA: Yes, Pandeus — I can vouch for that. You have been powerfully shaken in your hmm ... designs. But I shall console you with Sir Grant's new pills.

PANDEUS: This is horrible. And it was today that I wanted to begin revealing to him the ultimate mysteries of the highest understanding of life.

SIR THOMAS: And that is not all: my niece Nina, as your protégé himself confessed, kissed him on the lips today. He seemed to be quite mortified by the fact, but I believe he was pretending because he was afraid of me.

PANDEUS: By Aldebaran, no, Sir Thomas! Mr. Teerbroom: I am innocent.

Simply, quite simply the earth is slipping from under my feet. I feel faint. (*The young ladies hold him up.*)

SOPHIA: Pandeus, your initiations are a fraud. I know how it will end. You want to recapture your youth by conjuring up memories of your days at Harvard College. Remember, you disappeared from the horizon at that point. We know what happened: a year in the house of correction on Crippen Heath.

PANDEUS: Yes — I admit it. And from then on I have lived according to the laws of nature, although there are people who dare to maintain that the periods of the highest civilization are always closely associated with disregarding those laws. What I am dreaming of now is beyond your sordid suspicions. You judge it by your own standards, Sophie. Oh, yes — you are capable of the most atrocious things! I know you. But you won't get anywhere. You will be the last temptation for Quinnie, a temptation that he will conquer. And if he conquers you — there are no more temptations left for him in this world.

SOPHIA: I thank you for that acknowledgement. At least you are fair. But I advise you to be on guard against yourself. The subconscious always works that way. You do not know yourself. I am the only one who knows you. You still have satanic possibilities ahead of you.

PANDEUS: For example, the possibility of falling in love with you again!!! Ha, ha, ha!

SOPHIA: You never can tell. Pills — that's the last word of the mystery. But as for me, I have not yet sunk so low as to be the object of your idiotic experiments with your mediums.

NINA: A point of order: couldn't the two of you postpone this conversation until later? Liza, go pay your respects to your father. (LIZA *falls into* TEERBROOM's *arms; to* PANDEUS) These people are tired after their journey. Perhaps you could see about showing the guests their accommodations. I'll take care of the flowers for dinner.

PANDEUS: Of course you're quite right, Miss Nina. Please come with me. (*He goes towards the center door, from the right side* TARQUINIUS *runs in, dressed as before.*)

TARQUINIUS: Pandy! I have been looking for you all over the palace. I have horrible forebodings. That lady (*points to* SOPHIA) doesn't appeal to me in the least, but she upsets me terribly. (SOPHIA *angrily strikes her whip against her coat.*) I am in a state of total divergence among my most essential directional tensions.

PANDEUS: (*Gloomily*) You have betrayed me. Now I do not know if I shall succeed in saving you from life. You are no longer a pure spirit without memories.

TARQUINIUS: Oh, those girls, those girls have given me away! No—the men must have been the ones who told you. (*With tremendous fervor.*) It was nothing: those were superficial contacts which I no longer remember. You must initiate me right now. I am in a state of frightful inner tension. I could explode; I could swerve to one side or the other with all the force of a volcano. But I swear to you: at heart I am pure. Let's go to your slothroom.

PANDEUS: No—let's put it off until tomorrow. I'm not in the right frame of mind today, I am not sufficiently collected. First withstand temptation, prove yourself worthy. Have a talk with Madame Sophia first of all.

TARQUINIUS: (*Very disappointed*) Oh, so that's how it is. Now I'll tell you something dreadful: you don't believe in yourself, you don't believe in the truth of your system. You're afraid, you don't have the strength. You mask the pettiness of your desires behind a false little theory. Why can't you exist all by yourself? Why am I absolutely necessary to you? Admit that you still don't know what you are going to tell me. You are trying to find inspiration in me, inspiration so as to be able to believe in yourself, to fill the horrible void that makes your life so unbearable. But you don't even have the courage to grieve over it any more.

PANDEUS: (*With bitterness*) See what terrible havoc those supposedly superficial contacts have wreaked in your soul. I have been betrayed, hideously deceived and betrayed.

SOPHIA: Yes—Pandy has let his mask drop. I said the same thing.

PANDEUS: You have no right to speak on this subject, Sophie. I ceased to exist for you from moment I could no longer be a man in my relations with you. You too are letting your mask drop.

TARQUINIUS: But what will become of me? Life is rushing into my frenzied brain through all my pores.

SOPHIA: Poor boy! Enough. It will all be resolved by itself. We shall finally be freed from this cursed Pandeus Clavercourse problem. He is either a common charlatan, or the greatest metaphysical brute I have ever known. Let's go bathe, and then eat. (*She goes towards the center door, and the others follow her. The* CARDINAL *prays as he goes.*)

TARQUINIUS: (*To* NINA) Miss Nina, I have to tell you something. My ganglions are bursting with inexpressible thoughts. (*He grabs* NINA *by the hand and drags her off to the left.*)

PANDEUS: (*Shouts after him*) You may live to regret it! Watch out. (SOPHIA *burst out laughing and leaves. She is followed out by* PANDEUS *and the others.* SIR GRANT BLAGUEWELL-PADLOCK *remains behind and holds back* OLIPHANT BEEDLE.)

SIR GRANT: Do you understand? Everything is in my hands. (*Pulls a little box out of his vest pocket and taps it with his finger*) The green pills. All the same, when you think about it, life nowadays would be quite frightful if it weren't for drugs. I am the last benefactor of mankind in its declining days, unless of course, my pill proves mortal in its after-effects. I have not had the courage to try it on human beings.

OLIPHANT BEEDLE: Fine—but actually, what do we care about all that? You're all manufacturing artificial problems.

SIR GRANT: But she *must* be mine, today, instantly, whenever I want her. (OLIPHANT *makes a threatening gesture.*) Don't get excited, I'm saving the next pill for her and for you. It's an old, old story: instead of a po-tion—pills. And as for the Pandeus problem, it is not as insignificant as you think. On the basis of this example, I shall demonstrate certain eternal truths.

YOUNG FOOTMAN: (*Entering through the center door*) This way to the baths, Your Lordships. (*They go out quickly, passing in front of the* FOOTMAN *who holds the door open.*)

Act II
Scene 1

*The same room. Half past nine in the evening. Through the center door
enter* SOPHIA, *dressed in a black ball gown, accompanied by the two
young ladies.* NINA *dressed in green,* LIZA *in yellow.* SOPHIA *sits down on
the sofa which is now to the right of the fireplace, opposite the door (the
green fire continues to burn in the fireplace) and puts something which
she has been clutching tightly in her hand into a small powder box.*
NINA *sits down on her right,* LIZA *on her left. Offstage, protracted, prolonged, dismal roars can be heard from time to time.*

NINA: What are you doing there, Madame Sophia?

SOPHIA: That is the mystery of the evening. I have never been as strong as I
am now. I have found a counterweight to Pandeus' psychic perversity in
the person of that little boy. But that is only negative strength. I have
something else, ha, ha, I have something else!

NINA: A woman's strength is always negative even if it's not considered evil.

LIZA: Yes—I think so too. Women's strength is concave—their strength is
convex...

NINA: Wait a minute, Liza: Madame Sophia says that she has something
more, something positive. What do you have in that little box?

SOPHIA: (*Getting up*) I have Sir Grant's green pill. A new drug
which creates such horrible insatiability that, compared to those who
will take it, Messalina would seem a perfect angel. He dropped the pill
into my wine glass, the little rascal, but I noticed and held it between
my teeth. And then afterwards, I took it out without anyone seeing.
Whoever I give it to will love me as no one has ever loved anyone since

the beginning of the world.

NINA: Only please spare Tarquinius. I love him.

SOPHIA: You won't have the strength to overcome Pandeus' influence. You don't know with whom you're fighting. I am the only one who can conquer the fiction Clavercourse infected him with: his belief in a higher knowledge of life without love.

NINA: Yes, but while you're at it, you'll take him for yourself. I don't want that to happen.

SOPHIA: And how are you going to stop me, poor silly little hen? You don't know how I know them. I know every fibre of their seemingly complicated souls. There's not been one of them yet who could resist me.

NINA: (*Ironically*) Except for Pandeus against whom your negative strength no longer suffices.

SOPHIA: But it seems you love Clavercourse too. At least that's what they have been telling me.

NINA: If it hadn't been for the fact that he was my late mother's lover, I would love him just as he is—without Sir Grant's green pills. (*Imploringly*.) Please, don't take Tarquinius away from me. I beg you.

SOPHIA: All right: I shall simply prepare him for you. Only as much as he'll need in order to overcome Pandy's temptations. And not that much more. (*She shows the very tip of her forefinger with her thumb.*)

NINA: Thank you. (*She kisses her hand.*)

LIZA: How beautiful Madame Sophia is in everything she says and does! (*To* NINA) If anyone else talked the way she does, it would be revolting.

NINA: Unfortunately, men's actions have an absolute value. What a woman does is overly dependent on her face, her figure, and her clothes, and above all on whether or not she has pretty arms and legs. (*Through the door to the right enter* TARQUINIUS *in a frock coat,* SOPHIA *expands.*)

TARQUINIUS: I have come for the test of my strength. But I warn you that I am condensed as never before. Everything hangs by a single thread which has the holding power of steel cable.

SOPHIA: So much the better for me, Mr. Umbilicus. Do sit down.

TARQUINIUS: (*Sitting down between the girls*) You don't understand me, I was talking of essential things. I feel a loathing for you that almost borders on physical pain. In every word you utter, you are cynical and repulsive. In every statement you make, even of the most indifferent kind, some lecherous thought lies hidden. Your voice doesn't seem to come from your throat, but from the devil only knows where...

SOPHIA: That is the basis of my strength. Things said that way sink deep into the innermost recesses of your bodies and then it becomes as difficult for you to root them out as memories of sensual pleasure.

TARQUINIUS: (*Shuddering*) Oh, how disgusting! I detest you. (*He gets up.*)

SOPHIA: But all the while you felt that mysterious shiver you have never known until now. You know what I mean.

TARQUINIUS: How did you know? You're clairvoyant. (*The young girls lean towards each other and look at* SOPHIA *with adoration.*)

SOPHIA: Actually, I am dimvoyant, but I see with certitude. My secret eyes circulate along with the red globules of your young blood and spy upon the hidden springs of your being.

TARQUINIUS: You made a miscalculation there. That statement doesn't make me feel the slightest shudder. Artistically it's a failure. Your voice wavered and cracked. Don't try to fake something beyond your abilities, or you could take a spill.

SOPHIA: Oh—don't talk so crudely. Look at me—don't avoid my gaze. Now don't you feel monstrous despair at the thought of what will never, *never* be? At this instant the entire world has ceased to exist for you. All its colors have paled somewhere in the distance, and the forms of the most beautiful sights have shriveled into hideous wrinkles, withered and senile, as though a secret flame from the bottomless void had consumed them from within. All your feelings have become the expression of the most frightful inner boredom and the coming day seems to you an infinite desert, impossible to cross even to the end of all eternity. Look at me: now isn't that true?

TARQUINIUS: It is, it is—you see clean through me. My head is spinning.

SOPHIA: (*Pointing to* NINA) Just what is that poor little, pure little tender feeling you have for her, compared to the insatiability of all the desires you now feel? I can fulfill all that or walk out of here this very moment with a cruel smile and leave you, burned to ashes, paralyzed, rigor-mortized by the unspeakable torture of the enormity of your never-sated longing. Look into my eyes. You attract me.

TARQUINIUS: (*Drawing closer to her*) It's frightful—I can't resist. (*He looks around at the young girls.*)

NINA: (*Springing up*) I won't give him up. I love him—you only want to amuse yourself with him. Leave him alone at once.

SOPHIA: (*Gently*) Run along this instant, my child. Take Liza and off to bed with both of you. But before you go to sleep, talk it all over. (*Dejected,* NINA *takes* LIZA *by the hand and they both go out slowly to the left.* SOPHIA *and* TARQUINIUS *stare at each other. The moment the door slams shut,* TARQUINIUS *throws himself at* SOPHIA *who envelops him in a snake-like embrace. Kissing, they both fall on the sofa. At this precise moment enter* SIR GRANT *through the center door.* TARQUINIUS *and* SOPHIA *spring apart.*)

SIR GRANT: Madame Sophia. I confess to everything. I dropped the green pill into your wine. Once you promised me...It's starting to work already...Prematurely, unfortunately...According to my experiments on my guans, it shouldn't start working until four hours later at the earliest. I beg you...You gave your word...We're the only ones who can test it.

SOPHIA: (*Getting up;* TARQUINIUS *remains seated*) You are a consummate ass! I have your pills here—look. (*Shows him the small powder box.*) I held it with my tongue against my teeth. Go back to your guans. (*Roars louder than before are heard.*) Well—can't you hear them roaring? I shall take the pill when I feel so inclined, or I'll give it to whoever I fancy. That's better still. Do you understand, Mr. Poisoner? You can go now. (*She points to the door.* SIR GRANT *goes out, crestfallen, without a word.*)

TARQUINIUS: (*Pulling* SOPHIA *towards him on the sofa*) More...Give me your lips.

SOPHIA: (*Sitting down next to him*) No, my little one, now we are going to have a serious talk. I crave not only your lips, no matter how exquisitely you can kiss. You instinctively possess what it takes others years to learn. But I love you, I want your soul. You must be truly mine before you satiate your desires. Otherwise you will be poisoned by me the way the others were.

TARQUINIUS: Then you really love me?

SOPHIA: Yes—you must believe in your good fortune. I am yours. Learn to know me now so that later on you won't regret not having appreciated my true worth. I can be everything. All I need is to be loved very, very much. Perhaps my girlhood days when I was truly happy will return once more.

TARQUINIUS: (*Starting to make advances on her*) Then let me kiss you. Why are you pushing me away?

SOPHIA: No, no—not now. Now I want only your soul.

TARQUINIUS: (*Gloomily*) You know—it seems to me at this moment that I have no soul at all. (*In the voice of a child who clamors for candy.*) I want your lips.

SOPHIA: It only seems that way to you. Sit down here next to me calmly, lean your head against me, and talk. Talk to me the way you would to

Nina, or to him...to Pandy.

TARQUINIUS: (*Settling down next to her*) I don't have anything to say. I have forgotten everything. Come with me right now, to my room.

SOPHIA: No, I won't come. You are not in the least mine. You're only attracted to me. All the time you are thinking about him, about that cursed Pandeus.

TARQUINIUS: (*Getting up*) That's just what is so dreadful, I've forgotten about him. I feel horrible pangs of conscience. Not only towards him, but towards myself as well. I have betrayed myself. I am a fallen man.

SOPHIA: (*Getting up*) You child! You don't know who that Pandeus of yours is. He is the incarnation of the worst perversion combined with the filthiest cravings. Today for the first time you will see for yourself that all his theories about the higher life are a complete fraud. There really is no higher mode of existence. Those are only fictions, created by socialized cattle such as we. At the bottom of Pandy's soul there's nothing but masked desire for the commonest pleasure-seeking.

TARQUINIUS: (*Getting up*) You made a miscalculation. You didn't know with whom you were dealing. I am stronger than you think. And besides, I know more than you suppose. Give me concrete proof. I have not yet been initiated into the ultimate mysteries, but what I do know is enough to convince me that it is not a fraud. Give me concrete proof.

SOPHIA: I know—the principle of Intrinsic Individual Identity. Everything that exists is what it is and not something else. But we all know that. It's a barren truth and it's no accident that the greatest sages in the world overlooked it. What's strange about that?

TARQUINIUS: The principle is simple—that I admit. But its actual consequences can be remarkable.

SOPHIA: I know that too. Each moment for its own sake, surmounting life not through Nirvana, but by concentrating one's individuality—of course, another person is needed for that. Just let Pandeus succeed in experiencing it all by himself. I'd prostrate myself in front of him. But this is a doctrine which owes its sole existence to the very process of indoctrination. (*Angrily.*) It's all a fraud! Either there's one definite course of action, this particular one, and not any other—no matter whether it's creative work in art or in life—or else there's Nirvana. The rest is sham concocted by puny weaklings incapable of living.

TARQUINIUS: That's not true. I feel that beyond that there is something else which I cannot grasp. Not in words, but in the actual execution. It has to be carried out. It cannot be defined before it has been created.

SOPHIA: Bergsonian balderdash! You are both idiots. One deludes the other, and each deceives himself into the bargain. You will see what the carrying out will be like. You will see tonight. Remember what I have told you. Remember!

TARQUINIUS: All right. We'll see. If it turns out to be untrue, you can consider me your own personal property. In that case my life won't be worth a dead stinking guan.

SOPHIA: But I don't want you in the least. Not any more. That was a moment of delusion. For me you are only an antidote: a means of controlling myself so as to conquer him. I care only for him, for that stupid, deceitful master of yours. What am I saying; not for him, but only for his tangible outer appearance — his soul I've already had and I vomited it up a long time ago, it was so petty and disgusting.

TARQUINIUS: Now you have mortally offended both him and me. I no longer know what is true in me. Only chance — or rather destiny — can decide that.

SOPHIA: In whom do you wish to embody your chance destiny?

TARQUINIUS: In you. The idea is not as foolish as you think. That is exactly what life is: chance destiny. That expresses the initial contradiction inherent in existence. Those two viewpoints are irreconcilable, and yet life constantly reconciles them. By consciously creating the potential for chance, we challenge the workings of the universal law that everything is predetermined. (*He grows lost in thought.*)

SOPHIA: Come to the point, boy. You really do have a touch of strength in you, and that is beginning to intrigue me.

TARQUINIUS: I have caught hold of an idea that has been wandering lost in the unconscious depths of my ego. I know that you won third prize in fencing at the international competition in Melbourne. I am not a bad fencer myself. We shall fight over him and over me, and perhaps even over you as well. That depends on you.

SOPHIA: You know, that is a splendid idea! At two, this very night, immediately after the initiation, provided, of course, you don't lose faith once you have heard it all.

TARQUINIUS: Even then I shall be fighting over myself and over that something which I cannot fathom in you. I wouldn't be capable of seducing you just like that.

SOPHIA: (*With irony*) Seducing me. And something as messed up as you, dares to say something like that to me.

TARQUINIUS: Shut up! First of all I must come to know the higher law of my life, not the ordinary everyday petty rules and regulations. For me you are now only a means, a piece of litmus paper, with which I test the reactions of my soul. But you must promise me one thing: you will fight me without showing any mercy (*He holds out his hand to her.*)

SOPHIA: (*Giving him her hand*) But of course I promise. What conceit! I don't care about you in the least. The idea appeals to me as a totally new motif, interwoven into the tangled skein of all these sexual disorders. (TARQUINIUS *yanks his hand away from her.*)

TARQUINIUS: Horrid vixen! But all the same, certain conditions: if you wound me, and I have lost faith in Pandeus, I shall consider myself your property; if I wound you, you shall never cross my path again unless I expressly desire it. If one of us dies, the problems between us will, of course, be resolved all by themselves.

SOPHIA: Very well, my pet. You're starting to appeal to me again.

TARQUINIUS: Good-bye, until two, here in this room.

(*He goes out to the left. At the same time the entire company of men with* PANDEUS *at their head enters through the center door. The staff in frock coats. The* MANDELBAUMS *as previously.*)

SOPHIA: (*To herself*) I'm afraid I've taken an overdose of the antidote. That boy appeals to me a bit too much.

PANDEUS: How are your temptations going? Too bad I didn't see it. But Sir Grant got drunk as a skunk and told us such marvelous things about those concoctions of his that I simply could not tear myself away. But where is Tarquinius?

SOPHIA: (*Irritated*) He went to get ready for the ultimate initiations. Really, you do have hellish power over him. Nothing but torture could separate the two of you.

PANDEUS: (*In triumph*) So you see. I knew that Quinnie wouldn't betray me. Today I shall initiate him definitively.

SIR THOMAS: Our chances are increasing. I think that instead of squabbling among ourselves, we'll form an association of the worshippers of this new Astarte.

CARDINAL NINO: May God watch over us. I have a feeling that something frightful is going to happen.

(*Uneasy murmur from the* MANDELBAUMS. *From the left enter the two young girls in dressing gowns.*)

SOPHIA: (*Suddenly brightens up*) Mr. Teerbroom and you, Sir Thomas, allow my little girl friends to enjoy themselves for one last time today. You can be sure of my favor in return. (*Hesitation on the part of* TEERBROOM *and* SIR THOMAS.) Fine — then it's settled. Let us begin the orgy. Pandy, have them serve the very best you have. I'm not specifying the things I crave, lest I be suspected of trivial snobbery or bad taste.

(PANDEUS *goes out through the center door.* LIZA *goes over to her father. The men remain at the back of the stage.* SOPHIA *and* NINA *in the foreground.*)

NINA: Well, what happened? Did you seduce him?

SOPHIA: Nothing of the sort. I'm fighting with him at two in the morning, we're using swords. Don't be afraid, Nina. Nothing bad will happen to him.

NINA: You've given me your word. But what are you going to fight about?

SOPHIA: A mere trifle. He has to retrieve his lost — what does he call it — honor. He has to look into his innermost depths or something like that. Such subtleties are beyond my understanding. What amuses me is the fact itself.

NINA: You always amuse yourself, but what about me?

SOPHIA: Rest assured that I shan't do him any harm. I'll give him back to you even more noble than he was.

NINA: I was so sure that you had given him that pill — I was so afraid! But Liza and I didn't dare come in.

SOPHIA: Tarquinius does not need any pills. He is a wonderful boy. If it weren't for the fact that I really do love Pandeus and only him, I would take him away from you in an instant. But now listen to me, and after that pay close attention to what happens. I don't have anyone to confide in. I'll give Pandy the green pill today. In that way we shall discredit him in Tarquinius' eyes; as it is, the boy's faith in him has already been shaken. And then, free of delusions about the higher life, Tarquinius will be entirely yours.

NINA: How noble and beautiful you are in all you do! I thank you for everything!

(*She kisses her hand. Enter* PANDEUS *with a footman bearing wine and wine glasses. Wine is poured and drunk. The* MANDELBAUMS *stand sullenly in the background.*)

SOPHIA: (*Dropping the pill into her own glass*) Pandy, take this cup from me and empty it to the health of your protégé's and to his successful initiation into the doctrine of the higher consciousness of life, life without women. You are doing this not to reach Nirvana — we all know that — but to intensify even to the bursting point our wretched, filthy, socialized individuality. Hurrah!

PANDEUS: (*Taking the wine glass*) Now at last we shall live in friendship. Who knows — perhaps even you, Sophia, will convert to my faith once you have exhausted all the possible pleasures of the senses. But in the meantime, I drink to the greatness of the principle of Intrinsic Individual Identity which until the present moment I alone of all the philosophers in the world have fully comprehended. Amidst the rare specimens of our species long live the supreme, sexless happiness offered by the higher consciousness of life, without belief in the other world, without theosophy, without any fraud whatsoever! Hurrah! (*They drink.*)

SIR GRANT: (*To* PANDEUS) Don't drink that: the green pill may be in it. She...

(PANDEUS *stops and looks around with a questioning glance.*)

SOPHIA: Shut up! The old geezer has gone crazy! Drink up, Pandy — I have never betrayed *you*.

(SIR GRANT *retreats.*)

PANDEUS: Yes — I believe you absolutely, our souls never parted. (*Drains the cup to the bottom.*) And now let us go to the round room for the wildest of orgies. I must fortify myself with the sight of real-life swinishness before revealing the ultimate truths to Tarquinius.

(TARQUINIUS *runs in from the left.*)

TARQUINIUS: Pandy! I cannot stand it any longer. Let us go this instant. Initiate me, or I shall swerve all the way over to the other side.

PANDEUS: Very well — it may as well be now. I feel a strange force taking possession of all the creases in my brain, and mysterious shudders run through my torpid marrow. I think that even I myself may still have some new revelations. I shan't attend that orgy. (*To the guests.*) If you'll excuse me. (*To* SOPHIA.) Sophia, take them to the round room where we have experienced so many moments of fleeting sensual pleasure. Tarquinius and I will rejoin you in an hour or two. By then we shall be on the inaccessible heights of friendship and absolute knowledge. Like two parabolic mirrors turned towards each other, we shall reflect each other in ourselves, in closed Infinity.

SOPHIA: Ha, ha, ha, ha, ha, ha!

PANDEUS: (*Coldly*) What are you laughing for, Sophia?

SOPHIA: Oh, nothing — for no reason at all, for the sheer joy of it. (*To the staff and the* MANDELBAUMS.) Come, gentlemen, and you too, my dear young ladies. (*Embraces* NINA *who has been standing next to her until now.*) We shall amuse ourselves as never before, while awaiting further developments. (*She goes toward the center door with* NINA. *The crowd follows her. The* MANDELBAUMS *mutter between their teeth. Meanwhile* PANDEUS *speaks.*)

PANDEUS: Come, Tarquinius, only now will ultimate knowledge penetrate you. You won't lose your individuality, you will simply create yourself anew above the chance realm of day and night. You will be one and indivisible, unique for yourself and for me. Only as two can we accomplish this. Solitude kills the essence of the self and brings us closer to Nirvana. Only what I call hermetism of a higher order opens the gates of the mystery for those suffering from a raging thirst for the absolute. Neither art, nor any real deed, nor any faith can be higher than what we are going to create. The world will give way to Nothingness, leaving us in the cold, crystal sphere of truth about ourselves. We are unique.

TARQUINIUS: I must tell you something. I do not feel worthy — I've been kissing your Sophia.

PANDEUS: (*Interested*) So you've been kissing. I do not know why, but today even that gives you added charm. I love your soul. (*He embraces him.*)

TARQUINIUS: (*With a slight shudder*) She told me exactly the same thing.

PANDEUS: She's lying. Come, let us go to my slothroom in the north tower. I feel as though my mind were a cold dagger boring into the blazing womb of the Eternal Mystery. The solution lies neither in concepts, nor in systems of concepts, nor in intuitive evasion of reality. Nor is it to be found in the renunciation of life either. It lies in life itself, in the dual comprehension of the uniqueness and identity of each moment of duration in and of itself. (*They head towards the door to the right and go out. Offstage can be heard* SOPHIA's *wild laughter and the far-off growling of the* MANDELBAUMS — *then the roar of the guans.* SIR GRANT *rushes in through the center door and looks all around.*)

SIR GRANT: (*Screams*) They're not here! (*He runs to the door at the right. The* YOUNG FOOTMAN *appears in the door, with the* OLD FOOTMAN *right behind him, revolvers in their hands.*)

YOUNG FOOTMAN: Not one step further, Sir Grant. His Lordship ordered us to put a bullet through the head of anyone who'd dare burst into the north tower.

SIR GRANT: Too late, too late. (*He runs out through the center door.*)

Act II

Scene 2

The same room, in almost total darkness. The stage is empty for a moment. From the right someone can be heard running down the stairs at breakneck speed. TARQUINIUS *rushes in, wearing bright pajamas and turns on the light. Then he falls on the sofa and covers his face with his hands.*

TARQUINIUS: Oh, what a filthy beast! How dared he, it was all a lie. A cheap seduction on the part of a brazen-faced, perverted *roué*. Oh... (*Looks at his wrist-watch.*) Three minutes to two. She should be here any minute now. Everything has become so mixed up that I no longer understand anything at all. I have to fight. I have the feeling that everything will be decided that way. The truth will out. I don't know who she is or even who I am. All I do know — but I don't even know that for certain — is that he is a monster. But his monstrosity is such a frightfully complex mystery for me that I don't know what facts could serve to clear it up. (*Calling for her as he lies helplessly on the sofa.*) Madame Sophia, Madame Sophia! (*From the left enter* SOPHIA, *dressed in red tights. She is holding two swords in her hand.*)

SOPHIA: (*Calmly and quietly*) Easy, Mr. Quinnie. Easy. I'm here. I'm ready.

TARQUINIUS: (*Getting up*) Madame Sophia, what I've been through! This is the ruin of all my dreams, of my whole higher life.

SOPHIA: Calm down, baby. (*Strokes his head.*) Tell me all about it.

TARQUINIUS: (*In a different tone*) Oh — if only I could. But I loathe you too.

SOPHIA: What for? It never is possible to unite absolute truth with life in one living whole. What do you want from me? Love me, that's all.

TARQUINIUS: You're lying. You're thinking only of him. I know your principle of antidotes: the system of two significant lovers—not counting all the others.

SOPHIA: That's Pandeus' system: the principle of two mistresses. I was the only one he wasn't unfaithful to—nor I to him. I was the last.

TARQUINIUS: He wanted to be unfaithful to you, but he wasn't able to because I didn't want him to. Pass me a sword.

SOPHIA: (*Gives him his choice of swords, he takes one*) Why, certainly, certainly. If this duel is absolutely necessary for you to gain self-knowledge, then go ahead and fight. I should prefer you to kill yourself, I may hurt you badly. I promise you that I shall fight in earnest.

TARQUINIUS: Yes—and if I detect the slightest trace of pity in your eyes, I shall shoot you down like a mad bitch. And then myself, and him, I'll kill them all off and those cursed girls too for that matter. I have a revolver in my pocket.

SOPHIA: (*Coldy*) I imagine that you'll kill all the others first, and then yourself—it will be simpler that way. I too need a shock for my nerves after all these unsuccessful perversities and initiations. Pandeus must be mine. (*They position themselves:* TARQUINIUS *to the left,* SOPHIA *to the right, and begin to fight.*)

SOPHIA: (*After a moment, coldly*) Watch out, I'm starting to get hot.

TARQUINIUS: (*With fury*) Get hot and burn, you slut! Once I've run you through, there'll be nothing left of you but a pile of liquid putrefaction. Take that, and that!

SOPHIA: Ho, ho. His attack's not half bad. But now it's my turn. Back two steps; (*a couple of thrusts*) back three steps. Oh, that's it, oh, that's it! That's it, that's it, that's it. (*She pins him to the wall, to the left.* TARQUINIUS *falls in front of the door.*)

TARQUINIUS: I'm dying. My heart...all my insatiable longings...oh, how I wish I could live...(*Attempts to raise himself up and lunge at her;* SOPHIA *knocks the sword out of his hand; he falls again.*) I loathe you! (*He dies.* SOPHIA *stands motionless. Then she wipes off the sword on her right thigh, throws it down and lights a cigarette. A tremendous racket is heard, someone running down the stairs, to the right.* PANDEUS *rushes in, wearing bright pajamas.*)

PANDEUS: It's you, Sophia! I am young and healthy as a bull on the pampas. All those revelations are sheer rubbish. Truth exists only in life, without any philosophy, without any metaphysical friendship, without any identity. All that's impossible. Absolute truth is one and indivisible, beyond life — there it is pure. But here in real life everything exists only in division, in multiplicity, in plurality itself, in total disorder. Only chaos and the absurd are beautiful. Sophie, do you agree with me?

SOPHIA: (*Pointing to* TARQUINIUS' *corpse with her cigarette*) I was just saying the same thing to that protégé of yours. He didn't want to believe me. I had to fight with him in earnest, since he insisted on my promising him that I would. And there he lies insatiable, defiled by his last thought about his unfulfilled life, run straight through the heart by me.

PANDEUS: (*Without paying any attention to* TARQUINIUS) Sophie, forgive me for everything. But how could I ever have supposed that I would grow normal and healthy again. I love you and only you and I shall never abandon you.

SOPHIA: I have killed my sole antidote against you. I am yours and yours alone. Now for the first time I truly love you. Come.

PANDEUS: Wait, in a moment I won't be able to talk anymore from an excess of strength. An entire life turned upside down within my head is piling up into a pyramid of nonsense dancing with its bottom up. My marrow rears up like a giant anaconda. Now for the first time I see what wretchedness all that was: the higher consciousness of life and other such lofty morsels. Those are only swindles on the part of incompetent bunglers. My bones feel as if they were made of India rubber, and my muscles are bursting with savage power. Down with all purposeful actions. There is only one thing — pleasure-seeking. There is no greatness in anything, no wealth, no art. Those are only symbols for the great wretchedness that is existence, and he alone lives who seeks pleasure, and that in the most beastly way. All the rest is a social mask for the weak and the worn-out.

SOPHIA: That's enough speech-making. I am fed up with people too. For once in our lives let's be like two beasts, like two May flies.

PANDEUS: Yes, yes. But I had to become conscious of it. Higher consciousness of one's own animality is the highest form of life. It's quite another thing if one isn't aware of it: then it's plain, ordinary swinishness. (SOPHIA *leads him off the left.* PANDEUS *pushes* TARQUINIUS' *corpse out of the way, lets* SOPHIA *go ahead of him, and they both disappear through the door which they lock behind them.* SIR GRANT, *in pajamas, dashes in through the center door. He rushes to the left and crashes against the door trying to open it.*)

SIR GRANT: (*Not seeing the corpse*) Too late! Too late! Help! I gave her my pill, and she has given it to Clavercourse. (*He goes limp in the door. The whole pack rushes in, the staff in pajamas, and the* MANDELBAUMS *in clothes hastily slipped over their naked bodies, their shirts not buttoned or tucked in, and their hair disheveled.* TCHURNIN-KOKETAYEV *in an unbuttoned uniform,* CARDINAL NINO *in unfastened cardinal's robes, but with his hat on.*)

TCHURNIN-KOKETAYEV: What! Where?

CARDINAL: Who did what to whom?!!!

SIR GRANT: They both went in there! And he has the pill dissolved in his blood. She promised me. I shall go stark raving mad.

SIR THOMAS: Look! Tarquinius Umbilicus is lying there by the door dead. There are swords. There was a duel.

OLIPHANT BEEDLE: Clavercourse has murdered Umbilicus. How horrible! And all because he was jealous of our fetish. (*Murmuring in the crowd of* MANDELBAUMS *who surge forward. Offstage roars from the awakened guans.*)

SIR GRANT: (*Barely conscious*) Those are my guans roaring! Help me break the door open! (*The* CARDINAL *and* KOKETAYEV *rush to the door and help* SIR GRANT *break it open.* SOPHIA *appears at the door with her hair down, dressed in a green dressing gown; she comes out onto the stage.* KOKETAYEV *and the* CARDINAL *let her pass and dash into the room, to the left.*)

SOPHIA: He's dead. He died at the height of sensual pleasure.

SIR GRANT: (*Horrified*) What are you saying?

SOPHIA: Your pills kill, Sir Grant. Their effect is marvelous, but mortal.

SIR GRANT: So the guans could take it, but not the human beings! That's the end! My invention is worthless. (*With fervor.*) But for you, I'll even take three!

SOPHIA: Well, take them, you doddering old fool, and go die with your guans. I don't have any such intention, and without the pill, I'm incapable of loving you.

SIR GRANT: So that's it? Very well. (*He goes off to the right and blows his brains out. No one pays the slightest attention to him.* KOKETAYEV *and the* CARDINAL *carry in* PANDEUS' *corpse through the door to the left and put it on the sofa.*)

SOPHIA: Look, there is the greatest man of us all and of many others as well. He died like a beast, like an insect, conscious of the fact that to be a human being today is no longer worthwhile. I regret that I cannot devour him the way the female scorpion does her mate. (*The* MANDELBAUMS *mutter in the background.*)

TEERBROOM: But who killed that other one? Did *he* do it? Oh! These puny weaklings nowadays really do devour one another like insects.

SOPHIA: *I* killed that other one in a perfectly correct duel. The difference is that other one degraded himself by crying out for life at the last moment...while Pandeus died as he lived...

TEERBROOM: That is to say, like the lowest swine.

SOPHIA: You are mistaken, Mr. Teerbroom. He lived a lie, but he died with the truth on his lips like a true beast: he said he loved me. And I believed *him*, but I still don't believe *any of you*. You are all deluding yourselves, but if I should feel so inclined, you can be certain that the same thing will happen to you, provided fate allows you such happiness.

TEERBROOM: Yes, but then one can only live for one short moment...

TCHURNIN-KOKETAYEV: (*His Russian accent and syntax becoming more pronounced*) What does matter? Short moment, no short moment! Madame Sophia (*accented on the second syllable*), you are marvelous woman! *Yei-bogu!*

CARDINAL NINO: My villa! This hat...Everything! (*He flings the* CARDINAL's *hat from off his head.*)

SOPHIA: For shame, Your Eminence. You show your true colors as a disgusting, vulgar, old reprobate. (The MANDELBAUMS *mutter more vociferously.*) What I ask of you, gentlemen, is a little more sublimity — of the beastly, not the human sort. In all of you there is still too much humanity, which you take so much pride in, but which I so despise.

SIR THOMAS: That's all very well, but if it hadn't been for the green pill, even that Pandeus of yours wouldn't have died like a beast; he would have rotted away in his former lie. After all, these pills *are* the highest expression of human civilization. One step more in this direction, and we'll bring the dead back to life in order to kill them off still more cruelly.

SOPHIA: How can you talk such stale twaddle at a moment like this?

SIR THOMAS: Perhaps for you this moment is extraordinary. For us, it's an ordinary everyday sort of day. There only exist these two principles: preservation of the individual and preservation of the species. In the correct balance between these two elements lies the highest point in the evolution of mankind. The limit points are: the solitary beast, human or non-human, at the one extreme; and the human anthill at the other. The relativity of ethics results from the possibility of a differing balance between these elements....

SOPHIA: Don't poison my sole moment of happiness with doubt, wretched old man. I'd give a great deal to go the way he did, a beast conscious of his own beastliness, consciously surmounting human lies. That is something totally new. And besides, Sir Grant still has a whole box full. All right — any volunteers! Who wants to experience the supreme happiness of conscious beastification? Search the body and gulp down the poison. And then die! Die, the sooner the better, so that I shan't ever have to set eyes on you again. And who knows, perhaps what was too strong for him will be just right for you? (*With the exception of the* MANDELBAUMS, *they all throw themselves on* SIR GRANT's *corpse and, having found the little box* [SIR THOMAS *finds it first*], *they hurriedly divide its contents. Only* TEERBROOM *does not swallow his pill, but ostentatiously puts it in his vest pocket. The* MANDELBAUMS *form a tight circle and approach* SOPHIA, *who, busy observing the above scene, does not notice what they are doing. As soon as the others have finished, the tight circle of* MANDELBAUMS *surrounds* SOPHIA. *With a wild roar, the* MANDELBAUMS *throw themselves on* SOPHIA *and cover her completely.* [*At this point, the actress, having quickly thrown off her dressing gown, must crawl out behind the fireplace without being seen, or disappear through the floor by means of a trap door.*] *The roar dies down. Only panting can be heard. A single frightful cry from Sophia rends the air, then silence and panting.*)

TCHURNIN-KOKETAYEV: Gracious, zey are crushing her to death!

CARDINAL NINO: So much the better, my last temptation is over. Oh, God! My thanks to Thee! And the Villa Calafoutrini with all its priceless collections will continue to be mine! (*He kneels and prays.*)

SIR THOMAS: Perhaps it is better this way. She was torturing herself too by the life she led, as well as torturing you. Let her perish once and for all. I tell you, gentlemen, at last we shall breathe freely.

OLIPHANT BEEDLE: Gentlemen, you forget that we have taken the pills. Their effect may prove mortal not only for degenerates of the Clavercourse variety.

CARDINAL NINO: (*Interrupts his prayer*) What does it matter, gentlemen. We are all old men. Perhaps God will take pity on us. We have four hours left, either to make our peace with God or to enjoy life to the very end. (*From the left,* NINA *and* LIZA *rush in, wearing dressing gowns:* NINA *in blue,* LIZA *in red.*)

NINA: What's this? They're both dead!

LIZA: How horrible! Oh, God!

TEERBROOM: Liza! Come here this minute! For a moment, I had forgotten that I have a daughter. (LIZA *runs to her father and nestles up to him. The* MANDELBAUMS *get up and move to one side. There's not a single trace of* SOPHIA. *Only her green dressing gown lies on the floor. And possibly her stockings and slippers may also be there.*)

THE OLDEST MANDELBAUM: She is dead. That is what we call a lynching, carried out in the name of vengeance by the confused masculine background.

NINA: She does not exist and neither do I really. I shall take her place for you! I know everything already. I shall create a new type of Cybele or Astarte—it doesn't matter which. Follow me, gentlemen, for the final initiation without any identity or fraud.

SIR THOMAS: Nina dearest, you do not know that we have all taken the pills.

NINA: So much the better for them and for you, uncle. Doesn't anyone have a pill for me?

TEERBROOM: (*Obligingly*) Here you are, Duchess. There's nothing I could refuse a friend of my daughter's. (*He takes the pill out of his vest pocket and ostentatiously hands it to* NINA.)

NINA: (*Takes the pill*) Thanks. (*Swallows it.*) An abyss has opened within me. I shall fill it with our corpses. Now I know how life should be lived. (*She goes toward the center door.* SIR THOMAS, OLIPHANT BEEDLE, CARDINAL NINO *and* KOKETAYEV *follow her. The* MANDELBAUMS *try to make a move after them.* TEERBROOM *stops them.*)

TEERBROOM: Mandelbaums! Not one step further. We are going to create the new race of the future. I give you Liza. She will be the mother of the new breed. But I shall give her to the one I choose, to the one who will be the most essential incarnation of the race. After what she has seen here, she will be the best mother. Follow me. (*He takes* LIZA's *arm and goes to the left. The* MANDELBAUMS *follow them. On the stage there remain only the corpses of* TARQUINIUS, PANDEUS, *and* SIR GRANT, *and on the ground, in the middle of the stage, a small heap of clothes that belonged to* SOPHIA *of Abencérages Kremlínska.*)

END OF THE SECOND SCENE OF THE ACT
AND OF THE PLAY

Selections from Witkiewicz's Critical Writings on Drugs, Society, Philosophy, and Art

Portrait of Bruno Schulz, 1935

On Bruno Schulz

Translators' Introduction

Witkacy first met Bruno Schulz in 1925, but a lasting friendship between the two writers developed only at the time of Schulz's visit to Zakopane in 1930. From then on, they saw each other frequently in Warsaw during Schulz's trips to the capital from his native Drohobycz. Witkacy was a great admirer of both Schulz's drawing and prose, and after the publication of *Cinnamon Shops* in 1934, he arranged an interview, conducted by correspondence through a list of questions mailed to Schulz, in order to promote the book and call attention to the younger artist (seven years Witkacy's junior).

Witkacy's "Introduction" and Schulz's responses were published in *Tygodnik Il-ustrowany*, a popular weekly, on April 28, 1935, accompanied by a portrait of Schulz by Witkacy, executed the same year, and reproductions of three of Schulz's drawings: The Book of Idolatry, Humility, and Susanna. The article on Bruno Schulz's Literary Work appeared in two issues of the journal, *Pion*, in July and August of 1935.

Witkacy's writings on Schulz reveal the older writer to be a loyal and generous friend, eager to recognize the talents of others and to share his enthusiasms with the world, and a perceptive and far-sighted critic able to seize upon the endur-ing artistic and human values in the work of as yet unknown creators. With his uncanny powers of prophecy, Witkacy even predicts Schulz's tragic death, which occurred on November 19, 1942 when he was shot on the street in Drohobycz by the Nazis.

Witkacy finds in Schulz's drawings and prose writings those qualities that he most esteems and that constitute for him Pure Form in art: the ability to capture the metaphysical feeling of the strangeness of existence in banal, everyday reali-ty, and the power to express it directly through the interplay of images, sounds, and concepts in an autonomous and highly individual vision of the universe.

INTERVIEW WITH BRUNO SCHULZ
(Selections)

WITKACY [Introduction]

As a graphic artist and draughtsman, Schulz belongs to the line of demonologists. As I see it, the beginnings of this trend can be found in certain works by the old masters, even though in those days they did not make a specialty of it, for example in Cranach, Dürer, and Grünewald. With strange conviction and unbridled pleasure they paint subjects that have an infernal rather than a heavenly inspiration, finding a source of relaxation there after what often must have been for them boring compulsory pieties. Hogarth too I consider to be a demonist.

But the true creator of this trend in art [. . .] was Goya. Demonologists of the nineteenth century, such as Rops, Munch, or even Beardsley, are his direct descendants. And it is not a matter of the accessories of demonism (witches, devils, etc.), but rather of evil itself that lies at the basis of the human soul (egotism [. . .], greed, the urge to possess, sexual desire, sadism, cruelty, the will to power, oppression of everything and everybody around). [. . .]

These are the general areas in which Schulz works, his specialty in this field being female sadism and male masochism. In my opinion, woman by her very nature [. . .] must essentially be a sadist psychologically and a masochist physiologically, whereas man as a rule is a masochist psychologically and a sadist physiologically. Schulz has brought the expression of these two psychic combinations to the extreme possible limits of tension and almost monstrous emotional frenzy. For Schulz, the female instrument of oppression over males is the leg, that most frightful part of a woman's body, except for the face and certain other things. With their legs Schulz's females stamp on, torture, and drive to desperate, helpless fury his dwarfish, humiliated, and sex-tormented male-freaks, who find in their own degradation the highest form of agonizing bliss. Schulz's graphic works are epic poems on the cruelty of legs. [. . .]

In my opinion, Schulz is a new star of the first magnitude.

SCHULZ [On the philosophical meaning of reality in *Cinnamon Shops*]

Cinnamon Shops offers a certain formula for reality and decrees a special kind of matter. The matter that makes up this reality is in a state of perpetual fermentation, germination, potential life. There are no dead, hard, limited objects. Everything spreads beyond its own boundaries, remains but a moment in a given shape, only to abandon it at the first opportunity. In the customs and manners of this reality there is manifest a particular kind of principle: the pan-masquerade. Reality takes on distinct shapes only as a pretense, a joke, a game. Someone is a man, while someone else is a cockroach, but such a shape does not constitute an essence; it is only a role adopted for a moment, an outer skin that will be shed in another moment. In *Cinnamon Shops* an extreme monism of matter has been ordained, in the name of which individual objects are nothing but masks. The life of matter consists in wearing innumerable masks. This migration of forms is the essence of life. That is why an aura of pan-irony emanates from matter. Ever-present in *Cinnamon Shops* is an atmosphere of behind-the-scenes and back-stage, where the actors, after taking off their costumes, ridicule the high emotions of the roles they have just played. The very fact of an individual existence here on earth implies irony, trick-playing, sticking out one's tongue like a clown. (Here, I believe, is the common ground between my *Cinnamon Shops* and the world of your creative work in painting and theatre.)

BRUNO SCHULZ'S LITERARY WORK
(Selections)

I have referred to Bruno Schulz as a phenomenon just this side of genius, if he is not in fact quite simply a genius in embryo. This is no trite superlative if by a genius in art and literature we mean an individual who to the highest degree of intensity combines the following elements:

1. A worldview that has not been acquired secondhand, but which has sprung from the innermost guts of its creator.

2. An intellect sufficiently powerful so that this worldview can be presented conceptually or at least symbolically.

3. Talent, that is the ability to create sentences which are the synthesis of images, sounds, and conceptual content into almost homogeneous amalgams, provided that these are sentences whose arrangement of words, imagery, and sound patterns (in other words, form) are not a repetition of any previously known form in literature. I believe that Schulz possesses all of these qualities. [. . .]

Schulz has in prose what Miciński had in poetry: the ability to create alloys in which image and sound plus the conceptual aspect, both of itself and as the source of imagery and sound patterns, constitute an absolute unity: they create *new composite qualities.* That is why I consider some portions of Schulz's prose to be short compositions in Pure Form. [. . .]

For Schulz the chief element is the image, and I maintain that up until now there has never been such a master in Polish literature, and who knows, perhaps even in world literature. [. . .]

Like meteors, his sentences illumine new, unknown lands, which usually are submerged in a sea of banality and which we, deluged with mediocrity, are not able to perceive. [. . .] His sentences create for us a metaphysical vista on the world, a vista on the ultimate Mystery of everything in the universe, without which feeling there is no great literature or great art considered from the point of view of form.

Besides these artistic values, Schulz gives us purely practical values having to do with how we live our lives, and for certain of these we must be eternally grateful to him. [. . .] These precious gifts include, in my opinion: (1) A feeling of the highest, immaterial pricelessness of life, which it is so hard to maintain in a state of intensity in the ordinary course of everyday life with all its cares and complications. This feeling is a priceless treasure in and of itself, and whoever does not have it is a true beggar, despite all his other good qualities. This feeling comes through directly in almost every sentence of his, whereby Schulz with a kind of outright metaphysical lechery fingers each and every tiny nook and corner of his beloved reality. But this is not any kind of hackneyed sensuality or aesthetic gourmandise; this is *a true and great love* with which he also "inspires" us. (2) Out of this supreme love there grows a feeling of the ultimate incomprehensibility of the object of our love (as is probably always the case with great love), along with a sense of the incomprehensibility of the feeling itself as well as of the personality of which it is the expression. The most profound essence of Being is inexhaustible and boundless: we do not know what our own existence means or what the existence of the world signifies, we do not know what we are, we do not know anything about the meaning of our being in the totality of becoming. The Ultimate Mystery—expressed in primeval concepts not subject to definition—shines through the most ordinary everyday activities. [. . .] Schulz gives us this, and if we try to imitate him in this "insight" of his, we shall live differently, and even dream differently, once we have really got into his relation to reality. [. . .]

Schulz is the only writer who has given us a genuine description of the purely private charm of a dream, which as a rule is untranslatable into general symbols: he objectivified the dream, [. . .] made it intersubjective and intelligible in its "auto-individuality" for all. [. . .]

With Schulz we travel *everywhere*. Through his eyes, the earth is one of the strangest stars in the universe, and not a place of dirty business deals, underhanded schemes, abject poverty, exploitation, and degradation. [. . .]

In Schulz's writings we find a glimmer of hope that this invaluable strangeness can be shared by all; under what conditions still remains to be seen. Perhaps Schulz will explain it to us in his future works. After all, each one of us dreams about suddenly waking up on other shores, about changing the grayness of his existence, about taking a plunge into the unknown. [. . .]

And lastly, will he have strength enough to carry on and maintain the same form—even to bear himself with dignity if he should have to face a hideous, unsavory death?

Report About the Effect

of Peyote on

Stanisław Ignacy Witkiewicz

Translators' Introduction

The following account of Witkiewicz's experiment with peyote is the complete version of the abridged text which appears in Chapter V of *Nicotine, Alcohol, Cocaine, Peyote, Morphine, and Ether* (Warsaw, 1932). Witkiewicz himself purposely omitted passages of a frankly sexual nature which he felt might be offensive although he recognized that without them it would be difficult to convey the true character of a peyote vision. In the book he explains: "I won't be able to describe everything out of consideration for future readers as well as for myself. And I want this book to be read by everyone. But I don't know whether I shall succeed in conveying to the reader all the beauty and horror of what I have seen....For fear of outraging public decency I cannot enter into a detailed analysis of these visions. From time to time I like to see monstrous things, but peyote surpassed all my expectations. That one night gave me enough for an entire life-time."[1] Fortunately, the original report of the controlled experiment, recorded at the time first by Witkiewicz's wife and then by the playwright himself, survived in manuscript form and is given here in its entirety.[2] Whereas for Witkiewicz alcohol and cocaine are "realistic poisons," he considers peyote "a metaphysical drug causing a feeling of the strangeness of existence which, in a normal state, we experience extremely rarely — at moments of solitude in the mountains, late at night, in periods of great mental exhaustion, sometimes at the sight of something very beautiful, or listening to music."[3] According to Witkiewicz, peyote, by destroying rational self-control, makes it possible to penetrate into the subconscious. Further, in artificially lifting those who take it out of the sphere of day-to-day life, peyote produces a feeling of distance towards oneself and the world; this feeling is accompanied by an intense awareness of the uniqueness of the self which is the basis of metaphysical anxiety, so highly prized by Witkiewicz.

[1] *Nicotine, Alcohol, Cocaine, Peyote, Morphine, and Ether* (Warsaw, 1932), pp. 103, 115-16.

[2] First published in *Teksty*, edited and with an introduction by Bohdan K. Michalski, No. 6, 1972, pp. 175-187.

[3] *Nicotine*, p. 100.

REPORT ABOUT THE EFFECTS OF PEYOTE ON STANISLAW IGNACY WITKIEWICZ — June 20, 192-

At 5:40 W. took 2 ground-up pills of Pan-Peyote. After a few minutes he began to feel lightness and cold throughout his body and became afraid of being sick to his stomach. 6 o'clock — yawning and chills, pulse 88. 6:15 feels wonderful, nerves completely soothed. W. takes another dose (2 pills) and eats 2 eggs with tomatoes and drinks a small cup of coffee with just a drop of milk. 6:25 feels a little bit abnormal, like after a small dose of cocaine, pulse 80. The tired feeling after three portrait sittings disappeared totally. W. walks around the room with a steady step and closed the blinds on the windows tightly. 6:40 pulse 72 — feels slight, agreeable stupor and light-headedness. The inactivity bothers him, he's bored and would like to smoke a cigarette. 6:50 W. takes a third dose — stares with tremendous interest at an airplane in flight — then lowers the blinds again and lies down on the bed. Pupils normal, pulse 84. Strange feeling, waits for visions without any results, finally out of boredom smoked a cigarette but didn't finish it. 7:20 got up, took the last pill and lay down again. Starts to feel apathetic and disheartened. After lying down for half an hour, W. got up and felt sick, pulse a little weak, pupils somewhat enlarged, voice changed. Asked for coffee and stays lying down, as soon as he tries to get up, feels sick. 8:30 sees swirls of filaments, bright against a dark background. Next there start to appear animal phantoms, sea monsters, little faces, a man with a beard, but he still does not consider this to be visions, only the kind of heightened images that occur before falling asleep. Someone in a black velvet hat leans from an Italian balcony and speaks to the crowd. Definitely feels a heightening of the imagination, but still nothing extraordinary. Feels better, but when he gets up has dizzy spells and feels "odd", in an unpleasant way, at the same time a strange feeling in his muscles. 9 o'clock begins to see rainbow colors, but still does not consider this to be visions. 9:30 — various sculpture in sharp relief, tiny faces, feels "weird," but good. Sees rainbow stripes, but incomplete — the following colors predominate: dirty-red and lemon-yellow. Desire to forget reality. Huge building, the bricks turn into gargoyle faces, like on the cathedral of Notre-Dame in Paris. Monsters similar to plesiosauruses made out of luminous filaments. The trees turned into ostriches. A corpse's brain, abcesses, sheaves of sparks bursting out of them. On the whole unpleasant apparitions. On the ceiling, against a red background horned beasts. A gigantic stomach with a wound — the insides turn into coral at the bottom of the sea. A battle among sea monsters. Dr. Sokołowski turns into a cephalopod. Spatial "distortion." Cross-section of the earth. Fantastic luxuriousness of plant life. 10 o'clock languor continues. Stupor. Battle among senseless things. A series of chambers which change into an underground circus, some strange beasts appear, interesting class of people in the boxes, the boxes turn into (?). Impressions of two visible layers — the images are only black and white, and the rainbow colors are as it were separately. Land and sea monsters and frightful human mugs predominate in the visions. Snakes and giraffes, a sheep with a flamingo's nose, cobras crawled out of this sheep, a double-crested grebe with a seal's tail — bursting jaws, volcanoes change into fish. African vision. 11 o'clock terrific appetite, but at the same time total laziness so that eating a few tomatoes took over half an hour. With the monsters in the background a yellow pilot's cap appeared, then a uniform, then the face of Col. Beaurain in a yellow light. Out of the wild, chaotic coils a splendid beach came to the fore, across it along by the sea a Negro rides a bicycle and changes into a man with a small beard, and the toys which the Negro was apparently carrying turned into Mexican sculpture which, while looking at W., climbed up ladders. A series of female sex organs, out of which spill out guts and live worms as well as a green embryo turning somersaults.

W. HIMSELF WRITES THE CONTINUATION

Kogda perestanu kushat' pomidory (Russian: when I finish eating the tomatoes). A song. 20 before twelve. *Polosatiye* (Russian: striped) monsters at the side. The bottom of the ocean. A shark. Bubbles of gas. Sea anemone. A battle of sea-monsters to the left. Anonymous jaws. Previously about 10:30, hairy machines. Abstract creations, machinishly alive, ramrods, cylinders, grasshoppers and their battles. (Marvelous) Anteaters twisting backwards; spiny anteaters. Rodent covered with bristles of that kind etc. Col. Beaurain in a cap at 11 lighted in yellow. Zawadzka distorted giving someone a flirtatious wink. 12:10. Pulse 72. Time swollen. Metallic and precious stones. *Living* Indian sculpture (started with a gold miniature of Beelzebub). Hellish transformations of stylized mugs and animals (mixed up together) ending with a brood of snakes on a Grand Scale. Snakes in bunches uniting into monsters. Nina sleeping nearby changes into a mask *from staring at her,* moves her eyes in a horrible fashion (*en realité* goes on sleeping without moving). A second time — the same thing — monstrous moving masks.

Drugs create styles in sculpture and architecture. An elbow with a coat-of-arms. An arm turned into snakes (yellow and blue), conquered by discoloring monsters with crab-eyes. Green snake-worlds against a brown background. Worlds. Gruenewald's Iselheimer (Altar) and something like Lucas Cranach. Monsters of this sort mixed up with corpses in a state of decay. The Negro who rotted in my eyes, evaporated half-way in the form of a shaft of sparks. Often it all stays crosswise. A cross-section of earth in the tropics. Machines — turbines — the Center of the World and their brakes made out of fur. Monstrous speed. I had the impression that hours (days?) had elapsed — but it was a quarter of an hour. What can you do to enjoy yourself in such a short time? I drew just to "go through the motions," although the lines were something special. But it was a waste of time compared to what there was to be seen. (12:30).

Snakes too "good to be true." Stylization and colors. Pearly tanks of the Assyrian kings. (I often interrupt the visions in order to write them down). So many things vanish in this whirl. The portrait of old Kossak (hanging in my room) came to life and started to move.

I return to *that other* world. Such large numbers of reptiles (colored) are *monstrous.* Higher (metaphysical) acrobatics by chameleons. (How is it that they do not vanish in those somersaults too?)
Once again only a quarter of an hour. *La plante qui émerveille les yeux.* Brain-strain-storms. The vodka was tasteless. Hunger pains. Total contempt for cigarettes. Moving china made out of reptiles. Piggish monsters came out of Boren's eye. A pile of pigs came spilling out. A stage. Artificial monsters. Pigsnouts in green four-cornered caps (those worn by 18th-century Polish patriots).
12:55 — I am going to try not to write, and to enter more into the spirit of things. I put out the lights as an experiment. I cannot stand not writing it down: cross-section of reptile machines (of course this is scarcely a particle).

Desisterization of double sharks on water dolthives.

1:02 — I put out the light again.
1:15 — 2nd series of drawings. I roar with laughter.
1:17 — I lie down. (No — wander around and eat sweets).
1:25 — (Drawing with the Mokrzysies) Check what the M's were doing at this time. I shut my eyes for a second — I see an animal behind broken lids. Transformations of animals into people in a continuous fashion *à la fourchette.*

Portrait of Dr. Teodor Birula-Bialynicki
(Insincere Drawing, 1928)

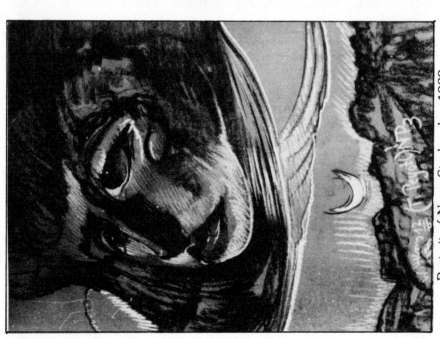

Portrait of Nena Stachurska, 1929

1:28 — I put out the light and decide not to write things down. I cannot do it. Centuries have elapsed, but by the clock it is 7 minutes after 1:30. It began with the Bolsheviks (Trotsky) and their transformations. Supergenitals in crayfish-red colors, sexual intercourse *in natura* and next the *incarnation of sexual pleasures* in various little monsters rubbing up against one another and fighting among themselves, in crayfish-red color. Sometimes cobalt eyes flickered on top of filaments — it ended in reptiles. 1:40 — pulse 68. Alien hands are writing. I close my eyes by the lighted lamp. Primeval matter with snakes. It started with a scene from *Macbeth* from the side and from below. A gigantic sister of mercy intersected with frightful genitals seen from underneath. I feel a bit like smoking. I stare at the childhood portrait of Nina. Nina smiles and moves her eyes, but *does not want* to look at me. I have had enough reptiles. Seals in a sea *thick* as grease. Whole series of brown-green sculpture representing peyote scenes. (Executed in a highly artistic way.) A monastery on the moon undermined by snakes and a monstrous female organ on a cliff, upon which a violet spark has descended. The monastery tumbled down on me into the sea. (Grabiński.)

1:52 — Seems that the visions are growing weaker.

2:05 — Centuries have elapsed. Whole mountains, worlds and flocks of visions. Too many reptiles. Finally a cave made out of pigs — out of a gigantic moving pig, composed of little piggish tiles.

The Chinese knew peyote. All Chinese dragons and all of India come from it. The initiated — the artists. *Eine allgemeine Peyote-theorie.* Panpeyoteism.

Peyote

the two branches of art

China, India, Persia   America-Mexico, Africa-Egypt

Our navel of decline. Perhaps peyote will resurrect us.

Music and a phonograph from down below destroy the importance of the visions. Should I turn on the light? At times there were red and blue dancing paper figures.

2:11 — One vodka and a few tomatoes. Notes. I close my eyes by the lamp. 2:15. A vision of Gucio Z. *snaked* (by snakes) yellow and black. And then realistically sleeping on his right stomach-side. Headache. Glass visions — criminal ones. Superscamps. The start of fantastic theatre. Alcor — double star — 2 suns (160 years a revolution) turned very fast.

2:30 — A madmans' brain with gurgling eyes in the clutches of a hellish snake-cephalopod.

After vodka sad and gloomy visions. A yellow eye pudent amid soot. *Superhuman* edifices with columns turned into mountain-genitals (big as Giewont) made of shining pink stones.

2:35 — Violet sperm-jet straight in the face, from a hydrant of mountain-genitals (down below superedifices).

2:45 — I eat Graham bread and butter. Looking out through the shades at disagreeable apartment buildings. Calling to mind a certain horrendous view of the Poldek's apartment building on View Street. Will there be visions? The Poldeks sleep *separately* under one quilt. Poldek on his back and Wanda on her right side, curled up (towards the window). Visions (renewed) of tiny little faces. The thought that Kotarbiński could use this world and my reptiles more than Rafał and I.

2:53 — Superasses keep on constantly pouring like waterfalls.

2:58 — Procession of elephants and a pearly camel (in a mask) in proportion (tremendous realism). Eyes peeping at and embracing female organs.

3:00 — A little fellow something like Miciński tearing off to the moon and his adventures after landing by parachute in a state of addle-patedness. Elves on a see-saw (Comic number). The Queen of Sheba's horny genitals in a planetary museum.

3:05 — I said "enough visions" and put out the light. Cadaverish sexual visions set in (*Macabre* number). A skull (which had dropped down) floating across the stomach — so hideous that I turned the light on as quickly as I could. Erotic rain of skirtish flowers (crocuses). Smiling man with a beard (Valois) locked in gigantic ox-snouts.

3:10 — Hades according to my conception of it. Skeleton in a circular desert and specters à la Goya. Goya must have been familiar with Peyote.

3:30 — Tiring visions. A battle of centaurs turned into a battle of fantastic genitals. Conversion, but not to any religion, rather in the realm of life. Renouncing drugs. Soulfulness. The crab of iniquity crawled out of the wound in a skull. The partridge-ification of a goshawk. The marvelously wise, goshawkly-human eyes grew dull and stupid, became duplicated and flew away in bird heads beyond the round horizon.

3:45 — A Pharaoh similar to me. Processions. Totemistic rites (somewhat goshawkly-reptilian). On shields — then floating away in the form of animal spirits. Reptiles in sexual entanglements. Minettes of iguanas.

3:50 — Snakes in desert springs. (Realistic number.) Again a vision (repetition with variation) of a madman's brain ulcerated to the point of gangrene (à *propos* no more drinking) and a bird-amphibian face pecking a monster's brain (and holding it in its clutches) lifted up its head in my direction and looked at me lasciviously. Sexual abyss with a blond wooly hippopotamus. In this eyes.

3:58 — Bristling concepts and from out of these concepts, instead of the truth (it stood with its back artificially turned to me), there came forth a strange animal, and then an ordinary wild pig.

4:05 — The birth of a diamond goldfinch. A rainbow-colored basset hound spurted into fireworks of black and pink butterflies on bent pink sticks. Egyptian and Assyrian processions. A female slave behind a column and from out of this there then came forth an unfinished palace tale, drowned in greasy genitals.

4:10 — In these visions I saw my entire inner wretchedness.

4:15 — Transformation of a skeleton into an ethereal body (diamond).

4:20 — Third series of drawings. I want to smoke.

4:27 — Drawings (2) finished (?).

About 3 o'clock processions mixed up in different styles, for example: rococo, present-day and antiquity. (Mélange of styles as though at the races — seen from below.)

4:30 — Crotch from Zakroczym. I cannot be completely saved, since I cannot renounce sex.

Nina's portrait won't look anymore, because I have lost my secret power over things. In the dark depths of the coils of my brain the remnants of visions are lying in wait (I have deserved these — the Indians are right, Peyote punishes the guilty).

4:40 — Slight headache. Fatigue from visions. Desire for sleep without visions. Pulse 72. Ordinary reality more and more often seems normal, and not horrendous as heretofore. Curving of space slowly vanishes. (Einstein put into practice).

4:43 — Vision of fat old women hanging in the mountains (Hala Gasiennicowa) on ropes. (Vision of unintelligible symbolism.) The Strążyskis in their living room on a sofa turned into a bed. He by the window with his feet towards the window, she on her right side with her head towards the library. Now she woke up, 4:49, he's asleep.

4:55 — Realistic eye of Piłsudski — it comes gently out from its eye-socket and springs (already ethereal) straight at me through space. It hits some point in the Ukraine and from there swarms of geometricalized, striped black worms pour out onto the entire world.

5:00 — The mysterious tale of a lady from the Eastern Provinces (a blonde), a gendarme, a Russian Orthodox priest, an old man in a nobleman's uniform. English Fieldmarshals — one a cuirassier of the guard, the other in a pointed hat — pulling a wagon with a Hindu statue through the rain (punishment). All these reptiles are monsters born in me due to alcohol and cocaine. There was so little of it, and so many reptiles.

5:04 — Hideous monster with whiskers, cat-like, crawling out of a fatty female organ — being born.

5:08 — Grim fleet with faces under the rudders. I have had *enough visions*.

5:11 — Rotting foot, the shoe disintegrates. Pink worms, similar to phalluses, crawl out, change into erect lingams. (Foot and shoe gangrene.)

5:18 — Ideal young lady slowly changed an ambling, bubble-shaped horror.

5:20 — I am perhaps the incarnation of the King of Snakes of the Tatra mountains. (Tatra vision.) The Small Meadow in winter, and it ended as a *monstrous* reptile on Przysłop Miętusi.

5:25 — I put out the light.

Zygmunt Unrug (a heretic), seen in profile, drawn into a vortex of snakes. A shield with a coat of arms grew into a snake and crashes down. Alongside, visions of another shield with a lion, his legs astride. Visit to the Sokołowskis in Brwinów. Slinking monsters; chocolate-colored with black and gold.

5:33 — Distortion of Nina asleep with her eyes open. Before that, transformation of the pitcher in the corner. I put out the light. Brighter and brighter in the room due to the daylight. Immediately thereafter vision of nicotine — small yellow eye in a corpse's skull. Next of alcohol — a marvelous humming bird snake crawls out; and Coco — a woman's eye, white as a pigeon's and from underneath a small woman's hand which grows into white snake reins, prodding and squeezing my neck. White feminine fluffy down and a beautiful eye, a blue one. An empty blister on the leg, sticking out into infinity.

5:47 — Vision of a deluxe reptile (dinosaur), *pour les princes.* Rather humorous number as an encore. Sunny knight under glass (after a geographic vision with the sun on the mountains from both *sides*). Caricatures of male characters in costumes. An affair of honor involving French officers and wild combinations with a young Russian. Frenchmen and Bedouins on Percherons fill in a well with monsters. General Porzeczko's ulcerated tits.

6:15 — Hydrocychnytine. Stinkotine. Music, a lower art, gave birth to itself — but only Peyote could have given birth to such a cunning thing as painting or sculpture, and then it went on its own — just like that.

6:17 — I take valerian. Desire to smoke. Mundane quarter-asses barked at by flying dragons (on a cone). Hideous reptile, *bleu acier,* at the bottom of shallow water, flat as a ray without a head, alongside but at the top . . . a snake peeped out from this. Disappearing towers and a gigantic mourner lights the sun of truth — a little metal figure with a bare backside. I, as a little boy on a catafalque, turn into a wild pig.

6:30 — Drank up the rest of the valerian. I have decidedly had *enough* visions. The total ugliness of naturalism compared to the riches of these forms. Sins against Mother. And here Peyote gave me a vision, although I thought that it would not dare. How my wrongs and sins are destroying my Mother's health.

6:38 — Parade of contemporary masks with duplications and caricatures *in the eyes,* constrictions, contractions, and repulsions. Realistic character of a harum-scarum (scared his harem).

6:50 — The Strążyskis start to wake up. Vision of the transformations of a marvelous woman, then sexual tentacular getting hooked. How much evil there is in me. And I consider myself good. Frightful visions of

Mother. Nina on her wedding trip with an unknown gentleman, in a hammock on the Riviera.

7:15 — Dozing without *real* visions. Normal sleeping dreams. Franz Joseph and Franek Orkan — one and the same. Marvelously indecent woman gives birth to a monster. Hideous sexual intercourse with a horde of reptiles. Once again . . .

8:15 — Morning activities. Fear of the light. However, state still highly abnormal. Pupils somewhat narrower than at the maximum. Dying visions of rainbow-colored whirls of filaments.

9:00 — Visions still, but weaker and not so awful. Many visions. *Reptiles.*

9:20 — Multiform flat green snake in a shallow pond.

10:00 — Remnants of visions.

10:15 to 12:00 — Sleep. Then relatively normal state. Slight stupor and spatial disorientation. Weak enlargement of the pupils.

New Forms in Painting

and

The Misunderstandings

Arising Therefrom

Translators' Introduction

New Forms in Painting and the Misunderstandings Arising Therefrom was begun
in St. Petersburg in 1917, finished in 1918 after Witkiewicz's return to Poland,
and published in Warsaw in 1919. *New Forms in Painting* contains all of
Witkiewicz's essential ideas on society, philosophy, art and reveals him to be a
prophetic thinker on problems of mass culture in post-industrial societies.
Witkiewicz's plays and novels are often directly derived from passages in *New
Forms in Painting;* in his imaginative writing the ideas acquire the dynamic and
colorful embodiment of the dream images which Witkiewicz experienced while
under the influence of peyote. The following selections from *New Forms in
Painting,* a very long and detailed work, present the fundamental argument.

PART I: Philosophical Introduction

... Artistic creation ... is an affirmation of Existence in its metaphysical horror, and not a justification of this horror through the creation of a system of soothing concepts, as is the case with religion, or a system of concepts showing rationally the necessity of this and not any other state of affairs for the Totality of Existence, as is the case with philosophy....

. . . .

PART III: Painting

Chapter I: General Considerations

... We live in a frightful epoch, the likes of which the history of humanity has never known until now, and which is so camouflaged by certain ideas that man nowadays has no knowledge of himself; he is born, lives, and dies in the midst of lying and does not know the depth of his own degeneration. Nowadays art is the sole crack through which it is possible to get a glimpse of the horrible, painful, insane monstrosity which is passed off as being the evolution of social progress; finding the truth in philosophy is virtually impossible since it has become so en-tangled in lies in the shape of empirio-critics and pragmatists. In the forms of the art of our age we find the atrociousness of our existence and a final, dying beauty which in all likelihood nothing will be able to bring back any more....

PART IV: On the Disappearance of Metaphysical Feelings as a Result of the Evolution of Society

Chapter I: The Evolution of Society

... The views expressed here are not those of some "social reactionary," for in fact we believe in the inevitability and necessity of certain changes which have as their goal justice and the common good. We are concerned only with the secondary effects of these changes, as to whose consequences, in our opinion, certain delusions are much too prevalent.... Starting with the most primitive community, the development of mankind moves in the direction of restricting the individual in favor of the group, while at the same time the individual, in exchange for certain sacrifices, obtains other advantages which he could not attain all by himself. Subordination of the interests of the single individual to the interests of the whole — this is the most general formulation of the process which we call social progress.... It goes without saying that vain are the dreams of naïve communists who want to resolve the problem by a return to certain primitive forms of social existence while retaining all the achievements of present-day civilization.... Mankind cannot deliberately retreat from the level of civilization which it has already attained; it cannot even stop, for stopping amounts to the same thing as going backwards. We cannot give up the increasing convenience and security of our lives, nor can we deliberately stop man's further domination of matter and the resultant organization of the working classes on the vast expanses of our planet.... We cannot say: that's enough civilization and comfort in our lives for the time being, now we'll set to work on equal distribution of civilization throughout the entire world and bringing happiness to all by means of what has already been accomplished. As long as there exists raw material which can be processed and as long as technology encounters no barriers of catastrophic proportions (which for a short period of time is quite doubtful given the ever-new discoveries of sources of energy), our demands will constantly grow in keeping with the dissemination of previous accomplishments, and halting civilization on a certain already attained level is an absolute impossibility. We cannot foretell what forms the life of society will assume with the passage of time — this is an equation with too large a number of unknowns — in any case on the basis of the already known segments of history we can say that the process of mankind's socialization is a phenomenon which is irreversible in the long run despite the fact that in the short run it can undergo certain relatively minute fluctuations.... The gray mob was only a pulpy mass on which grew monstrous and splendid flowers: rulers, true sons of powerful deities, and priests holding in their hands the frightful Mystery of Existence. Today, with the astonishment of true democrats, we cannot understand how this mob could have endured so much suffering and maltreatment of "the dignity of man" without protest and revolt, or why they did not establish some kind of communistic regime. But the traditions of such realms are still alive even in our own times in the form of the great nations which succeed in placing their own honor higher than the lives of millions of individuals. The present-day ruler is only a ghost, a wretched caricature when compared to his ancestors—he is only the embodiment of all the people's power and strength which in the past was the privilege of a person or a small group, but today is the property of whole nations. But we live in times in which, as the ghosts of nations depart into the past, there appears a shadow threatening for everything that is beautiful, mysterious, and unique of its kind—the shadow of that gray mob kept down for centuries, and it is growing to frightening proportions embracing all of mankind. This ghost still is not strong enough yet, but like a spirit at a spiritualistic seance it is materializing more and more; already its grazing touch and first contact can be felt which, transformed into hard blows, will avenge the torments of all those wretched beings out of which the mob took shape. Now terrified of this shadow, rulers humble themselves before the people, begging them for the power which in the past they derived from themselves, from the deities who gave birth to them . . . . This frightful shadow makes the rulers of the world tremble, threatens to destroy all understanding of the Mystery of Existence by making philosophers the servants of its demands, and hurls.artists into the depths of madness. As it grows organized, this mass of former slaves, whose gigantic stomach and desire to enjoy all that they have been deprived of until now, becomes the law of existence on our planet. . . .

Whereas for the former ruler the mob was only pulp which he shaped according to his own will and he alone accomplished great deeds following his own bizarre notions and using the mob as though it were an obedient tool devoid of a will of its own, now the powerful master of times to come will be (and perhaps already is in an embryonic state) only a tool in the hands of the mass which strives for material enjoyment and a sense of its own power . . .

We turn our eyes from the past in shame and from the future in dread at the coming boredom and grayness, or we create artificial narcotics with which we hope to awaken the long since dead feeling and fervor of individual strength, we create artificial mystery and artificial beauty in art and in life. It's all in vain—beauty resides only in madness, truth lies at our feet torn to pieces by contemporary philosophers, and of this trinity of ideals, for us there remains only goodness, that is, the happiness of all those who have not had the strength to create beauty, or enough courage to look the mystery in the eye. What awaits us is the monstrous boredom of mechanical soulless life through which the little people of the world will swim in moments of leisure produced by reduced work loads . . .

The people of the future will need neither truth nor beauty; they will be happy—isn't that enough?... The people of the future will not feel the mysteriousness of existence, they will have no time for it, and besides they will never be lonely in the ideal future society.

What then will they live for? They will work to eat, and eat to work. But why should this question upset us. Isn't the sight of ants, bees, or bumble-bees, perfectly mechanized and organized, a reassuring one? Probably they are totally happy, all the more so that undoubtedly they never could think and experience what we have during the four or five thousand years which we have endured with a consciousness of the mystery of being.... The physical and spiritual forces of the individual are limited, whereas the strength of organized humanity can grow, at least for the time being, without limit.... The first step on the way to a total leveling of differences is the standardization of civilization which, since the perfection of the means of communication and interchange of information, grows, at least in Europe, at an absolutely frantic rate. Abstract inequality and individual differences are being wiped out by the specialization of work, and at the extremes the machinery of the whole system will iron them out perfectly. In comparison to present-day cultural interaction, former civilizations were totally isolated, and most significantly, they developed extremely slowly. Nowadays whatever any genius discovers instantly becomes the property of all, and even the most individual deeds, quite independent of the will of the person who did them, add to the growing power of the mob of gray workers fighting for their rights....

In our period, wars—once a splendid manifestation of the wild strength of nations—are neither spontaneous outbursts of hatred caused by essential differences between nations and a direct desire for domination personified by powerful rulers, nor a battle over ideas whose concrete embodiment was not a matter of material utility, as for example, the wars of religion. War nowadays is nothing but cold, mechanical, systematic murder of one's fellow man, devoid of spontaneous emotional motivation, and it has as its goal the acquisition of financial profits carefully calculated and contrived by diplomats, businessmen, and industrialists. Instead of picturesquely dressed knights fighting breast to breast over what to us are completely fantastic issues, we have reduplicated crawling wretches who murder one another from a distance and poison one another with hideous gases....

At the moment when the old world died, a world based on the monstrous torments of the greater part of mankind, but which nevertheless bore the most splendid flowers of creativity, and the new transitional regime of moderate democracy based on parliamentary principles failed to produce universal happiness and simply led to exploitation, in another guise, of the same lower strata of mankind, without being able to bring forth anything which could be compared to the former creativity, it can only be wished that the process of mechanization and the leveling of individuality will be accomplished as quickly and as un-catastrophically as possible, out of regard for the cultural values already achieved....

Since there is no doubt but that life tends to more and more social justice, to the elimination of exploitation, to an even distribution of burdens, to comfort and security—for every one, not only for excep-tional individuals—it might be assumed that the whole mass of until now wasted energies will be turned in another, more important direc-tion than mutual slaughter and torture, and that now for the first time there will appear, perhaps in the near future, a kind of golden age of mankind ... This, it seems to us, is a delusion to which in our times men of good will succumb since they wish to see the future in every aspect through rose-colored glasses.... Today's liberals see the future of the broad masses through the prism of their own present psychology.... The mystery of existence, unless it appears in the horror of daily life, loses its true significance.... Nothing can be achieved without paying for it, and universal happiness is no exception to the rule. Creativity of a certain kind must be lost as the price of this happiness, creativity which has its source in the tragic sense of existence which future people will not be able to feel.... While we recognize the necessity of social change and the absolute impossibility of going backwards to former times when millions of the weak were oppressed by a few of the strong, we never-theless cannot close our eyes to what we will lose through socialization, and perhaps this awareness will at least permit us (as long as we are not able to adopt artificial naïveté in our thinking) to experience in a significant fashion our contemporary artistic creativity which, although it may make inroads on the world of madness, is all the same the sole beauty of our age.

Chapter II: The Suicide of Philosophy

In our times the educational function of religion has come to an end once and for all, and religion itself is slowly taking a secondary position. In fact today the only religion which has any validity is the cult of socie-ty. Today any one may worship whatever fetish he wants in his own home or celebrate black masses as long as he is a good member of socie-ty. Religion still exists for the masses, but in the form of automated rites which have little in common with the essential metaphysical moment.... With unparalleled ease the masses are discarding all the dead weight of religion in favor of doctrines which propose alluring solutions to problems of property and the general welfare. The progress of science and the dissemination of discursive philosophy contributes to the decline of religion. Science, especially for enlightened minds which do not understand its essential value, is taken as the final explaining away of the Mystery of Being, on the basis of one theory or the other, or some "synthesis" of them.

As society evolves, as life becomes more and more comfortable, more certain in its outlines, more automatic and mechanical in its functions, there is less and less place in man's soul for metaphysical anxiety. Our life becomes so defined that man is brought up from the start to fulfill certain partial functions which do not allow him to grasp the whole shape of phenomena, functions which so consume his time with systematically organized work that thinking about ultimate matters which have no immediate utility ceases to be something important in the course of his everyday life. . . .

From a certain point of view, all philosophies, all systems are only a certain appeasement offered on the subject of the inexplicable Mystery. . . . Each epoch has the kind of philosophy which it deserves. In our present phase we do not deserve anything better than a narcotic of the most inferior sort which has as its goal lulling to sleep our anti social metaphysical anxiety which hinders the process of automatization. We have this narcotic in excess in all forms of philosophical literature throughout the entire world. . . .

The loneliness of the individual in the infinity of Existence became unbearable for man in the as yet incompletely perfected conditions of societal life, and therefore he set out to create a new Fetish in place of the Great Mystery — the Fetish of society, by means of which he attempted to deny the most important law of Existence: the limitation and uniqueness of each Individual Being — so that he would not be alone among the menacing forces of nature. . . . Metaphysical truths are pitiless and it is not possible to make compromises about them without producing inconsistencies. Given the way the problem is posed now, the only way out is to forbid people to search for the truth as though that were a kind of fruitless unhealthy mania from which mankind has already suffered long enough throughout the centuries.

This is exactly the position which has been adopted by contemporary philosophy which deserves the name "philosophy" even less than the most primitive or the most new-fangled religious systems. Even a person possessed by an unhealthy religious mania could be considered incomparably higher than a true pragmatist, Bergsonite, or follower of Mach. . . .

Our blasé intellect is only able to take cognizance of certain things passively, we can absorb information, but we are no longer able to say or create anything new on the subject. We have a complete choice of masks which we can wear in an hour of deadly boredom, but we cannot feel or experience anything as at least some of our ancestors did. . . .

The proof that the Great Mystery has stopped existing for us once and for all and that we have lost the ability to feel it in its entirety lies in the search for half-mysteries, which, it is hoped, will provide life with some new magic now that the old has been taken away by the exact sciences, social stability, and metaphysics itself in its debased form.

The creation of artificial petty mysteries is a symptom of the disappearance of metaphysical anxiety. The same thing applies to all those mystical beliefs which contemporary America abounds in, despite all its sober approach to life: they are tiny symptoms of an anxiety that something has disappeared which needs to be restored *deliberately,* because without it, for some people, the grayness of tomorrow which is bearing down on us is simply too monstrous. But even these tiny symptoms will soon disappear and from then on mankind will sleep a happy sleep without dreams, knowing nothing in truth about the beautiful and menacing reality which has been its past.

Chapter III: The Decline of Art

In the closed cultures of antiquity the great artistic styles whose beginnings are lost in the mists of history developed extremely slowly; these styles consisted of two fundamental elements: ornamentation and the presentation of religious images under pressure from the menacing conditions of life and the profound, pitiless beliefs. The religious content of the sculpture and painting which adorned temples was directly connected to the form; there was no difference between Pure Form and external content because, being close to its primeval source, metaphysical feeling in its purest form, the directly expressed unity in plurality was not divided from its symbol: the image of a fantastic deity. At that time there were not, in our sense of the term, any separate artists forging a style of their own. Rather there was a throng of workers within the context of a style which evolved slowly as the result of a collective effort to which each of them contributed certain relatively minor alterations . . .

As religion grew superficial and gods were likened to men and the intellect developed in pace with social democratization, there was an immediate effect on art. This process reached its height in Roman sculpture, and then there was a total decline of Art. . . . When Christian mysticism arose, there was a fertilization of the human spirit with regard to art. . . But from our point of view the Renaissance was a defeat for true Art. . . . Painting declined rapidly, and its ideal became fidelity in copying the external world. . . . An important revival of Pure Form took place in the last decades of the nineteenth century in France starting with the Impressionists who, however, did not leave behind them works of great value besides a riotous outpouring of color which had been previously killed off by classicism. Despite the fact that it stopped being a soulless and even sentimental imitation of nature, painting during this period was not connected with a generally valid metaphysics in the form of religion, but was rather the expression of a private, secret, and more or less deliberate metaphysics on the part of individual artists ... The value of a work of art does not depend on the real-life feelings contained in it or on the perfection achieved in copying the subject matter, but is solely based upon the unity of a construction of pure formal elements.. . .

Today we have come to Pure Form by another road; it is, as it were, an act of despair against life which is becoming grayer and grayer, and for that reason, although art is the sole value of our times—excluding of course the technology of living and universal happiness—present-day artistic forms are, in comparison with the old ones, crooked, bizarre, upsetting, and nightmarish. The new art stands in relation to the old, as a feverish vision in relation to a calm, beautiful dream.. . .

Nowadays an overworked person has neither the time or the nervous energy for any thoughtful absorption in works of art, the understanding of which demands leisurely contemplation and inner concentration proportionate to the slow maturation of the works themselves. For people nowadays, the forms of the Art of the past are too placid, they do not excite their deadened nerves to the point of vibration. They need something which will rapidly and powerfully shock their blasé nervous system and act as a stimulating shower after long hours of stupefying mechanical work. This can best be seen in the theatre, which as most dependent on an audience, has most rapidly reached a point of decline from which most probably nothing can ever rescue it, despite efforts at restoring certain old forms.. . . Today's theatre cannot satisfy the average spectator ... Cabaret on the one hand and cinema on the other are taking away most of the audience from the theatre.. . . Cinema can do absolutely everything that the human spirit might desire, and so if we can have such frantic action and striking images instead, isn't it well worth giving up useless chatter on the stage which nobody needs anymore anyhow; is it worth taking the trouble to produce something as infernally difficult as a truly theatrical play when confronted by such a threatening rival as the all-powerful cinema?

Today, like every one else, the painter as artist is compelled to live in the same atmosphere as other people.. . . He is subject to the general acceleration of life ... and even if he were to live in the country, drink milk, and read only the Bible, he is carried along by the feverish tempo of all of life; and due to the influence of his blasé nerves, metaphysical anxiety in his works assumes forms at the sight of which the average audience ... without understanding their profound substance, roars with laughter and the critic talks about the decline of art.. . . Such an artist either dies of hunger, embittered by the world's failure to understand his tragedy, or one or more gentlemen appear to take him on as an enterprise and launch his career ... and make a pile of money out of him; and then the same critic who previously had virtually wiped the floor with him ... now will write about him with wild enthusiasm, while the artist himself, after having created his own style at the age of twenty-eight, will long since have been in the cemetery for suicides or in the hospital poisoned by some drug, or calmed down in a strait-jacket on a bed, or, what is still worse, alive and well, but imitating himself in ever cheaper editions for business purposes.... Nowadays painting is teeming with hyenas and clowns, and it is often very hard at first sight to distinguish between clever *saltimbanques* and the true geniuses of our rabid, insatiable form....

We do not maintain, however, that to be a genius one has to drink oneself to death, be a morphine addict, a sexual degenerate or a simple madman without the aid of any artificial stimulants. But it is frightful that in fact whatever great occurs in art in our agreeable epoch happens almost always on the very edge of madness....

In our opinion, true artists—that is, those who would be absolutely incapable of living without creating, as opposed to other adventurers who make peace with themselves in a more compromising fashion—will be kept in special institutions for the incurably sick and, as vestigial specimens of former humanity, will be the subject of research by trained psychiatrists. Museums will be opened for the infrequent visitor, as well as specialists in the special branch of history: the history of art—specialists like those in Egyptology or Assyriology or other scholarly studies of extinct races: for the race of artists will die out, just as the ancient races have died out.

Drawings, 1933

The S.I. Witkiewicz

Portrait Painting Firm

Translators' Introduction

Established in 1924, after Witkacy renounced painting as an art forever, the S.I. Witkiewicz Portrait Painting Firm was a complex intellectual and artistic ploy expressive of the writer's deepest impulses and in many ways comparable to Marcel Duchamp's abandonment of art for a program of irony and destruction. Like a Dadaist provocation, Witkacy declared his career as an artist finished and created a mock-capitalist enterprise with a brochure (published in 1928 and re-issued in 1932) designed to attract bourgeois customers.

The firm's clientele fell into three groups: first, the outsiders or paying customers—merchants, bureaucrats, officials—who wanted the most conventional likenesses; second, women with striking and unusual faces, whom Witkacy regarded as "mediums" offering inspiration and as fit subjects for repeated sessions; and third, friends—doctors, philosophers, artists, and writers—for whom Witkacy did wildly distorted protraits *gratis*. The deformed work he always signed as Witkacy; the straightforward portraits as Witkiewicz.

Type C, painted under the influence of alcohol and drugs, proved to be the most interesting of the firm's output. These were usually non-commissioned portraits of friends, characterized by distortion and abstraction and accordingly closest to Pure Form. Witkacy's experiments with drugs, particularly in the period 1929-32, gave these psychedelic portraits an oneiric and mystical quality. Different drugs or combinations of drugs were used by the artist to produce widely varying effects. What Witkacy called the metaphysical, or antisocial drugs—peyote and mescaline—called forth the strangeness of existence, as opposed to the realistic narcotics: eucodal, ether, cocaine, nicotine, and alcohol. The portraits painted under the influence of peyote utilize the colors red, violet, blue, and lemon-yellow and contain geometric forms, reptiles, and monsters. These peyote heads, executed in detail, often hang suspended in the air, above mountain landscapes, or surrounded by mediumistic nebulae. Hashish, on the other hand, produced doubles, of both people and things. The combination of peyote, cocaine, and alcohol led to strong deformation of the face and dark colors: black, brown, violet, and red with thick, heavy lines.

The uncanny self-portraits that Witkacy executed shortly before his suicide, in the period 1938-1939, were called forth by small doses of cocaine and beer. In all cases, Witkacy indicated on the protrait in abbreviations the type of drug which he had been using, and also the number of smoking (P) or non-smoking (NP) days, as well as the number of drinking or non-drinking days. For Witkacy, these artificial means were an attempt to recapture, if only briefly, the metaphysical feelings that had been lost with the advance of civilization.

Bibliography

Irena Jakimowicz. *Witkacy—Chwistek—Strzemiński*. Warsaw: Arkady, 1978.

Andrzej Kostołowski. "Firma Portretowa 'S.I. Witkiewicza,' *Miesięcznik Literacki*, No. 3 (1970), pp. 59-66, and No. 4 (1970), pp. 62-64.

RULES OF THE S.I. WITKIEWICZ PORTRAIT PAINTING FIRM

Motto:
The customer must be satisfied.
Misunderstandings are ruled out.

The rules are published so as to spare the firm the necessity of saying the same things over and over again.

#1. The firm produces portraits of the following kinds:

1. Type A — Comparatively speaking, the most, as it were, "spruced up" kind. Suitable rather for women's faces than for men's. "Slick" execution, with a certain loss of character in the interests of beautification, or accentuation of "prettiness."

2. Type B — More emphasis on character, without, however, any trace of caricature. Work making more use of sharp line than type A, with a certain touch of character traits, which does not preclude "prettiness" in women's portraits. Objective relationship to the model.

3. Type B + s. — Intensification of character, approaching the caricatural. The head larger than natural size. The possibility of preserving "prettiness" in women's portraits, and even of intensifying it in the direction of a certain "demonism."

4. Type C, C + Co., E, C + H, C + Co + E, etc. — These types, executed with the aid of C_2H_5OH and narcotics of a superior grade, at present ruled out. Subjective characteristics of the model, caricatural intensification both formal and psychological are not ruled out. Approaches abstract composition, or what is known as "Pure Form."

5. Type D — The same results without the use of any artificial means.

6. Type E — And its combinations with the preceding kinds. Free psychological interpretation according to the firm's discretion. The effect achieved may be the exact equivalent of the result produced by types A and B — the manner by which it is reached is different, as is also the method of execution, which may vary, but never exceeds the limit(s). A combination of E + s. is likewise available upon request.

Type E is not always possible to execute.

7. Children's type — (B + E) — Because children never can sit still, the pure type B is in most instances impossible — the execution rather takes the form of a sketch.

In general the firm does not pay much attention to the rendering of clothing and accessories. The question of the background concerns only the firm—demands in this regard are not considered.

Depending on the state of the firm and the difficulty of rendering a particular face, the portrait may be executed in one, two, or from three to five sittings. For large portraits showing the upper body or full figure, the number of sittings may even reach twenty. *The number of sittings does not determine the excellence of the product.*

#2. The basic novelty offered by the firm as compared to usual practice is the customer's option of rejecting a portrait if it does not suit him either because of the execution or the degree of likeness. *In such cases the customer pays one-third of the price, and the portrait becomes the property of the firm.* The customer does not have the right to demand that the portrait be destroyed. This clause, naturally, applies only to the pure types: A, B, and E, *without supplement(s)*—that is, without any supplement of exaggerated characteristics, or in other words, the types that appear in series. This clause was introduced because it is impossible to tell what will satisfy someone else. An exact agreement is desirable, based upon a firm and definite decision by the model as to the type requested. An album of "samples" (but not ones "of no value") is available for inspection at the premises of the firm. The customer receives a guarantee in that the firm in its own self-interest does not issue works which could damage its trademark. A situation could occur in which the firm itself would not sign its own product.

#3. Any sort of criticism on the part of the customer is *absolutely* ruled out. The customer may not like the portrait, but the firm cannot permit even the slightest comments without giving its special authorization. If the firm had allowed itself the luxury of listening to the customers' opinions, it would have gone mad a long time ago. *We place special emphasis on this section, since the most difficult thing is to restrain the customer from making remarks which are entirely uncalled for.* The portrait is either accepted or rejected—yes or no, without any explanations whatsoever as to why. Inadmissable criticism likewise includes remarks about whether or not it is a good likeness, observations concerning the background, placing one's hand over part of the face as painted in order to imply that this part really isn't the way it should be, comments such as, "I am too pretty," "Do I look that sad?" "That's not me," and all other opinions of that sort, whether favorable or unfavorable. After due consideration, and possibly consultation with third parties, the customer says yes (or no) and that's all there is to it—then he goes (or does not go) up to what is called the "cashier's window," that is, he simply hands over the agreed-upon sum to the firm. Given the incredible difficulty of the profession, the firm's nerves must be spared.

#4. Asking the firm for its opinion of a finished portrait is not permissible, nor is any discussion about a work in progress.

#5. The firm reserves the right to paint without any witnesses, if that is possible.

#6. Portraits of women with bare necks and shoulders cost one third more. Each arm costs one third of the total price. For portraits showing the upper body or full figure, special agreements must be drawn up.

#7. The portrait may not be viewed until it is finished.

#8. The technique used is a combination of charcoal, crayon, pencil, and pastel. — All remarks with regard to technical matters are ruled out, as are likewise demands for alterations.

#9. The firm undertakes the painting of portraits outside the firm's premises only in exceptional circumstances (sickness, advanced age, etc.), in which case the firm must be guaranteed a secret receptacle in which the unfinished portrait may be kept under lock and key.

#10. Customers are obliged to appear punctually for the sittings, since waiting has a bad effect on the firm's mood and may have an adverse influence on the execution of the product.

#11. The firm offers advice as to framing and packing portraits, but does not provide these services. Further discussion about types of frames is ruled out.

#12. The firm allows total freedom as to the model's clothing and *quite definitely does not voice any opinion in this regard*.

#13. The firm urges a careful perusal of the rules. Lacking any powers of enforcement, the firm counts on the tact and good will of its customers to insure the carrying out of the terms. Reading through and concurring with the rules is taken as equivalent to *concluding an agreement*. Discussion about the rules is inadmissable.

#14. An agreement on the installment plan or by bank draft is not ruled out. On account of the low prices the firm asks for, any demand for a reduction is not advisable. Before the portrait is begun, the customer pays one third of the price as a down payment.

#15. A customer who obtains portrait commissions for the firm — that is to say, who acts as an "an agent of the firm" — upon providing orders for the sum of 100 zlotys receives as a premium his own portrait or that of any person he wishes in the type of his choice.

#16. Notices sent by the firm to former customers announcing its presence at a given location arc not intended to force them to have new portraits painted, but rather to assist friends of these customers in plac-

ing orders, since having seen the firm's work they may wish something
similar themselves.

Warsaw, 1928   The "S.I. Witkiewicz" Firm

Portrait, 1924

Unwashed Souls

Translators' Introduction

Witkacy's socio-psychological study, *Unwashed Souls*, was written in 1936, but not published until 1975, although a few short excerpts had appeared during the author's lifetime (in 1938 and 39) in the literary magazine *Skawa*. Frankly personal and autobiographical, *Unwashed Souls* is a highly eccentric work that shows Witkacy in an informal, chatty mood, indulging in reminiscences, confessions, and polemics. Designed as a practical guide to everyday living in the Poland of the 1930s, Witkacy's pseudo-scientific treatise offers both medical advice and moral exhortation in a series of digressions and strange appendices, postscripts, and addenda about such diverse subjects as remedies for hemorrhoids, ways to stop smoking, best soaps for the skin, and treatments for dandruff. "The book as I see it," Witkacy writes, "will contain only digressions; it will simply be one big digression."

Witkacy was a lifelong admirer of Freud as a theorist of human nature, although he had serious doubts as to the therapeutic value of psychoanalysis and confesses that he never finished reading *The Introduction to Psychoanalysis*, which he found boring and ineffective. However, by applying Freud's psychoanalytical method to contemporary Polish attitudes and institutions, Witkacy is able to develop his own theory of culture. A large part of *Unwashed Souls* is devoted to a consideration of the inferiority complex (which, Witkacy argues, has existential roots in man's strivings to cope with the infinite and can therefore be a stimulus to creativity), as well as to an historical psychoanalysis of the Polish national character and its shortcomings. According to Witkacy, the typical Pole of his day suffers from delusions of grandeur, inner falsity, intellectual laziness, and worship of sham. An unwashed soul, in Witkacy's terminology, is an arrogant poseur, singularly lacking in self-knowledge (and thus unlaundered) who "frequently inveighs against everything and everybody, criticizes the whole world (unproductively), and delights in tearing down — as this is his sole means of raising himself above both himself and others." It is against such enemies and detractors that the playwright-philosopher battles aggressively in *Unwashed Souls*.

Bibliography

Anna Micińska, "Na marginesie 'Narkótykow' i 'Niemytych Dusz' St. I. Witkiewicza," *Twórczość*, No. 11 (1974), 30-47.

Małgorzata Szpakowska, *Światopogląd Stanisława Ignacego Witkiewicza* (Wrocław: Zakład Narodowy im. Ossolińskich, 1976).

The Nitwit's Smirk

My voice sounds as faint as a mosquito's buzz in comparison to the banalizers' megaphones, but the fact is that I issued warnings many times against various things: the excessive acceleration of life, the decline of theatre and literature (as a result of sucking up to a public which grows more moronic from one day to the next), anti-intellectualism, and the threat of total guanification of people's brains. No one was even willing to discuss these matters with me. When the ideas that I had developed entirely on my own began to penetrate to us in the form of Spenglerism and Huxley's literary caricatures, even those circles which had previously scoffed at my predictions began to grow somewhat *bedenklich* [German: suspicious] about these matters. That's the way it is with everything: harass home-grown originality, but welcome the same thing several years later when it comes from abroad. Słowacki already wrote about this phenomenon, and the situation is getting worse and worse. Of course, the nitwit's smirk is just as much a manifestation of an inferiority complex as every other bit of self-puffery. I call special attention to it only as a singularly virulent, but on the surface and in small doses, supposedly harmless form of dealings, in which we are so proficient, *nous autres Polonais.* I know in advance what the reaction will be on the part of the smirking nitwits to what I am now writing: "Mr. W., deservedly unrecognized because of the small value of his works and embittered on that account because of a lack of certain amenities of life that money brings, pours forth his bile in this fashion, seeking revenge on those who refused to let themselves be taken in by him."

The NS Problem*

The most critical issue: the *no-smoking* question.

After the publication of my book about narcotics, I stopped smoking for eight months, then I smoked again for a month, then I stopped smoking for half a year and I smoked again for two weeks. Since that time (October, 1932) I have not smoked for over three and a half years (now it's the fifth year) and I'm just extremely pleased about it. My reversions to smoking have always been linked to a general decline in energy and productivity, not to mention hideous psychic and even physical depression . . .

Naturally, some irresponsible scum have spread the rumor (I wonder if after my death these horror stories invented on my account will come to an end) that I am only faking when I claim to have stopped smoking for five years without a break and that in fact I inhale the filthy stinking stuff in secret or during drinking bouts (infrequent, by the way). Now that's what they call an "arrant" lie. *I have not had that foul stuff between my lips for five years less one month.* But once when I was cocainized and so drunk I was scarcely conscious (unfortunately such infrequent excesses still used to take place; besides, I am only opposed to all forms of *addiction* — a true titan of work can from time to time allow himself a binge, but he must be a titan really and truly), a lighted "weed" was stuck into my mouth, but the "friends" who did it could not force me to inhale the smoke.

After you stop smoking, you have to count on between three and four months of lessened productivity and "creativity," but after a year not a trace of this remains; the intellect works far better than in your smoking days, only a change in schedule occurs. Work at night falls off. The non-smoker goes to bed early, but the magnificent morning hours (in summer starting at 5 a.m.) are at his disposition for accomplishing the most difficult assignments.

Sleepiness and increased appetite, as well as the weight-gaining that accompanies it — which various people, especially chubby dames, use to explain the impossibility of NS — totally cease after half a year. Of course, if a war or some other historical cataclysm comes along, it's quite possible that I'll start smoking cigarettes again and inhale that stuff, but whoever sees me under normal circumstances with a weed stuck in my mouth is entitled to say that either temporarily or for good and all I have given up all higher intellectual and spiritual ambitions.

*In Polish, NP (Nie-Palenie), a notation used frequently by Witkacy on his portraits to indicate non-smoking days.

Chained Dogs

The sight of a dog on a chain is capable of spoiling my good humor while out on a walk for at least two hours, if not more. A creature expressly created and brought up to be man's friend is, through no fault of his own, sentenced by heartless scum to imprisonment without any fixed term; the situation is all the worse, because in this imprisonment he, unlike the normal prisoner, is not isolated from the world and its temptations, but through sight and smell, so strong in a dog, is susceptible to their most powerful impact. It is as though a human being were kept for his entire life in a cage on the floor of a four-star dance hall full of high-class broads without any possibility of taking part in the eating, drinking, conversation, and fun.

Production of Plays in this Volume

The Beelzebub Sonata	Bialystok	Studio 66	1966
	Lodz	Teatr Nowy	1967
	Wroclaw	Teatr Polski	1968
	Poznan	Teatr Polski	1968
	Warsaw	Ateneum	1969
	Rzeszow	Siemaszkowa Theatre	1970
	Honolulu	Kennedy Theatre	1974
	Wroclaw	Wroclaw Opera	1977
	Gdansk	Teatr Wybrzeze	1979
Tumor Brainiowicz	Cracow	Slowacki Theatre	1921
	Olsztyn	Jaracz Theatre	1974
	Paris	Theatre Mouffetard	1977
Dainty Shapes and Hairy Apes	Warsaw	Student Theatre IWG	1967
	Cracow	Cricot II	1973
	Edinburgh		
	Cracow	PWST Theatre School	1977
	Jelenia Gora	Cyprian Norwid Theatre	1978
	Richmond	Virginia Commonwealth University	1978

Translators' Biographies

Daniel Gerould is a playwright, translator, and critic who teaches Theatre and Comparative Literature at the Graduate Center of The City University of New York. His critical study, *Witkacy*, will be published in the Fall. He has also published two other volumes of plays by Witkiewicz, and is the author of *Twentieth-Century Polish Avant-Garde Drama*.

Jadwiga Kosicka is a translator and historian, formerly with the Polish Academy of Sciences in Warsaw, who writes about European intellectual history. She is currently preparing a volume of plays about the Warsaw Ghetto uprising and a collection of essays by Polish authors.

PERFORMING ARTS JOURNAL PLAYSCRIPTS

THEATRE OF THE RIDICULOUS
Plays by Kenneth Bernard, Charles Ludlam, and Ronald Tavel.
$9.95 (hbk); $4.95 (pbk).

ANIMATIONS: A TRILOGY FOR MABOU MINES
Plays by Lee Breuer, with 70 illustrations.
$35.00 (limited signed); $12.95 (hbk); $7.95 (pbk).

THE RED ROBINS
Play by Kenneth Koch.
$7.95 (hbk); $3.95 (pbk)

THE WOMEN'S PROJECT
Plays by Joyce Aaron/Luna Tarlo, Kathleen Collins, Penelope Gilliatt, Rose
    Leiman Goldemberg, Lavonne Mueller, Phyllis Purscell, Joan Schenkar
$14.95 (hbk); $6.95 (pbk).

Other publications:

PERFORMING ARTS JOURNAL
LIVE (Performance Art)

Write to:

Performing Arts Journal Publications
P.O. Box 858
Peter Stuyvesant Station
New York, N.Y. 10009